# INEVITABLE DETOUR

# INEVITABLE DETOUR

AMAZON BESTSELLING AUTHOR

## S.R. GREY

Inevitable Detour (Inevitability #1)

Copy Editing: Katherine
Cover Design: Arijana Karčić, Cover It! Designs
Interior Design: E.M. Tippetts Book Designs
ISBN-10: 0692222170 (print edition only)
ISBN-13: 978-0692222171 (print edition only)

# CHAPTER ONE

I STARE at the computer screen. It's my last exam of spring semester, and there are only five questions left on the Strategic Management final before me.

My eyes are glued to words, forming a single question. I know the answer. Yes, I do. But then my vision blurs, and I think, *ugh, whose idea was it for me to major in business?*

Not mine.

The cursor on the screen blinks over answer choice B. Like I said, I know the correct answer, and it sure as hell isn't B.

*What to do…what to do…*

With a sly grin, I choose B and hit next.

I am feeling particularly defiant today. My parents left me a voice mail this morning, telling me in no uncertain terms that any thoughts of heading up to New York City this summer with my best friend and roommate, Haven Shaw, are best put to rest. So much for thinking it'd be fun to hang out in the Big Apple with Haven while she worked on finding an agent, making acting contacts, and generally just doing whatever it is a person needs to do when preparing to land a part in a play someday.

And not just any play.

"Broadway, here I come," Haven said the other day when we were discussing her big-city dreams.

She's a bit theatrical, but that's to be expected. She's a theater major, after all. Her goal is to eventually make it as an actress on the Great White Way.

Conversely, my dreams are much smaller. My primary longing lately is for something—*anything*—to happen in my mundane life. I thought New York would be a promising start. Guess not. Thanks to my parents and their aversion to anything fun for Essa, there will be no excitement in my life this summer. Nope. Just like the two previous summers, I'll be lulling away the time here at Oakwood College. Excitement for me will consist of chilling in the coffee shop on the edge of the tiny Pennsylvania town my small college is located in. My after-class afternoons will include exciting activities like staring out at cows and farmland, sipping on a mocha, and wishing and hoping for something more.

And that's just not right.

I'm a damn straight-A student, for God's sake. I don't need to spend the summer at Oakwood, taking stupid summer classes. Unfortunately, my parents don't care about my wants and needs. They believe their only child should apply herself year-round. Forget that I'm already a model daughter.

Well, more or less. But that's neither here nor there.

Bottom line is that my parents will not, as they put it in their terse message, have me "veering off course."

Oh, really? So they think…

My defiance hits full throttle, and I purposely choose the wrong answers for the next four questions.

I hit submit and think, *take that, Mr. and Mrs. Brant.*

Despite my actions, I'll still receive a solid A for the class. My GPA will not suffer in the slightest. Still, it feels kind of good to be bad.

*That's sad, Essa, that choosing a few wrong answers on a final is the best defiant act you can come up with.*

Sighing, I click a button to indicate I am finished with the exam. I then grab my purse from the back of the chair and head for the door. "You're pathetic," I mumble to myself as I step out into a warm, stuffy hallway that smells of varnish and books.

I kind of like the smell as it wraps around me. It's the smell of students seeking knowledge; it's the smell of youth. Despite all my protestations to the contrary, I do like college. I would just prefer to be studying something of my own choosing.

I stand and ponder. Not only does the smell of school envelope me, but the heat of the day does as well. The second-floor hall I'm lingering in is about ten degrees warmer than the classroom was. Dropping my purse to the floor, I shrug out of my olive-green mock-army jacket. I'm down to two layered tanks, blue over white, but I am still roasting.

"Blech," I pant, fanning myself as I bend down to pick up my purse. The button on my pants threatens to pop, and I let out a curse. I really should have worn a pair of nice, loose shorts instead of squeezing my ass into overly stylish skinny jeans this morning.

*Maybe if the jeans were a little looser, I'd be more comfy.*

I do a funny little dance in the thankfully empty area outside the classroom. Sadly, the jeans don't feel a single inch looser.

Damn designers. Don't they realize we're not all model-perfect? When I exhale, the button squeezes once again at my middle, and I remind myself that I need to lay off the sweets.

Yeah, right. A girl has to have some kind of indulgence, right? And since I'm no exception, sugary treats are it for me. Otherwise, I'm fairly straight and narrow. I don't do drugs, and I don't smoke. I also barely drink—two drinks are my limit when I do imbibe—and I'm not promiscuous.

"Far from it," I mumble.

I've only had sex once, in fact. And what a disaster *that* turned out to be. The memory alone, from one of the few nights I deviated from my two-drinks policy, at a Saint Patrick's Day party two months ago, leaves me feeling nauseated. Yeah, the thirty seconds spent with the senior who was cowriting an article with me for the online *Oakwood College Gazette* just wasn't worth the time it took to take off my clothes. All too clearly, a fuzzy memory of him grunting on top of me, sweaty and harsh, comes to mind. I kept regretting that this was how I was losing my virginity. I still regret it. But what can you do? Last time I checked there were no time machines.

So, yeah, forget about sex. That's my motto. I'll stick with sugar-laden goodies for now. Like cupcakes. Haven made a batch to celebrate our surviving finals week. Her homemade buttercream frosting is far better than sex any day. Not to mention it's more orgasm-inducing than the thirty seconds that had me asking, "What? That's it? Why bother?"

I sigh. I need to get back to the apartment and hit up those awesome cupcakes. But my feet are far from moving. I can't believe I daydreamed away five whole minutes. Or maybe it's been ten.

Retrieving my phone from my purse, I send Haven a quick text:

*Leaving Byers Hall. Don't eat all the cupcakes.*

A few seconds later, she texts back:

*Oops. I got hungry and ate the rest for dinner. Sorry.*

*Bitch*, I reply.

*Whore*, is her response.

I call her a bitch again and laugh. She's laughing too. I'm sure of it. Haven knows my texts are sent with love. She is so not a bitch, and I would never think such a thing for real. Nor do I suspect she sees me as a whore. I am far from it, as established. Well, unless we're talking sugar. Then, I'm a full-blown slut.

Haven sends another text.

*Just kidding, Es. I didn't eat all the cupcakes. I know you love them, so I left the rest for you.*

Aww, Haven is the best.

*You're super sweet,*

I text back, and then I start down the hallway. Finally.

As I amble along, I think of how Haven is definitely one of the better parts of my life. Throughout the course of the past three years, we've become best friends. We met at a freshman orientation. It was an early one, held during the spring prior to matriculation. We sat next to each other and clicked immediately, which is kind of amusing, since we're so different from one another. Somehow, though, we just work. Bottom line, I love Haven, and I'd do anything for her. She's certainly done some selfless things for me, no doubt about that. As a result, we're close, thicker than thieves some say. I tease Haven all the time; tell her she's my sister from another mother. Since her own mom passed away years ago, she usually replies that she'd let my mom adopt her. But then she adds the qualifier, "that is, if she wasn't so damn overbearing."

Understatement of the year.

Just the other day, after I received a call from my mom—she was checking in on my studying—Haven joked, "If your mom took me in she'd probably insist I change my major from theater to business."

"She probably would," I agreed.

It's true. My mother means well, as does my dad, but both my parents have a tendency to focus on practicality. And to the Mr. and Mrs. Brant, practicality means majoring in business.

"It's always smart to major in something marketable," Dad likes to say.

"Like business, honey," Mom always adds with a smile. "You're making smart choices, Essa."

Too bad they're not *my* choices.

Wishing I was more like Haven, who answers to no one, I round the corner and run smack dab into one of Haven's acting professors. To my dismay, it's the shitty professor who broke my friend's heart two weeks ago.

"Hi, Essa," Professor Walsh says cordially while pretending to step out of my path.

He remains in the way, of course. Still, I manage to slip around him. He nonetheless stays with me, turning and watching me the whole time.

*Ugh.* It is so hard not to snipe, "Get the hell out of my face, you fucking douche bag."

Since I lack the courage to say such a thing, I hold my tongue.

But when Professor Walsh reaches out and touches my arm, halting my progress, I twist from his grasp and snap, "Really?" I raise both brows and take a step back. "Please tell me you did not just lay your hand on me."

"Now, now," Douche Bag Walsh says in a sickly, patronizing tone. "There's no need for such a venomous retort. I don't know what Haven has told you—"

"Try everything," I interrupt.

Haven and her thirty-five-year-old professor had a three-month fling. It was all hot and heavy, not to mention illicit as hell, until he ended it in a not-so-nice way.

Concern fills the professor's light-brown eyes as he taps his foot and stares at me. It's not concern for the girl whose heart he's broken. It's purely concern for his own ass. Oh, the trouble he could get into for fucking one of his students.

"Don't worry," I say, just to get him to stop staring and, hopefully, go away. "Haven won't let me go to the disciplinary board, and God knows she'll never do it herself, so your secret is safe."

The professor, more confident as soon as he hears I plan to keep my mouth shut, lazily brushes back a lock of wispy, dirty-blond hair that's fallen to his forehead. He's boyishly handsome, and this is a move he's obviously perfected.

Too bad it does absolutely nothing for me.

Undeterred, he says in a low voice, "Everything that happened between me and Haven Shaw was consensual. She's twenty-two years old, Miss Brant. Last time I checked that makes her an adult."

I feel like screaming in his smug face. "You were her freaking professor, prick. Not only did you violate school policy, but you violated her when you let her fall in love with you and then callously walked away."

But there's no point in lashing out. Haven is still hung up

on the guy, shady though he is. She doesn't want him to get into any trouble. And someone might hear me if I start going off in defense of my friend. The halls are empty, but many of the classrooms are full.

So I don't say a thing. I do, however, scowl at the man. And then I walk away, leaving him standing in the middle of the hall. I feel his eyes on me, probably checking out my ass. His hooking up with Haven wasn't some fluke. It's common knowledge that Professor Walsh has a thing for college-age girls. Until Haven, he was known as a one-and-done kind of guy. But he was really into Haven, for a while…until he wasn't.

It's really no surprise he liked her as much as he did in the early days of their fling. Men find Haven irresistible. And why wouldn't they? The girl is gorgeous. She is far prettier than I am. Haven is tall, with a model-like body. I am short, not super thin. Haven has big, expressive aquamarine eyes and shiny, raven-black hair. I have boring hair that can't even decide what color it wants to be. Some days it appears light brown, other days it's more of a dark blonde shade. Not that I pay much notice. I usually just pile the long, unruly tresses up in a sloppy bun, or twist the mess into a ponytail.

I'm not saying I'm unattractive. I just don't really stand out in a crowd. Not like Haven does.

Despite all she has going for her, Haven is far from conceited. She's unassuming and genuine, loyal to the core. That's why I maintain that she didn't deserve to be treated the way Professor Walsh treated her. He used her for sex, strung her along, and then unceremoniously dumped her with no explanation two weeks ago.

My ire at the jerk professor escalates. By the time I reach the stairs, I am smacking my hand down on the dark wood railing in anger. Quickly, I spin around, intent on stomping back and having one last word with the guy.

But he's long gone.

"Chickenshit," I murmur.

Sighing, I step over to a wall and lean back against it. There's a classroom a few feet away, in session. Leaning my head back, I listen to the soothing murmur of voices, thus allowing myself a few minutes to calm down.

Soon, I am relaxed. I also find I am fully engaged in listening to the lecture. Not surprising since the instructor, her voice light and feminine, is speaking on a subject I find fascinating—the role of fate in our lives. I walk over to the door and press my ear up against it.

"Wonderful," she says. "You've all shared some great insights. But now that we've dissected Shakespeare's use of fate in *Romeo and Juliet* and *Macbeth*, I have a question for you, a question regarding *your* lives."

The class titters, she chuckles, and I step back to where I'm able to lean against the wall. After a minute or two, I slide down to a seated position.

"What I want to know," the instructor continues, "is who here believes that real lives—*our* lives—are influenced by fate?"

"I do," I whisper. *At least I think I do.*

The professor calls on someone in the class, a girl. She responds, "I believe all of our lives are influenced by fate. And I firmly believe in destiny."

"Is there a difference?" the instructor questions.

The girl replies, "Yes, I think so. I've always heard that fate refers to the bad things that happen in our lives."

"And destiny?" the instructor prompts.

"It's the good stuff."

"That is a commonly accepted belief," the instructor concurs. There's some shuffling of papers.

"What it all comes down to," the instructor continues, "is that every person's life is destined for a certain path. We may not realize it, especially when it's happening, but we *will* end up where we're supposed to be."

Wow. I think about my own life. I believe in concepts like fate and destiny. But, to my chagrin, I don't feel as if either has ever touched my life. In some ways, I suppose my parents have prevented *things* from happening by the way they've structured everything for me. Still, I hold out hope that something that is "meant to be" will eventually occur. If that doesn't happen, what will become of me? My biggest fear is that I'll graduate from college next year—with my shiny, new business degree—and move right back to my hometown of Philadelphia. Maybe I'll become an accountant, like my mom and dad. And maybe, like Mom and Dad, I'll never really *live*.

"Ugh." I place my face in my hands. I don't want to be an accountant. I'd rather eat pocket lint, I swear. If I had my way, I'd much rather work as a writer, a journalist of some sort. I find joy in writing articles for the school paper. But, really, if I dare to dream big, I see myself as an investigative journalist. The kind that seeks out exciting stories, stories with an element of danger.

Who in the hell am I kidding? I'm play-it-by the-rules Essa Brant. "Let's be real here," I whisper.

Sighing, I return my attention to the instructor and her big words on fate.

"Remember," she says. Her tone is so very serious, so very

ominous. "Just because you think fate or destiny hasn't yet guided your life in some noticeable way doesn't mean it won't happen. I promise you, my friends, you will end up where you're supposed to be. And how can I say that with such certainty? The answer is simple: You can't escape your destiny."

*Okay, so where will fate lead me? What is my destiny?*

On a roll, the instructor goes on. "Things happen in our lives that are predetermined, whether we realize it or not. Often it's a series of small events that slowly and methodically lead us to where we're supposed to be. But sometimes it's a big, cataclysmic event that changes the course of everything. Even so, you may not realize your life is changing at the time. Something may happen to someone you know, perhaps someone close to you. Their 'something' ends up affecting you. *Your* life is now altered; *you're* set on a different path." The instructor pauses, and then she says, "Think of this path as an inevitable detour of sorts."

Everyone in the classroom is so quiet you'd hear a pin drop if someone were inclined to drop one. Guess everyone is deep in thought, wondering what "inevitable detour" is in store for them. And how will this "detour" alter their lives. God knows that's what I'm thinking.

"We have about ten minutes left," the instructor announces, breaking the trance she was holding everyone in, including me. "Are there any questions, class?"

A lively Q&A ensues, and I know it's high time I get up off my ass and go home. But I can't leave, not yet. I need a minute to take in all I've heard. It's like when someone puts something in your head, and that's all you think about. Now, I can't help but imagine an inevitable detour of my own. Maybe I should take charge and make one happen next week. I could defy my parents and go to

New York City with Haven. It might be worth my parents' ire to finally venture out of the only state I've ever known. Not only would my bestie and I have a great time tearing up the town, but I'd be staying with Haven in her older brother's apartment. And there's a good chance that though Farren Shaw travels a lot for some crazy-secretive job he has, I'd finally have an opportunity to meet him. Possibly, I could even spend some time with him.

*Gah.* A thrill shoots through me at the thought of spending even a mere minute with Farren. Now there's an inevitable detour I'd like to take. Much like his sister, Farren is gorgeous. He has the same raven-black hair, same model-perfect features, like full lips and high cheekbones. His eyes, however, are not aquamarine. They're better; they're a unique and stunning shade of green. Not that I've had the pleasure of viewing these stunning green eyes in person. Only in pictures have I seen them, since, sadly, I've never actually met Farren. He's not around much. He was in the military for years, special ops according to Haven. And though he was discharged over a year ago, he still spends a good deal of time in other countries for his "work." Consequently, he's never visited Oakwood College campus. That's why I've never met him. And that is why I'm so incredibly upset about New York. That would have been my chance. Travel or no, he'd have to stop home at some point.

Oh well. Guess I'll have to continue to rely on pictures and short videos of Haven's incredibly handsome brother to fuel my libido. And by fuel, I mean on all cylinders. I may not have much of an interest in sex, but I am still a woman. And, as a woman, I sense a man like Farren could change my mind on the sex-thing. He's like some dream guy—tall, dark, and too handsome for words.

So, yeah, I'm into him. It's mostly a secret, though. However, I must confess that once, several months ago, Haven caught me uploading pictures of Farren from her computer to my phone.

"Cyberstalking my brother, I see," she teased as she walked over to where I was seated—rather uneasily at that point—on the sofa in our living room, her laptop in my hands.

"No, no," I stammered while trying to close all the open windows…of Farren in uniform, Farren standing next to Haven, and Farren—a recent shot—in a finely tailored suit.

"He does look good in that one," she said, tapping the screen before the picture of her brother in a dark suit disappeared.

She was right. Farren in a business suit was all kinds of serious hot, so I had to agree. Then, I turned from the computer and asked, "Does he have to wear suits for his new job?"

She shrugged. "I don't know, Essa. I guess."

"What exactly *is* his new job?" I pressed. "You said he's some kind of personal security contractor, right? What does that mean, exactly?"

"I don't really know," Haven admitted. Then, with a laugh, she said, "All I know is whatever Farren does he gets paid a lot of money."

"I hope it's nothing illegal," I mumbled under my breath.

Hey, it's not so farfetched to think such a thing. Not only does Farren fund his sister's college education—as well as all her expenses—but he also has plenty of money for himself. He owns some of the best real estate in the world, including a luxurious New York City apartment. The place is sweet, very sweet, located on the Upper West Side of Manhattan, in a high-rise building right next to Central Park. I've seen pictures, and it looks like the kind of place a celebrity would live in. Not that I care about

13

the money Farren has, but the fact that he has so much of it does make me curious.

See, Farren and Haven Shaw were not born into any kind of money, not like the level of wealth Farren currently possesses. Their childhood circumstances were far from ideal and not anywhere near upscale. Their dad, a man named Alan Shaw, disappeared, seemingly into thin air, when they were very young. At the time, Farren was ten and Haven was only three. Their mom was left to struggle on her own to support her two young children. And she was doing okay, until she was killed in a car crash. Seventeen-year-old Farren and ten-year-old Haven were sent to live with their aunt—someone who absolutely did not want the burden of her sister's kids. Her aunt was cold and indifferent. Haven has said many times that her aunt was far from nice. That's why Farren joined the army the day he turned eighteen. He left and started sending Haven money right away. Their aunt was always cheap with them, buying the kids only the bare essentials. Despite all of those things, to this day, Haven still craves family. She tries so hard to maintain a relationship with her aunt. But the woman rarely—if ever—returns Haven's calls.

My phone vibrates, bringing me back to the present. It's another text from Haven.

*Where are you? You better get your ass home soon. We're still going out tonight, right?*

*Of course,* I type back. *I haven't forgotten that we're celebrating the fact we survived our third year of college.*

*We did, didn't we?*

*Hell, yeah,* I type back. *Seniors next year. Woohoo.*

*I'll drink to that,* Haven replies.

*Me, too.*

*Hey, by the way, I hope you're planning on having more than two beers tonight. Rules are out the window.*

*Ha-ha. And, yes, rules are out the window.*

*Good,* she texts. *Who knows, Essa, maybe you'll get so loosened up that you'll end up meeting your fantasy man.*

If only she knew it's her brother who stars in my fantasies. Just thinking about the man—and he is a man, not some fumbling college boy—gets me all worked up. But it's ridiculous to continue on like this. I'll surely never meet Farren, seeing as New York City is off the table.

Resigned to live my parent-directed life, which certainly does not include hot guys, I push all thoughts of my secret fantasy, Farren Shaw, to the back of my mind. Gathering up my purse, I stand. But before I leave, I think about the lecture I listened in on.

*Fate…*

*Destiny…*

What's in store for me? Where will these so-called predetermined events lead me? Somewhere, everywhere, nowhere. The possibilities are endless. Still, I have to wonder if there will ever be an inevitable detour in *my* life.

"Yeah, right," I quietly scoff. The only inevitability in my future is that my life will continue as planned. But the instructor's words resonate in my head, reminding me that we can't escape our destiny and that we always end up where we're supposed to be.

Of course, for that to happen, it may require a bit more defiance on my part. Particularly when it comes to my parents and where they expect me to spend this summer.

*Good, okay.* That's fine with me.

'Cause I think I'm finally ready to start pressing B every chance I get.

# CHAPTER TWO

THE Mexican-themed bar, located a few blocks from the tiny frame house where Haven and I rent a second-floor apartment, is completely packed. I shouldn't be surprised. The lone bar in the otherwise quiet and sedate tree-lined neighborhood—located just off campus—is always busy. But with tonight bearing the distinction of being a Friday *and* the end of finals week, Señor Frog's is utterly crazy.

"Looks like everyone decided to celebrate here tonight," I yell over to Haven.

It's hot and sweaty in the bar, the small dance floor is packed, and a heavy bass beat is practically shaking the whole building.

Haven spins on her barstool to face me, her aquamarine eyes widening in agreement. She nods and takes a sip from her frothy margarita. Lowering the salt-rimmed glass, she yells back, "I know, right?"

The track changes to something less rowdy, and I'm finally able to speak without having to scream. Just as I'm about to say something to Haven in a nice, normal tone, some jock saunters over and oh-so-obviously bumps into her shoulder.

She almost spills her drink, but still manages to smile. Not in a flirtatious way, she's just being nice.

Jock-boy says, "Oh, hey, sorry 'bout that."

He reaches out to touch her arm, but Haven smoothly shifts and avoids his grasp. "No worries," she says tightly, still smiling.

The jock finally gets the hint and moves on with a shrug.

Haven rolls her eyes my way and mouths, "Men."

I just nod back, since I'm used to guys hitting on my friend. It's pretty much like this every time we go out. Haven is beautiful and sexy, especially tonight in her distressed denim miniskirt, black combat boots, and a clingy red sweater with one shoulder down. Her bra strap is exposed, black, a perfect match to her fishnet stockings. Only Haven could successfully pull off such a hot, urban look in such a rural and conservative town.

I, on the other hand, am dressed like most of the other girls in the bar. I have on dark skinny jeans, a lacy black shirt over a white tank, and a pair of flat sandals that I threw on before leaving the house. As a concession to Haven, I let her do my hair and makeup. That's why my blondish locks are down, all wavy and bouncy, and my whiskey-colored eyes are lined with lots of smoky color.

That reminds me…

I swipe a finger under my lashes, rubbing twice, just in case I'm smudging.

Haven's own smoke-lined eyes slide to me, and she says, "So, let's review. Tell me again what your parents' crazy reasoning is for why you can't come to New York City this summer?"

"Ugh, Haven." I cover my face with my hands and speak through my fingers. "What do you think? It's the same as always. They want me to stick around campus and take summer classes."

Haven tugs my hands away from my face. When I acquiesce, I see she's frowning. She shakes her head slowly, and a lock of raven hair falls to her cheek. She tucks it behind her ear.

"That's bullshit, Es," she says. "You, of all people, do *not* need summer classes."

"I know," I lament, since my parents' stance is unbelievably ridiculous to me, too.

Haven sighs. "You're a twenty-two-year-old woman. You need to take a stand at some point. You should just tell your parents to go fuck themselves."

I'm in the middle of taking a drink from my bottle of beer, and I practically spew Corona Light all over the polished-wood bar.

"Um, right," I mutter. I nod to her margarita and say, "Just how much tequila is in that drink, anyway?"

I'm only half-serious, but Haven replies without missing a beat. "Three shots of Patrón."

"Sheesh, good thing we walked here," I mumble.

Haven doesn't disagree. "For sure," she says with the glass halfway to her mouth.

After taking a sip, she adds, "So, what are your plans? Are you going to defy or comply with Mr. and Mrs. Brant?"

I let out a long sigh. "I'd like to defy," I admit. "But you know I'd get cut off. That would mean no more school, no more anteing up my share of the rent for our cute apartment—"

"They wouldn't stop paying for your classes," Haven

interrupts, her voice soft despite her cutting me off.

"That's probably true," I say. "But I'd definitely be back in the dorms."

Haven shudders. "I know, sweetie. Your parents probably would cut out anything they deemed unnecessary."

"Which would mean most everything," I say, sighing.

With a genuinely apologetic tone, Haven says, "I shouldn't have said anything, Essa. Besides, all is not lost. You can always drive up to the Big Apple and visit for a few days."

I don't say anything, but I doubt a visit to New York will ever really happen. I'm too chicken to take a chance like that. What if something went wrong? My parents would flip.

For Haven's sake, though, I smile and nod.

Haven smiles back and then motions for the bartender. "Hey, let's do a shot," she says to me. "We need to lighten the mood. We're supposed to be celebrating tonight, right?"

"Right," I agree, before I tip back my bottle and finish off what's left of my beer.

Haven eyes me curiously.

Since it looks like I will, indeed, be abandoning my two-beer rule tonight, I declare, "Let's get fucked up."

She replies, "Hell, yeah. I'm all for that."

A mere minute later, we're downing shots of tequila. Another round of shots follows, and then Haven and I hit the dance floor. I am officially drunk, so when Haven initiates a bump-and-grind routine with me, I roll with it.

Soon, half the bar is watching us—the male half. Haven leans in and whispers in my ear, "Hey, let's give them a show."

Before I know what a "show" involves, Haven's lips are on mine. There's nothing romantic or erotic about the kiss, however.

My best friend's lips feel warm and soft as they press against mine. I know the intent behind her action is born purely from affection, so I kiss her back. Soon, though, there's whooping and hollering and calls to "touch each other's tits."

"Okay, that's enough of that," I murmur, breathless and dizzy as I take a step back.

Haven laughs. And we continue to dance, albeit with less grinding, until the song ends.

When the next song begins and it's nothing we like, she grabs my arm. "Come on, Essa," she says. "I think we need more shots."

My head is spinning, and everything is kind of fuzzy. But who am I to ruin our good time? Intent on being a good sport, I heartily agree that more shots are what we need. On our way to the bar, though, a sense of uneasiness creeps over me. Even in my inebriated condition, I feel as if Haven and I are being watched. Some deep intuition warns me that these are not college-boy stares.

Glancing up to a raised portion of the bar overlooking the dance floor, I spot two men in business suits watching as Haven and I make our way through the crowd. The men, who are clearly older than us, try not to be blatantly obvious. When they catch me staring at them, they turn away quickly and engage in conversation. I assess them. Maybe they're not so bad. They're both nice-looking, and compared to the rest of the guys in the club, these men ooze suaveness and sophistication.

Feeling brave from the alcohol, and with clearly impaired judgment, I lean in close to Haven and whisper loudly in her ear, "Two hotties at three o'clock."

Her eyes dart over to where the men are seated at a high table, giving them a commanding presence.

"Oh, hell, Essa," Haven gushes over her shoulder to me. "Good pickup. Hmm, wonder what two guys like that are doing here. They're not kids," she continues, stating the obvious. "They must be at least thirty."

"Yeah, I'm sure," I muse.

Stopping in the middle of the crowd, she spins to me, bounces on her toes, and says excitedly, "We should go talk to them. This could be your chance, Essa. Maybe you'll like one of them."

"Whoa, slow down," I say.

This is a level of enthusiasm I don't know what to do with. Personally, I'm nervous as hell at the thought of actually meeting these strange men. Suddenly wishing I'd kept my mouth shut, I step around Haven. Over my shoulder, I say lightly, "Jeez, Haven, didn't you get enough of older men with Professor Douche Fuck?"

She catches up to me, leans in, and says quietly, "Aww, you're just nervous."

"Damn straight," I reply.

"Trust me, Essa," Haven continues. "If you're fortunate enough to experience an older man—one who knows what he's doing—then you'll understand."

I make a scoffing noise. "No thanks. Older, younger, the same age, I'm really not interested. You know I've sworn off sex."

Haven stops and levels me with an are-you-kidding-me expression. "I never thought you were serious," she says.

We've reached the bar, and we wedge our bodies in between two standing patrons. Haven is facing me, inches away, as she hisses, "You need to forget about that God-awful, three-thrust experience you had with the study-partner dude."

"He wasn't a study partner," I mutter, just as the song in the background is changing. "He was cowriting an article for the school paper with me."

"What?" she yells over the now very loud music.

I yell back, "He wasn't my study partner."

"Whatever," Haven says, shrugging her slender shoulders. "In any case, you need to dust yourself off and get back on the horse." She nudges my arm. "Like, literally, Essa."

"I don't know…" I'm glad it's dark and she can't see me blushing. "…maybe."

Despite my embarrassment, I can't deny that Haven has a valid point. I sometimes think the same thing. Maybe that's why I'm still taking birth control pills, even after the Saint Patrick's Day bad-sex debacle. I lie to myself. I tell myself I stay on the pill for clearer skin. But, really, there's one guy I'd scrap my no-sex-ever-again plan for—Haven's brother, Farren. And maybe that would have been in the cards, if New York was happening.

But it's not, alas…

My gaze flickers to the two men in the bar. They are both older, like Farren. One has dark hair, the other is a blond. From far away like this, and with inebriation blurring my vision, I start to think the dark-haired man could pass for Farren. Maybe.

Dark-haired Man catches me staring. He nods and lifts his drink—something that looks like whiskey in a rocks glass.

Beer goggles or not, while staring at the Farren look-alike, I dreamily murmur to Haven, "Hmm, maybe you're right. Maybe I should, uh, how did you put it? Get back on the horse, right?"

I don't dare add that I may be drunk enough to pretend my dark-haired admirer *is* Farren. I'd never tell my friend—who's currently staring at me, mouth agape—that I lust this hard for her brother. She'd probably think I'm crazy, considering I've never even met Farren.

Losing the shocked expression, Haven clears her throat and says, "You know what, Essa. I'm proud of you. You're being daring." She studies me, glances at the guys, and then returning her gaze to me, says, "You like the dark-haired one, don't you?"

"He's okay," I say, shrugging.

Jesus, I hope she doesn't notice the man's resemblance to her brother.

But I don't think she sees the connection, since she starts pulling me in the direction of the men. "Come on," she says, laughing. "Let's go get you laid."

I grimace. I may talk big, but am I drunk enough to have sex with a stranger?

Haven, taking notice of my slowing steps and troubled expression, backtracks quickly. In an understanding tone, she says, "You don't have to do anything you don't want to do. You know that, right?"

I nod.

"Do you want to at least go talk to them? I think the dark-haired one likes you. We can get a drink with them and see how things go."

"What about you?" I say. "Are you okay with hanging out with the blond one?"

I don't want Haven wasting her time talking to someone she's not into just for my sake.

"Sure," she says, nodding in his direction. "Look at him. He's really cute. Plus, God knows I can use a distraction. I need *something* to help me forget about the professor."

I'm about to say teasingly that I'm shocked my dance-floor kisses didn't make her forget about her broken heart. But then

I see how sad she really is, and I say nothing at all. *Poor Haven. Professor Walsh really messed with her head.*

In that moment, I decide to be a good friend and roll with whatever happens tonight. After all, this evening is supposed to be about fun and good times. So we maneuver our way past two girls chatting on the steps that lead to the raised area above the dance floor and close in on the older men.

*It's like they're our prey*, I think, giggling at the thought. But then I see the way the blond man is eyeing Haven, hungry and cold, and I worry someone in this scenario is prey.

And it's not either of the men.

Just then, I notice I'm being watched as well. The man with the dark hair is sizing me up. Not in any hungry or cold way, but rather in a seemingly thoughtful manner.

"Hey." Haven bumps my shoulder with her shoulder. "Check out the hot Scandinavian features on Blondie. I didn't notice it from far away, but he could totally pass for Eric on *True Blood*."

Haven and I are *True Blood* junkies. We binge watch past seasons when we're bored. Hmm, maybe that's why the blond man initially looked like a predator to me. The whole vampire thing and all.

"Shit, Hav," I reply. "He really does look like Eric."

And he does. Blondie is Viking-tall, blond, and very obviously buff. His toned body moves fluidly in his smartly tailored suit.

"I think I want him." Haven sighs dreamily. "Just look at his smooth, confident ways. It's like he really is Eric."

"Great," I mumble. "He'll probably end up wanting to drink your blood or something equally kinky."

"Ooh, let's hope he's kinky," Haven purrs. "I will so let him do whatever he wants."

Haven, despite her ill-advised fling with the professor and her girl-gone-wild behavior tonight, is not promiscuous. She's just a girl hoping to mend her broken and stepped-on heart. Alas, if drinking and sex are what she needs to feel better, I can play along.

When we are about five feet from the men I've temporarily christened "Eric" and "Almost Farren," I sadly come to the conclusion that the dark-haired man falls far short of the real Farren. He's not as built as Haven's muscular brother, nor does his face compare. His cheekbones and jaw aren't as finely sculpted, his lips are too thin, and his eyes appear to be brown, certainly not green like Farren's. The guy is a good-looking man, don't get me wrong. He's just no Farren Shaw.

With Haven in the lead, we saunter up to the high table. After a flirtatious greeting, the dark-haired man asks me, with a wave of his hand, if I'd like to take a seat. "Eric" asks Haven the same question, only he is gentlemanly enough to pull out one of the tall chairs for her. Haven sits down, straightens her skirt, and proceeds to engage the men in conversation. "This is Essa"—she gestures to me as I'm sitting down—"and I'm Haven."

The blond man speaks first. "Nice to meet you ladies," he says. "We noticed you dancing out there." His ice-blue eyes slide to the dance floor. "Nice moves, by the way," he adds with a smirk.

Clearly, he's referencing the kiss Haven and I shared or possibly all our grinding.

Haven laughs, and after a pause, the blond-haired man holds out his hand and says, "I'm Eric."

"No way," Haven exclaims, touching his outstretched hand.

Her eyes meet mine, and though we try like hell not to giggle, a few snickers do escape. I mean, come on. What's the chance of

"Eric" really being named Eric? I almost ask him if he ever gets mistaken for the actor who plays Eric Northman on the show, but the dark-haired man speaks first when he says, "What's so funny?"

His tone is devoid of humor, so I conclude it's probably best not to share.

Twisting in my seat till I'm facing him, I breezily reply, "Oh, nothing."

He smiles, his deep-set eyes crinkling at the corners. His smile softens his appearance, making him seem a whole lot friendlier than a few seconds ago. Still smiling, he says, "I'm Vincent, by the way."

"Nice to meet you," I reply.

After chatting for a few minutes, I warm up to Vincent. But maybe, like everything tonight, my soothed feelings are due to alcohol. Just as I'm thinking I should probably switch to water, a waitress comes around and Eric orders a round of shots for everyone.

"Patrón for the two of you?" He raises a blond eyebrow, directing his question to Haven.

*Huh, interesting.* For Eric to know what kind of shots we were taking earlier, he must have been watching us carefully. I can understand his noticing the kissing and the grinding on the dance floor—after all, he is a man—but this is a bit much.

*Has Vincent been just as observant?* I wonder. Apparently so, I conclude when he leans in close to me and asks, "Would you like a Corona Light to chase your shot?"

"Yeah, sure…" I trail off, uncertain anymore of what to think. Sure, I may be drunk, but, like at first, I have an unsettled feeling about these two men. Their ages, the way they are dressed…

They just don't fit. Why would they be hanging out in *this* college bar in *this* rural town? Clearly they are not from around here.

Emboldened by beer and tequila, I inquire, "So, since you two are quite obviously beyond college age, I sincerely doubt you attend Oakwood. Where are you from?"

Vincent glances over at Eric, like he's waiting for some sort of guidance.

"It's not that difficult of a question," my drunken ass adds.

I immediately regret my words when Eric shoots me a look that leaves me ice-cold. I shudder, and not in a good way. "New York," he replies, his tone flat.

Haven, not noticing anything is amiss, says excitedly, "Like, the city?"

Eric places his hand possessively and firmly on my friend's black fishnet-covered knee. He gives me a smug smile and replies, "Yes, like the city."

Haven takes no notice of his hand or the fact that his fingers are currently intertwining in the net pattern.

"My brother lives in Manhattan," she tells Eric. "I'll be staying at his place this summer. Maybe we could meet up sometime after I get settled in."

*Uh-oh, she's smitten already.*

"Yes, I think that could be arranged," Eric replies as he smiles wolfishly at Haven.

I shudder again, and Vincent, taking notice, places a hand on my shoulder. "Are you okay, Essa?"

I wave him off. "Yes, yes, I'm fine."

Eric and Vincent buy another round of shots, plus more drinks, and before long, I'm beyond hammered. When we finally stumble out of the bar—well, Haven and I stumble; our male companions appear more or less fine—Vincent asks how we plan to get home.

"You're too drunk to drive," he states firmly.

"Um, we only live a few blocks away," I shoot back, slurring my words. Spinning in place, I point in what I think may be the direction of our street. "We walked from our apartment. Wherever that is," I mumble, unfocused.

"I don't want to walk all the way back," Haven protests, pouting. "Maybe these nice men can drive us home." Smiling up at the very tall Eric, she adds softly, "That'd be okay, right?"

"Absolutely," Eric says, satisfied, like this is all going according to some plan.

What plan, though? Seducing Haven? Is the only thing on Eric's mind the seduction of a young woman? I don't know. But I do know there's something about him that bugs me. Too bad I'm too inebriated to figure out why that is.

Vincent drapes his arm around my shoulder, ripping me from my wayward thoughts.

Glancing forward, I see Haven and Eric are already several feet in front of us. "Our car's over there," Vincent says as he guides my steps.

I'm a bit unsteady, but he helps me stay upright. "I didn't mean to get so drunk," I whisper.

"It's okay," he replies. "You'll be fine."

He tightens his arm around my shoulder, and I get a waft of men's cologne...and just man. I can't deny that I feel a little turned on. With my inhibitions lowered, I slide my hand under the back edge of Vincent's suit jacket and grasp onto his dress shirt for more leverage.

I suppose that's a green light for him. When we get into the backseat of their car—some supernice luxury sedan—Vincent wastes no time in pulling me onto his lap. He's strong. I don't resist. I do the exact opposite, in fact. I'm the right amount of drunk and lonely that I maneuver until our faces are mere inches away. This close, if I squint and create more blurriness than what I'm currently experiencing, I can pretend Vincent is Farren.

"You look a little bit like someone I know," I say.

"And who would that be?" Vincent's lips trail along my jaw and up to my ear. "A boyfriend?" he whispers lightly.

*I wish.* "Um, no, just a guy." *A guy I wish you were right now.*

I shake my head slightly to clear my crazy thoughts. The movement doesn't deter Vincent. His lips continue their assault, traveling down my neck and over my collarbone.

"I don't really *know* know the guy you kind of look like," I continue, babbling now.

Vincent's hands move down to my ass and then up under the back of my shirt.

"It doesn't matter, anyway," I gasp, succumbing to the lusty feelings this stranger is awakening. "He's not here."

"No, he's not," Vincent says softly as his lips brush over mine. "But I am here."

"Yes, yes, you are…"

I then proceed to make out with a man whose last name I don't even bother to ask for. When I venture a quick glance to the front seat, I see Eric is driving. Haven is sprawled over his shoulder, her hand moving rhythmically in his lap. She's clearly jacking him off. His eyes are half-closed, and he's inching down the street where our place is located at a snail's pace. Thankfully, we reach the little frame house we live in before he finishes.

Eric nudges Haven's hand away, zips up his pants, and opens

the door. But he doesn't get out right away. He asks Haven, his voice even, "Do you rent the whole house?"

*What an odd question.*

Haven appears to be as confused as I am. "Um, no, we live on the second floor," she answers,

"Anyone live on the first floor?" Eric wants to know.

"No," Haven says. "The student who lives there during the school year moved out, like, days ago."

This seems to satisfy Eric. "Okay," he says, nodding. He then gets out of the car, as does Haven.

When Vincent and I stay put, Eric pokes his head back in and asks, "Coming?"

Drunk as I am, I find Eric's question hilarious. "No, but it sure looked like you were about to on the way here," I retort.

I'm still perched on Vincent's lap, and I feel his chest rumble. He's trying not to laugh. Okay, maybe this guy I've spent the past ten minutes sucking face with is not so bad. Maybe I should throw caution to the wind and sleep with him.

Those are my intentions, but by the time Vincent and I make it to my bedroom, everything is spinning.

"I don't feel so good," I mutter as I fall back onto the bed.

Vincent fumbles with the straps on my sandals and gently slips them off my feet. I try to sit up to remove my lacy top, but I fall backward. Vincent props me up and tugs the black material over my head, leaving me in just a tank and skinny jeans.

"Are we going to have sex?" I bluntly ask.

Vincent chuckles. "I don't think so, Essa." He looks around the room. "Do you have a bucket? You don't look so good."

I slur, "Yeah, there's a bucket in the bathroom."

Our apartment is small enough that I feel confident he'll have no trouble finding the bathroom. It's located right between my bedroom and Haven's bedroom.

"I'll be right back," he tells me when he's near the door.

My head is pounding, so I ask him to grab some aspirin, too. "Sure thing," he replies.

I assume Haven is in bed with Eric. He's probably pounding all thoughts of Professor Walsh out of her body by now. But, oddly enough, I swear I hear Vincent talking to Eric outside my bedroom door. I can't hear what they're saying—they're speaking too low— but it does lead me to consider Haven may be as fucked up as me. Maybe she needs a bucket, as well.

I fade in and out of consciousness. When Vincent returns, he has to prop me up so I can swallow the pill he gives me. It tastes bitter, much more so than aspirin, but I have no chance to question why.

A minute later, I lose consciousness.

# CHAPTER THREE

I WAKE up with a blinding headache. "Oh, God," I mumble, wincing from the pain.

I assume it is morning, but when I roll toward the alarm clock on the table next to my bed, big red LED numbers inform me it's two in the afternoon.

"Shit."

I try to sit up, but everything around me wavers and tilts, forcing me to lie back down.

"Ugh," I mutter as the events of the evening rush back to me. "Vincent?"

I glance around my room. Where is he?

*Well, he's not in here*, I conclude. I can't imagine he stayed long after I passed out. Just to be sure, I take a quick assessment of myself and my surroundings. The bed I'm lying on top of appears to have barely been slept in. I must have hardly moved from the position I passed out in. I rise up slightly. There's an indentation from one body only, mine. It's a relief to know I was not violated in any way last night. Because, let's face it, it was pretty stupid bringing home two strange men. Further indication Vincent did not touch me in any inappropriate way is that I still have the same clothes on.

And, Jesus, do they ever reek. The smell of dried sweat from dancing, as well as grinding in the car on top of Vincent, pushes my uneasy stomach a bit too far. I lean over the edge of the bed and promptly throw up in the bucket Vincent left there for me.

When my stomach settles somewhat, I flop back on the bed, wiping my mouth with the back of my hand. I'm so glad Vincent isn't here. It would be embarrassing to have him see me like this.

Then again…I suddenly realize he could very well be around. What if he had to wait for Eric? *Crap*. An image of him out in the living room, listening to me yakking and having a good laugh over how lame his seemingly "sure thing" turned out to be, fills my mind.

Then I remember the pill Vincent gave to me before everything went black. Was it really just an aspirin? The white tablet tasted different. And it sure made me sleep for a long time. The few other times I drank too much, I experienced a restless sleep, with lots of waking and tossing. Last night I was dead to the world.

Slowly, I force myself to stand. When I'm more or less upright, I waver left, then right. I'm still far from sober. Consequently, it takes me longer than usual to reach the door. When I do, I have to lean my forehead against the cool wood for a few seconds. It helps to soothe my pounding head.

"I'm never drinking again," I vow.

Finally, I open the door and take a tentative step out into the living room. Thankfully, it's empty. There's no laughing Vincent, like I feared.

Our apartment consists of a modest living room, a galley kitchen you can see from the living room, a tiny bathroom, my room, and Haven's room. Glancing around, and noting that the kitchen is empty, I think, *three rooms clear, two to go.*

On unsteady feet, I make my way over to the bathroom that is nestled between my room and Haven's.

I swing open the door.

"Empty," I whisper as I breathe out a sigh of relief.

It's then that I realize I have to pee like crazy. After I relieve my bladder, I wash my face and hands, and then linger in front of the sink. The aspirin is kept in the medicine cabinet, the one right in front of me. Last time I checked, there were only four pills left in the bottle. I'm sure of this because I clearly recall telling Haven that we needed to restock.

Tentatively, I rest one hand on the edge of the sink. Using my other hand, I open the medicine cabinet.

There's the aspirin bottle, in its usual spot. And there are four round white pills settled in the base. Four, not three.

*Oh, no.*

Now, I panic. Hell with queasiness and an aching head. I race out of the bathroom like the place is on fire and skid to a stop in front of Haven's closed door. Tapping out a slew of frantic knocks, I shout, "Haven, are you awake? Is it okay if I come in?"

Silence.

"Hav, I'm coming in," I announce in a loud voice.

I'm hoping not to walk in on her and Eric in some compromising position. But I need not worry. When I push open the door, there is no sign of Eric. In fact, the bed appears as if no one has slept in it, let alone engaged in *other* things. A quick survey of the room—neat and tidy, as always—leads me to surmise everything is in place. But the one thing glaring me in the face is that there is no Haven.

I know then that my best friend has been taken.

A N hour later, I am arguing with a burly cop named Officer Knowles.

He rubs his beefy hand over his bald head, while he listens to me say, "Haven did *not* just leave. I know my best friend, and she'd never take off without telling me. Plus, I've called her cell, like, a hundred times, and it keeps going straight to voice mail. She wouldn't turn off her phone like that. And, again, she wouldn't pack up and leave the apartment without telling me."

I'm adamant, but unfortunately, all signs do seem to indicate Haven has done exactly that. Not only is her car gone, but when Officer Knowles's partner returns to the living room after searching the apartment, he reports that nothing is amiss.

"There are certainly no indications Haven Shaw was abducted," he states firmly, his gaze sliding to me pointedly.

"What did you find?" Burly Knowles inquires.

"Absolutely no sign of any struggle," the partner says. "In fact, there's nothing to indicate anyone was ever in her bedroom with her. Everything appears to be in perfect order." He pauses then turns to speak solely to me. "A few missing clothes, Miss Brant, doesn't mean your roommate was abducted."

His reference to the clothes I told him were missing doesn't sway me. "It's more than just a few," I firmly state. "A *lot* of Haven's clothes are gone, a bunch of her shoes, too. And her suitcase, the big one that holds a lot, isn't in her closet. Half the makeup that was on her vanity is no longer there. Plus, her cell phone and purse are gone."

I suspect that if Eric and Vincent abducted my friend—and I'm sure they did—they took the time to make it look like she left of her own volition. But I don't have a chance to add that theory to the mix, as Officer Knowles, before I can speak, says gently, "I'm sorry your friend took off without telling you where she was heading. But these things happen all the time. The semester is over, finals are completed, people are anxious to take off, and—"

"Haven wouldn't just leave in the middle of the night," I interrupt, my voice but a whisper.

*They don't believe me,* I think. *And nothing is going to change their minds.*

Officer Knowles clears his throat. "Bottom line, Miss Brant, is that there's absolutely no sign of foul play. I'm afraid there's nothing more we can do."

*They're going to leave. They're going to walk out that door, and you'll never find Haven.*

"What about the men we brought home last night?" I blurt out. "Maybe you should talk to them. One of them could have driven Haven's car. Maybe that's why it's missing. The other guy probably took her in the car they were driving. I gave you the description of the vehicle, right?"

"Yes," Officer Knowles replies, sighing. He's sounding put out now.

Still, I continue. "Just because her clothes and belongings were packed doesn't mean *she* packed them. Even if she did, maybe she was forced to. Like, at gunpoint."

There, I got that theory out. But all the officers do is roll their eyes.

I hurriedly add, "What about the aspirin the one named Vincent gave me? I think it could have been something else. I mean, I passed out immediately. And then I slept, like, forever."

Officer Knowles shakes his head. "Miss, you told us all of this. And need I remind you that you also said you and your friend were out drinking last night. Perhaps that's why you passed out and slept in so late." He eyes me warily, sighs, and then concedes, "But we can talk to these two men, if it will make you feel better. Who knows…maybe your friend mentioned to one of these guys where she was going."

Officer Knowles removes from his shirt pocket the small flip tablet and pen he used to take notes earlier. "What are the names of these two fellows?" he asks, huffing.

"Eric and Vincent," I say. I begin to provide a quick description of each, but realize there was nothing distinguishing about either one of them. Sure, they were hot, and Eric did look like *True Blood*'s Eric. But still, when all is said and done my descriptions sound very general.

Officer Knowles dutifully jots down the info, and then he prompts, "Last names?"

"Uh…" I bite my lip, scrunch up my face.

"Miss Brant?"

"I don't know their last names," I admit.

He shakes his head and flips his tablet closed. "You said they were from out of town, though. Is that right?"

"Yes," I reply. "They said they were from New York City."

"Do you happen to know where in Oakwood they're staying?"

"They never said."

"Maybe nowhere," Knowles's partner muses.

"What do you mean?" asks Officer Knowles.

"They could have just driven in and driven back."

"Hmm," says Knowles. "That is a possibility. New York City is not that far away. They could have driven in yesterday and drove back last night."

"Yeah, with Haven," I cry out.

Both men shake their heads, and then Officer Knowles says, "I'm sorry, but there's no proof of anything like that happening. No proof at all."

"I just have a feeling," I whisper.

To which he replies, "We operate on evidence, Miss Brant, not feelings."

As the weekend progresses, I discover, to my chagrin, I am on my own in my search for Haven. I call a few of our mutual friends, but no one has heard anything from Haven. Everyone sounds rushed, and why wouldn't they be? They're all packing up and leaving for the summer. It doesn't help that Haven's quirkiness and spontaneity are common knowledge. No one sounds too concerned to hear she's missing. They believe as the police do: Haven Shaw just up and took off.

*No way.*

I consider contacting Haven's aunt, but I know in my heart that she doesn't care what happens to Haven, not really. She'd probably just feel bothered if I were to call. It's sad, but true.

I discard that plan immediately, and instead I try to contact Farren. Only problem is that the number Haven gave to me—for emergencies—is no longer in service.

"What next?" I ask myself on Monday morning.

Forty-eight hours have passed since Haven went missing. I've always heard the more time that passes the less chance there is of finding the person who's missing.

Well, that is not an option.

With the town of Oakwood more or less empty, I climb into my little rust bucket of a car and embark on my own investigation. In the interest of self-protection, in case Eric and Vincent decide to return to take me too, my first stop is at a convenience store. There, I buy a container of pepper spray to put on my key chain. I'd rather be safe than sorry.

Next stop is Señor Frog's. Sadly, I have no luck in finding any answers there. None of the employees who were working Friday night recall the two strange men. They don't even remember me and Haven.

"Thanks, anyway," I say dejectedly as I leave.

Discouraged, but determined, I drive over to the part of town where all the hotels and motels are located. I'm hoping to find out if Eric and Vincent stayed in any of them. But, again, no one knows anything. Maybe the two men did just drive in on Friday. But why would they bother to come to a place like Oakwood? Were they looking to hook up with two college girls? Recalling their stares, I question whether they specifically planned to meet us. Or, more specifically, was their plan to meet Haven?

I shudder.

Why in the world would Haven Shaw be a target?

On my way back to the apartment, I consider that the men may have been lying about many things. Perhaps they weren't even from New York. Why, though, would Eric say such a thing if it wasn't true? Looking back at our interaction with the men

Friday night I find it flat-out weird. Like how New York was so easily injected into the conversation. It's like the men knew all along that by saying they were from New York City it would appeal to Haven. Was Eric's intent to make her trust them by creating a bond with her? Eric certainly had her attention, and the mention of New York seemed to seal the deal.

"Oh, Haven, where are you?" I whisper as I park in front of our apartment.

*Where would Eric and Vincent take Haven? And why would they abduct her in the first place?* These are my thoughts as I lock up my car, and then slowly climb the stairs leading to the second floor. When I reach the door to our apartment, I take out my key and slide it into the lock.

As soon as I step inside, I know something is off. I sense I am not alone in the apartment. Slowly, I flip the safety switch on my newly acquired pepper spray. Attaching it to my key chain directly after buying it was a damn smart move.

But I have no time for self-congratulations, as I hear faint noises coming from Haven's bedroom. It sounds as if drawers are being opened and closed. Quietly, I tiptoe over to the door to her room. For a minute, I feel elation. Maybe Haven has returned. Maybe she's the person opening and closing the drawers. I want so badly for that to be true that I start to call out her name. But then a sigh emanates from the room, a clearly male sigh.

My mouth snaps shut. Hope turns to fear.

My hearts starts to pound as I debate whether to run or confront whoever has broken into the apartment. Every instinct urges me to take off, get the hell out of the apartment. But if I run, I will probably never find out who was on the other side of the door. On the other hand, if I stay, I am potentially placing myself in harm's way. What if Eric or Vincent has returned? Worse yet, what if both men are behind the door? Even if that's the case, this may be my only chance to find out where my friend is.

So I stay.

I step closer to the door and find it's not completely closed. It's slightly ajar, but the crack is far too narrow for me to peek in and see who's on the other side. *Shit.*

Uncertain, I stand completely still and just listen.

There's more movement in the room, someone walking around. I conclude from the single set of steps that there's only one man in the room. Since I've not yet been discovered, it seems the element of surprise is on my side. Maybe I can take this guy out with my new weapon.

Emboldened, I push the door open slowly. Very, very slowly. At the same time, I raise the can of pepper spray to what I assume will be eye level for this breaking-in mofo. When there's enough space for me to slip through, I quickly and quietly duck into the room.

Instantly, a hand, a very strong hand, covers my raised one, the one holding the spray canister. Uh-oh, I'm screwed.

*Ouch!* One sharp squeeze and I drop my only weapon.

The intruder is standing behind me. How did he so quickly get from one end of the room to the other? I swear his steps sounded not anywhere near the door.

I twist my hand from the man's grasp and start to scream, "Help—" But the man quickly covers my mouth.

From behind me, he leans down and whispers in my ear, "Settle down, Essalin."

*Huh?* This man—who happens to smell amazingly good— knows me?

Slowly, my nice-smelling assailant removes his hand from my mouth. I spin around to face him. And when I recognize the face—a face far more gorgeous than in pictures—I squeak out, "Farren?"

*Holy crap*!

I quickly forget about being afraid.

Oh, my heart still pounds. But this pounding is caused from something entirely different than fear. Haven's photos and videos did *not* do her stunning brother justice. In person, Farren Shaw is beyond stunning. He's male perfection. From his tall, commanding stature to the way his presence fills the room, he makes the space we're sharing feel small, very small. It's suddenly just me and him, man and woman. I've never felt full-on lust like this before. I mean, I guess that's what I'm feeling. All I know is that I'm breathless and bothered in a way that urges me to thrust out my chest, open my mouth, and arch my back. My body tells me to make myself available to this man.

Of course, I'm not crazy. My brain cuts in and keeps me from doing any of those nutty things. Still, I can't fully escape my body's visceral, raw, and primal reactions to Farren Shaw. Damn, the man personifies sex. No wonder I fantasized about him. But fantasies are nothing compared to the reality before me. My gaze shamelessly travels from his strong, jean-clad legs up to his wide shoulders then down his veiny, muscular arms. Damn, his biceps are bulging, straining at the short sleeves of the snug black T-shirt he's wearing. Farren is all man, toned and hard. And now, before me, his carnal beauty slays me at his feet. I want more. I wish I could have more. My brain finally gets on board with my body and I imagine what it would feel like to writhe beneath his hard body, begging him to—

"Essalin?"

His smooth words, accompanied with a cock of the head and a knowing smirk, rein in my lust-fueled imaginings.

"Huh?" I so eloquently respond. Glancing up at his face, I find myself staring into the most beautiful green eyes I've ever seen. I knew they were stunning, but *oh my*.

Farren clears his throat, and I quickly avert my gaze.

"I was just saying…" he begins.

Was he talking? Huh, I missed that.

"I'm sorry for letting myself in to the apartment," he continues. "I should have waited for you to return, but I had no idea how long you'd be gone. In any case, I didn't mean to frighten you."

My ire goes up a little. That's right—Farren broke into the apartment. That's what I tell myself, but, truthfully, I'm embarrassed he has me so flustered. To hide my carnal weakness, I lash out at the source.

"You didn't just *let* yourself in," I say accusingly. "You *broke* in."

Farren smiles like he's up for this game. He's fully aware I was checking him out two minutes ago. And he surely knows how incredibly handsome he is. He's blessed, and he knows it. He probably thinks he'll win this battle, and he may. He'll most likely trounce my anger with his powers of seduction.

But I raise my chin defiantly. *Let the games begin*, my expression dares.

Smoothly, he counters, "Technically, I did not break in." Holding up a key, he adds, all smugly, "Haven sent me a key to this apartment the day you two moved in."

"Oh."

I'm fumbling already. Farren knows he has me.

With a smile surely designed to melt panties, he says silkily, "If you had been home, Essalin, I certainly would have knocked first."

My panties *do* just about melt, damn him. To save face, I snap, "Quit calling me Essalin. Everyone just calls me Essa."

Farren replies. "Well, I'm not everyone, now am I, *Essalin*."

*You sure as hell aren't*, I think. But I don't dare let him know how much he's gotten to me. The man is far too cocky already.

Still, I like him. He has a fresh and fun air about him. I have to admit I'm enjoying the banter we're engaging in. It's an escape from everything that has happened this weekend.

But reality crashes down on me when Farren says softly, "What happened to my sister, Essalin?"

"You know she's missing?" I whisper.

"Yes, I know."

"Who told you?"

He scrubs a hand down his face. "It doesn't matter how I found out. What matters is that I need to find her. And find her quickly."

I can't really argue with that logic. Plus, I'm smart enough to recognize that Farren is my only ally. He believes Haven is missing, just like I do. And, really, that is all that matters. I feel confident this clearly alpha-male man will stop at nothing to find his sister. He has the resources—money, special-ops background. Not to mention, skills obtained in whatever shady business he's been involved in lately. Yeah, Farren Shaw is my best bet for finding Haven.

Taking a deep breath, I dispense with any further smart-ass behavior. Instead, I share with him the details of my last night with Haven. I tell Farren how after finals had ended we went out on the town to celebrate. I explain that we got really drunk and met two men who weren't from around here. Farren raises his hand when I rush through that last part.

"Whoa, wait," he says. "Back up a little. Give me a description of the man who was with my sister. Leave out nothing. No detail is insignificant, Essalin."

I blow out a breath. "Okay…"

I proceed to tell Farren everything. I even share with him how we thought businessman Eric looked like *True Blood* Eric. That particular detail doesn't seem to amuse Farren in any way, shape, or form.

"Guess you had to be there," I mumble.

"What about the man you brought home?" Farren wants to know. He crosses his arms across his chest, making his arms look huge. "What did he look like?"

I blush, not only because Farren looks hot as hell with his biceps bunched up and bulging, but also due to how very much I don't want to tell him *why* I was attracted to Vincent.

But when he prompts, "Essalin," I know I have no choice but to answer his question.

In a voice a hair above a whisper, and with eyes downcast, I say, "Um, he looked a little bit like you."

I'm rewarded with a knowing smirk when I glance back up at him. "And you slept with this man who looked like me?" he says.

*Cocky, smug, arrogant man.* There are so many words at my lips, but I stick with one. "No."

Farren shoots me a look of disbelief, and I snap, "It's really none of your business what went down."

"Nothing is insignificant," he reminds me, one brow raised.

I lower my gaze and murmur, "Okay, okay. Truthfully, I

probably would have slept with him. But I didn't, because I, uh, passed out."

I expect a smart retort, but when I glance up, instead of laughing or smirking, Farren is eyeing me concernedly. "What do you mean you passed out?"

I tell him about the "aspirin" Vincent gave to me and how there were still four in the bottle when I checked the next day. "Do you think I was drugged?" I ask.

Farren replies somberly, "Most likely."

I swallow hard. "Who are these people, Farren? Do you have any idea? I mean, why would they abduct Haven?"

I sense Farren knows more than he's letting on, especially when his response to my questioning is a one-shoulder shrug.

When my story is complete, Farren turns away. He stands at Haven's dresser for several minutes and then resumes searching through the drawers like I'm not even there.

I step back to the doorway and lean on the frame. "So, what happens next?" I inquire.

Farren glances over his shoulder, but then continues searching as he says, "I'm going on the road as soon as I'm done here. Whoever took my sister, they've been using her credit card, making it look like she's stopping for gas, staying at motels. Whoever has her is heading west."

I know Farren pays Haven's bills, so it's no surprise he has this info.

"Where was the card last used?" I ask.

"Indiana," he replies, "near Indianapolis."

"That's a few hundred miles away," I remark. "We should probably get started soon."

Farren turns slowly, until he's fully facing me. He raises an eyebrow. "We, Essalin?"

"That's right," I state. "I want to go with you."

Said out loud, I realize my statement is true. In fact, I not only want to go with Farren, I *have* to go. To hell with my parents' wishes; fuck summer school. I'll deal with the fallout later. In the meantime, I have enough money in the bank to pay my own way. It's not a lot, but it's enough to pitch in for gas, eat on the road, and rent my own hotel room when we stop. In my heart, I know this is what I'm meant to do. Finding my best friend is my destiny. Fate has set me on this path. An inevitable detour led me here, to this turning point, and this is the juncture where I choose how to respond.

With newfound conviction, I say, "I want to help, Farren. I can't just sit around here and do nothing. I love Haven, too. She's not just my roommate; she's my best friend."

Hearing my voice crack, Farren's expression softens. His lips press together, forming a grim line, and I'm led to believe he's actually considering it.

Helpfully, I offer, "I'll be safer with you than if I stay here. What if Eric and Vincent return? They might, you know. After all, I have seen their faces."

I'm just trying to get Farren to agree to let me accompany him. But the serious look he shoots my way tells me that all I've said is a distinct possibility. "Shit," I mutter.

"You can come with me under a few conditions," he says at last.

"Okay, I'll agree to anything."

That remark causes him to raise an eyebrow, but he refrains from any smartass retorts. He just lays down the parameters. "First, we'll be taking my car. Your car stays here."

I nod, agreeing. "That's fine."

He continues. "Second, we do this my way. There are things only I know"—*aha, Farren does know more than he's saying*—"and if I tell you to do something or not do something, believe me, it will be for a damn good reason."

With a raised eyebrow of my own, I ask, "Is that all?"

"For now," he responds.

"I can live by those rules," I declare. And then I add, "What should I do now?"

Farren smiles a smile that, unbeknownst to him, melts not just my panties, but me into a thousand pieces.

"Pack some things," he says. "We need to leave as soon as possible."

Nodding, I conclude that despite the dire circumstances, I am in for one hell of a wild ride with Mr. Farren Shaw.

# CHAPTER FOUR

"TIME is of the essence, Essalin. The abductors have more than a two-day lead on us."

Farren's words from before I left him in Haven's room so he could continue to search for clues resonate in my head. I'm in my own room now, tossing an assortment of summer clothes into an open suitcase I dragged from my closet to the bedroom floor.

I work fast, especially when I hear Farren leaving the apartment. Minutes later, I am making my way down the inside stairs that lead to the front door on the first floor. Farren turns from his position at the base of the stairs. His hand remains on the doorknob, but he watches me amusedly while I bounce my heavy, overloaded suitcase down each individual step.

With a suppressed grin, he eventually lets go of the doorknob and steps onto the lowest step. "Here, let me help you with that," he says, reaching out.

His stretch is long, reaching me easily even though I'm a few steps away. I gladly relinquish the heavy bag and follow Farren down to the door.

But when I linger, Farren asks, "What's wrong? Did you forget something?" He hoists up the suitcase and sarcastically adds, "Seems unlikely, considering the weight of this thing."

"Very funny," I retort. "And, no, I didn't forget anything. It's just that I was thinking about things I should do before we leave town. I don't have much money on me, but I do have a small savings at the bank—"

Farren clears his throat, interrupting me. Softly, he says, "You don't need to take money out of the bank. I'll cover all our expenses."

I start to protest, but he shushes me. "Don't argue with me, Essalin. Just because you're going to be safer on the road with me than if you stayed here alone doesn't mean the trip is without risk. This isn't some vacation. We could run into trouble. Real trouble..." He trails off, giving me no more.

I arch an eyebrow, hoping to prompt him to continue, but all I get in return is stony silence. Just like I suspected when we were upstairs in the apartment, I sense Farren knows more about what's really going on with this situation involving Haven than he's saying. But since I can't make him talk, I sigh and agree to let him pay for everything.

"But, if expenses get out of hand, I'm paying you back," I state resolutely.

"Whatever, Essalin," Farren replies, chuckling. "I think I can handle it."

True, Farren is loaded, but I refuse to take advantage.

With a trip to the bank deemed unnecessary, I start to walk

past him. But then his hand touches my arm lightly, sending a delicious rush of warmth through me. I falter and stop. He removes his hand, much to my chagrin, and steps back.

Though it was only the lightest of touches, I liked Farren's hand on me. Just like when he covered my mouth in Haven's bedroom, after he grabbed my hand and I dropped the pepper spray, his touch was gentle, yet firm. It held promise, promise of how I've always dreamed of being touched. Touched by a man, not a boy.

"There is one more thing I should mention," Farren says.

I cross my arms to appear nonchalant. No need for him to notice he's affecting me again without even trying. "What's that?" I casually inquire.

"If there's anyone you'd like to talk to before we leave, you should call them now."

"Why?"

"I can't allow you to take your cell phone on the road, so there will be no calls from here on out. In fact, you need to give your cell to me before we leave."

"W…what?" I sputter. "Why?"

Farren drags a hand through his neatly trimmed dark hair. Though it's short, the strands appear silky and soft, making me wonder what it would be like to run my fingers through the raven locks.

"Your phone can be tracked, Essalin," Farren says as explanation to my question.

And suddenly I can't take it anymore.

"I told you to call me Essa," I snap. The stress is wearing on me, clearly. I miss my friend, and I want answers. Not to mention I'm afraid of this unknown journey I'm about to embark on.

Damn. But what has me so edgy and lashing out is that I'm far too attracted to this man I'm supposed to be partnering with, *professionally* partnering with.

I start to apologize, but before I can, Farren bites out, "Okay, *Essa.*"

Guess he's not immune to the stress of the situation, either.

"I'll give up my phone," I concede, my voice apologetic. "But can I ask you something?"

Farren remains silent, but he's not saying no, so I forge on. "What aren't you telling me? Do you know Eric and Vincent? I just don't get why they would they do something so...so...sinister." My eyes implore his beautiful greens. "You know something, don't you? Personally, I think this whole thing has something to do with you." He raises a brow, and I add, "I'm telling you, Farren, I thought about it all weekend, and I can't come up with one single reason why my best friend would be abducted."

Coolly holding my stare, he asks in a low voice, "And how, Essa, would her abduction be tied to me?"

"I don't know," I admit.

And then he touches me again, differently than before. His fingers graze my jaw and linger on my cheek. Holy hell, this is seduction. His hand on my arm was nothing, just a prelude. I close my eyes and allow myself to enjoy how a man who obviously knows how to touch a woman can make me feel. I don't care if Farren is just doing this to placate me.

His seduction works—soft touches, softer words. When he whispers, "Just let it go, Essalin," I nod into his hand.

"I'll let it go," I murmur.

"No more questions," he says.

I nod again. "No more questions." *Oh, please keep touching me.*

But he lowers his hand from my face, and like a spell that's been broken, I open my eyes. After a long silence on both our parts, most of which, for me, is spent recovering, Farren says, "So, what about those calls? Do you have any you'd like to make?"

"Um, yeah"—I sigh—"I should call my parents."

Farren nods an assent, but warns, "Don't mention anything about Haven being gone."

I frown. "I wasn't planning to."

"And don't tell your parents how far away you may be traveling."

My eyes meet his. "You don't think we'll find Haven in Indianapolis, do you?"

Pain flashes in eyes as vibrant and green as emeralds, and I have my answer—Indianapolis is just a starting point, a place to search for clues.

I take out my phone and sit on the bottom step. Farren goes outside to give me some privacy, and I then call my parents.

Regardless of his warning, I never intended to disclose all that has happened. But, because I am an adult—like Haven reminded me during our last night spent together—I do finally take a stand.

When I inform my mom I won't be staying on campus this summer, which means no summer classes, she flips. "What the hell, Essa? Your father and I already told you no to New York City."

"I'm not going to New York," I calmly reply. It's true.

Sounding confused, Mom says, "Where do you plan on spending the summer then, if not at school?"

*Like there are no other options*, I think to myself with a roll of my eyes.

My silence results in my mother continuing. "Don't even think about coming home for the summer."

*I wouldn't.*

"Your father and I are not going to put up with you lazing around the house."

*As if.*

"Not when you could be doing something much more productive."

*Productive?* Wonder if searching for my missing best friend qualifies as productive? As far as I'm concerned, it's sure as hell a lot more meaningful than taking classes I don't even need. Bottom line, Haven is in danger and rescuing her trumps everything, including my parents' priorities.

"I'll be helping out a friend this summer," I tell my mother. Another truth told.

She doesn't ask for elaboration. All I get is a sigh and this: "Do what you want, Essa. But know that there will be repercussions come fall."

The rent is paid up on the apartment until September, but I suspect said repercussions will include a move back to the dorms for me, just like I told Haven.

"Whatever," I say, sighing. And then I add, "I have to go." One final truth uttered.

I do have to go. I so very much do.


TALKING with my mom leaves me feeling kind of down, so I don't have much to say as Farren and I walk to where he parked his car a few blocks away. I spend the time trying to distract myself by imagining what kind of fancy car he may have brought to Oakwood. Haven is always going on and on about how Farren loves expensive sports cars. He supposedly owns more than a few.

When Farren stops next to a white, boring midsized sedan, I am sorely disappointed. He laughs when he catches me frowning. "Expecting something different?" he asks. He turns away and pops open the trunk.

"Yeah," I admit, hanging back. "I kind of was."

His muscular body blocks my view of whatever he's messing with in the trunk's interior, but I'm cool with that. God, his ass looks amazing in blue jeans. I prefer that view to whatever is in the trunk.

"Like what?" he asks, back still turned, and oblivious to my ogling.

"Um, I don't know"—I clear my throat and try to focus— "maybe something a little sportier."

"Sportier?"

"Yeah, you know, like a Ferrari or something."

Farren coughs out an amused laugh as he places my suitcase in the trunk. With ease, I take note as I watch his rather impressive arms flex.

He slams the trunk shut and turns back to me. "This is just a rental," he explains, gesturing to the car. "We'll be changing out vehicles every few hundred miles." He starts toward the driver's door and tosses out over his shoulder, "But, hey, I'll work on getting us that Ferrari."

I assume he's joking and roll my eyes. But, damn, I like his witty retorts.

Yeah, you could say Farren is surpassing everything I ever

dreamed he'd be. Even when he's kind of a cocky smartass—which is often—I like him. In fact, I like that he's not a pushover or some jerky college boy. I like that his face is stunning to look at, and I like that he has a body to drool over. I like his confidence; I like his style. And, truth is, I like that he's a little dangerous… and a whole lot mysterious.

I just wish the circumstances that have brought us together could be different.

# CHAPTER FIVE

MY arm is out the window, my hand swishing through the air. It may not be a sports car, but, damn, I'm making the most of the miles Farren and I are covering in the boring white sedan. We've been on the road for a few hours and most recently passed a sign indicating we've crossed in to the state of Ohio.

"Ooh"—I point to a lush, green field dotted with cattle—"check out those cows. Those two by the big oak tree over there are totally doing it."

Farren hunches down to squint through the windshield to the spot I'm indicating. "Yep," he agrees, "they sure are."

And then, we both burst out laughing at the inanity of it all.

"Get a room," I yell out the window.

Yeah, it's stupid and silly, but I'm having fun. So far, I like traveling with Farren. He's surprisingly easy to be around. Or maybe that's just how he is with me. We seem to just kind of click. We haven't said a whole lot, but that's fine. Farren's been busy driving, and I've been enjoying the sunshine and fresh air coming in through the lowered windows. My arm has been out the passenger-side window more often than not. I now pull it back in and glance down at my black shorts and hot-pink tank top layered over a black bra. I hold my arms out in front of me, side-by-side. My right arm is clearly tanner than my left.

Just for the heck of it, and in the interest of an even tan, I ask Farren, "Do I get to drive at some point?"

Farren shrugs his wide shoulders. "I'll think about it," he replies.

His tone is light and teasing, so I mumble "smartass," and then take a playful swat at his hand on the steering wheel. He's way too fast, though, and I end up tapping the wheel and not him.

When he laughs, I playfully warn, "I'll get you next time."

He replies, "Good luck with that."

I have a feeling he's right. His reflexes are fast, far quicker than mine.

A few minutes later, we begin to pass a long line of trucks. The road noise becomes unbearable with the windows down so I hit the control to raise them. Without taking his eyes off the road, Farren turns on the air conditioning. I smile over at him, and when he feels my gaze on him he glances my way and smiles back. It's too hot in the car when the windows are up, so we've devised this synchronized routine—alternating between fresh air and AC, me on window duty, and Farren in charge of interior climate control.

"We have a good system," I remark, just to see what Farren will say.

He doesn't look over at me again, but his lips curve up into a grin, and then he replies, "We do."

A few minutes later, I pull my left knee up, place my foot flat on the seat, and rest my cheek against my knee cap. This position affords me a comfortable, resting view of all the farmland and countryside we're passing.

"You sure are enjoying yourself, Essa," Farren says.

I lift my head and turn to him. "I am enjoying myself." I then explain why. "It's because I've never been anywhere."

"Not even to Ohio?"

"No, this is the first time I've ever left the state of Pennsylvania."

"You're kidding me." Farren sounds surprised. And why wouldn't he be? I'm a twenty-two-year-old woman, not a child. I'm sure he figured I'd traveled at least a little bit before today.

But I haven't. This is a first.

I try to explain to Farren, "Yeah, my parents were never into traveling."

"No family vacations?" he asks.

"Nope." I sigh. "They were always too busy working, and when they had time off they preferred to stay home."

"What about you?" Farren asks. "You could always travel with friends, or by yourself even."

"I guess I've always been too afraid to go anywhere by myself," I admit. "And none of my friends have ever invited me to go anywhere with them." *Except for when Haven asked me to come to New York City this summer*, I think, but don't add.

"Well, you're traveling now," Farren says quietly.

"True. And I can totally count this as traveling with a friend, right?" I pause, and hurriedly add, "I don't mean to assume anything, Farren."

He looks over at me. "Of course I'm your friend, Essa."

I mark that point in time—this is the moment my friendship with Farren Shaw officially begins.

A little while later the subject of family arises when Farren asks, "Do you have any brothers or sisters?"

"No, it's just me."

I almost add that Haven is like a sister, but I'm hesitant to say something so presumptuous to her only sibling. I don't want to intrude on their relationship. Farren and Haven are exceptionally close, thanks to their rough childhood. I can't even imagine what it was like, having their father disappear forever. There one day and then gone the next. And then, a few years passed and they lost their mother in a car accident. How terrible. My parents are a pain, yes, but I do love them. Sure, they're tough on me, but that's just their way. I know they ultimately want the best for me. Unfortunately, they just don't always know what that is. Not that I'm all that sure either, but I'm trying to figure it out.

Suddenly, something up ahead catches my attention—a really odd building that's in the shape of a giant basket. And when I say giant, I mean huge. It dominates the flat surrounding countryside.

"Damn, I wish I had my phone," I say longingly as we pass the basket building. "That would have been a great pic."

Farren doesn't acknowledge my phone comment, but he does smile over at me.

"What?" I ask.

He shakes his head. "It's nothing."

"Oh, come on," I urge.

"Okay, okay." He laughs. "It's just your enthusiasm is reminding me that I need to try harder to savor the little things when I travel." He frowns, though he still manages to look gorgeous, even when he adds sourly, "Not that the places I go to are much worth remembering."

"Is it because those trips are for work?" I venture.

"Yeah," Farren mutters, "something like that."

I clear my throat and softly inquire, "Where all have you traveled to?"

"All over," he says. "You name it, I've probably been there."

"What about recently? Where have you gone?"

"Well," he says slowly. "I spent some time in South America last month. And before that I was in Thailand."

I twist in my seat, stretching out the seat belt so I can face Farren more directly. "Wow, I've always heard those places are beautiful."

Staring straight ahead, and in a low tone, he replies, "The parts of those countries I was in were far from pretty, Essalin."

*Hmm…*

I settle back in my seat. If I wasn't convinced before, I'm convinced now that whatever Farren's job is, it's shady. Hell, he's done nothing to dispel my earlier assertions that his sister's disappearance is somehow connected to his work. That let-it-go comment was far from reassuring.

Both of us grow quiet, and like the sudden mood in the car, things outside start to cloud up.

"Looks like rain up ahead," I observe.

"Yeah," Farren replies, sounding distracted. "It sure does."

Fat, squishy droplets begin to pelt the windshield, and then it starts to pour.

With the rain ominously pounding in the background, Farren asks, "So, the two men at the bar—Eric and Vincent—

how did they approach you and my sister?"

"Um, they didn't," I admit. "*We* went to where they were seated."

Farren's gaze slides sharply to me, his green eyes flashing. "What made you go to them? You both had to have realized they weren't students."

"Um, that was kind of the appeal." With heated cheeks, and a fair amount of cringing, I explain to Farren how his sister was urging me to "try out" an older man.

"And what would make her encourage you to do something like that?" he wants to know.

"Um, maybe because she's had experience with one," I offer.

Farren shakes his head and rolls his eyes. "Please tell me this wasn't something she pursued regularly."

"Well…" I scrunch up my face. I so don't want to have this discussion.

But when Farren says "Essa" in a chastising voice, I fess up. "Okay, okay. Haven likes older men. There, I said it. Are you happy now?"

He shakes his head. "Not particularly."

I hasten to add, "There is a reason, though."

"A reason for what?" he asks flatly.

"A reason for why she was so willing to approach Eric and Vincent Friday night at the bar."

"This, I can't wait to hear," Farren mumbles sarcastically.

Sighing, I try to explain, "It's because she was hurting. Her acting professor broke her heart recently. That night at the bar, she was hoping someone could fix it, help her forget about him."

Farren is silent, and I venture a peek over at him.

*Shit.* His posture is tense, and a muscle is twitching in his jaw.

"How old is this professor?" he asks, his tone inscrutable. "And what's his name?"

"Um…" I hesitate. I mean, I despise Professor Walsh, yes. But I don't wish to see him dead or anything. And the expression on Farren's handsome face—brutally handsome at this point—gives me pause about sharing what I know.

I assume, though, that Farren has other ways to find out what he wants to know, so I go ahead and spill. "His name is Professor Walsh. And he's about thirty-five."

Farren's only response is a quick nod, like he's storing the info for another day.

The next few miles are spent in silence, until Farren flips on the car stereo. He tunes in an indie rock station, and eventually— thank God—things begin to lighten up.

As time passes, we discover we like many of the same songs. When a Heather Nova song comes on, one that I love, I can't help but sing along. A few of the lines are provocative, and Farren chuckles and shakes his head as I belt them out.

When the song ends, he turns down the volume and asks, "What was the name of that song?"

"'Walk This World,'" I tell him.

I then realize how many of the lines could apply to me… and him…and him and me together. Next thing you know, I am blushing profusely. And I swear that man must have listened to every line and lyric—or else he knew the song already—since the smug look on his face tells me he knows exactly why I'm blushing.

Thankfully, though, Farren seems to sense I'm genuinely embarrassed and changes the subject.

"So, Essa," he begins, "why Oakwood College for you? Haven

told me she was lured by their stellar theater program, but you're a business major, right?"

"The business program at Oakwood is very well respected," I spout in a monotone voice. It's the same rote spiel I've uttered a hundred times before. I've learned it well from my parents.

Farren glances over. "Hmm, that didn't sound rehearsed at all."

I let out a humorless laugh. "I know, right? Let's just say a business career is my parents' dream, not mine."

Softly, Farren inquires, "What is your dream, Essa? What do *you* want to do?"

I stare out at rain that is lessening to a gentle shower. "Nobody ever asks me that," I say as gently as the falling rain, "so I don't really know for sure."

"You must have an idea," he says.

I take a breath. Should I dare to share my dream with Farren? Since I have nothing to lose, I go for it.

"If it were up to me," I say. "I'd choose a major geared to writing. I write for the school paper, and I contribute articles to a monthly business review." After a beat, I softly add, "And I really enjoy those things."

"I'm sure Oakwood has a journalism program," Farren replies matter-of-factly. "You can always switch majors."

Slumping down in my seat, I say, "No, I can't."

"Why not?"

"You wouldn't understand," I mutter.

"Try me."

Farren sounds sincere, so I tell him the truth. "I only have one year left for the business degree. It's too late to change."

"Hey," he says, his tone serious. "It's never too late to do anything, Essa. You can change majors, start over, do anything you want. You just have to be brave enough to take that first step."

Farren's words are passionate, and he makes me reconsider. I'm always doing what my parents want me to do. Always following their instructions on how things are going to go, never speaking up. If that continues, how will I ever find my true calling?

I'm silent, and Farren says, "Do you want to know what I learned after I survived my first day of active combat?"

I nod. "Yes."

With his eyes on the road ahead of us, he says, "If you're still breathing, you can change your life. You can always alter your direction, embark on a different route. You just have to be brave enough to do it." He glances over at me. "You decided to join me on this trip, right? That was pretty brave."

"I had to, Farren," I reply. "I had to for Haven."

But it's more than that. This is my first inevitable detour. Fate led me here. Maybe I need to let destiny have her chance, let her put me where I need to be. When I head back to school in the fall, I think I'll change my major. Then again, maybe I'll really shake things up and apply to a different school, maybe one that's out of state.

With these thoughts in mind, I say, "I think I may change things up, do some things differently."

"You should," Farren replies. "People set limitations on themselves all the time. Everyone makes excuses. Change is scary, I know. It's hard. But don't let anything—or anyone—keep you from your dreams."

Farren is so impassioned, and as we're leaving Ohio and entering Indiana, I can't think of anything but where my life is heading. I like this burgeoning change in my thinking. I already took a stand by coming on this trip. I didn't stay at Oakwood. I'm not enrolled in summer courses, and I'm not planning to be. In fact, I'm not going back to the way things were at all. I don't think I can.

I share my thoughts with Farren, telling him all of these facts.

He says softly, "Haven told me she invited you to New York this summer. Are you going to come up to the city with her once she's rescued and things are back to normal?"

I like Farren's confidence that Haven will definitely be rescued. And I like his softened tone when mentioning me and New York City. "I think so," I tell him.

"Good," he says, nodding once.

I stare straight ahead, smiling and feeling empowered. Way off in the distance, across acres of farmland, the sun is melting into the horizon. The sky looks as if someone took a brush and painted it with fiery reds, sharp oranges, and muted purples. The beauty before me has me wishing I could somehow capture this moment—this moment with Farren, this moment in my life. If I had my phone, I could take a picture of the beautiful sunset and have it to look back on and remind me of this talk, this day, these decisions—my decisions.

"I wish I had a camera," I mumble.

Farren throws me a contemplative glance and then returns to focusing on the road. A few seconds later, we're slowing down and merging into an exit lane. "Why are we stopping?" I ask.

"We need gas," Farren says. "And we haven't eaten for a while. We'll grab something while we're here."

My stomach rumbles at the mention of food. I'm reminded that the energy bar I picked up earlier when we stopped for a bathroom break has long been digested.

"Good plan," I say.

Minutes later we pull into a parking spot in a rest-stop lot. Farren and I go our separate ways when we reach the restrooms inside, but I rejoin him where he's in line for fast food a few minutes later.

"There aren't a lot of options here," he says as I nudge in next to him.

"That's fine," I reply. I peruse the menu board. "I'll think I'll go with the number-three combo."

"Burgers and fries it is," Farren says. "I was thinking the same thing."

I glance around and spot a small drugstore a few doors down from the burger joint. It gives me an idea.

"Maybe I should grab us two bottled pops instead of us buying drinks with our meals." I point toward the drugstore. "I'm sure they sell refrigerated pop in there. And this way we can save the bottles and refill them with water at our next stop."

"Great idea," Farren replies. "Plastic bottles will hold up better than paper cups." He reaches for his wallet to give me money, but I stop him.

"I think I can handle it," I say playfully, echoing the words he said to me when I told him I'd pay him back if expenses got out of hand.

He laughs and says, "Touché, Essa, touché."

We meet back up at the car ten minutes later. Well, actually I have to wait a few minutes for Farren. My stop at the drugstore was quick, so I made it out faster. It's a nice evening—we left the rain behind long ago—so when Farren walks up with the food, I suggest we eat at a picnic table in a nearby grassy spot.

Minutes later, in the middle of eating and enjoying our fast-food meals, I notice a small brown bag on the bench next to Farren. "What'd you buy?" I ask.

"A couple of things," he says. He pops a french fry in his mouth and pulls two prepackaged cell phones from the bag. Handing one to me, he says, "Burner phones. I bought one for each of us."

"Thanks," I murmur. I turn the very basic, bare-bones phone over in my hands. "I think."

"Only use it if there's an emergency," Farren continues. "Like"—his eyes hold mine when I look up—"if we were to get separated for some reason."

I shudder. We are only two states away from Pennsylvania, but already I am fully aware of how huge this country really is. I hate to admit it, but I'd be lost without Farren. Like, literally. He doesn't need GPS, and he barely looks at the maps I noticed on the backseat. In fact, when I asked about the GPS in the car, he told me he disabled it. Like with my cell phone, he doesn't want us being tracked.

So, yeah, if I were to get separated from Farren, even without the threat of danger, things would get pretty damn scary real fast. But to find myself on my own, with the possibility of encountering Eric—or Vincent, who drugged me—I'm certain I'd die on the spot from fear alone.

As I take the burner phone out of its packaging, I assure Farren, "I think I'll pretty much be staying by your side throughout this entire trip."

There's not an ounce of humor in his voice when he responds with, "That would be wise."

We resume eating our burgers and fries, and I find myself

assessing my travel partner. His tall height and muscular body make me feel secure. Plus, I'm well-aware he knows how to take care of not only himself, but me, as well. As long as I remain close to him, nothing bad will happen. Farren will protect me. Hell, he could probably protect ten of me if he had to.

I exhale a relieved sigh, content that—for now—I am in no danger.

"What else is in the bag?" I ask. I nod to the bag the phones were in. It's clear it's not empty.

"Oh," Farren replies, all nonchalant. "I bought you something else."

Whatever it is, it's making him smile. And a Farren Shaw smile is priceless. His green eyes soften. Wow, it warms me to see that whatever he has bought me, giving it to me is making him happy.

Invisible strings tug at my heart. I like Farren Shaw as a person and as a man. I like him beyond his great looks and his kick-ass bod. He really is becoming my friend.

But, boy, if my heartstrings were being tugged before, they pull with abandon when he hands me the gift he's bought for me.

"It's a disposable camera," I say, staring down at the plastic camera in awe. It's not the camera itself I'm all worked up about. It's the fact Farren was thoughtful enough to pick one up for me.

"It's not much, I know." He shrugs one shoulder, like he's not sure I like his thoughtful gift.

But he needn't worry. "I love it," I say, backing my words up with a huge grin.

The smile he gives me in return, frankly, blows me away, even more so than the other times. God, he is stunning.

"I figured you might want to take some pictures of all the

scenery you've been enjoying so much. You said when we saw the sunset earlier this evening that you wished you had a camera. And since you don't have your phone…" He trails off.

I sense that for all Farren's confidence and swagger, he's unsure in areas of the heart. So, after thanking him again, I say, "This is a great gift, Farren. Really, it is. I can't wait to start taking pictures with it."

Unfortunately, since it's almost dark, I have to tuck the camera in my purse for now.

"Picture taking shall commence tomorrow," I say playfully, patting the side of my bag.

Farren laughs, and then we clean up our bags and fast-food wrappers. We gas up before we leave the rest stop. And then we are once again on our way.

# CHAPTER SIX

A FEW hours after leaving the rest stop, Farren is shaking me awake.

"What?" I jump, jerking forward. The seat belt snaps me back, and I utter a pained, "Ow."

Farren leans over and digs for the seat belt release so I won't be snapped back a second time.

"Where are we?" I ask. My voice is thick with sleep. "Indianapolis?"

"Just outside of," Farren replies. "We're in a town called Avon. We'll be stopping here for the night."

It's then that I notice we're in a budget-motel parking lot. I'd probably notice more, but with Farren leaning so close to me, it's hard to concentrate on much else. He has no idea his proximity, as he undoes my seat belt, has me basking in the warmth emanating from his hard body.

He doesn't catch on, either, when I say in a rush, "Oh, okay. Avon, Indiana. Huh, that's great."

I take a breath. God, must this man smell so good, so…male? Thankfully, for my now-racing pulse and this little ache I begin to feel at my core, Farren releases the seat belt and settles back in his seat.

"While you were sleeping," he says, nodding to the three-story brick building in front of us, "I ran in and checked us into two rooms next to each other. If you need anything, I'll be close by."

*If I need anything?* I think of how good it would feel to have Farren's strong arms around me. What would it be like if he held me, kissed me, touched me? Spending the day together, talking, listening to music, and traveling, those things have left me feeling especially close to him. Not to mention his thoughtful gesture. Giving me a gift, even if it was just a disposable camera, touched me.

Farren hands me a key card, breaking me out of my sleepy, emotion-laden reverie. "Anyway," he says, "Haven's credit card was used at this motel on Saturday night."

I glance up at the building. There's a bright yellow sign on the side; a black eight dominating the center. Haven was here, at this very location, and only forty-eight hours ago. Now, instead of racing, my heart aches. I miss my best friend. Spending the day on the road has kept my mind occupied, but everything now comes rushing back to me.

"Are Vincent and Eric using her card to make it look like she's traveling on her own?" I ask.

"Most likely."

Farren sighs. I notice he looks tired. His sister's disappearance is taking a toll on him, even if he barely lets it show. But late at night like this, defenses down, I see it.

"Hopefully," he continues, regaining his usual cool composure, "I'll know more once I check things out."

This is all so sad. I'm saddened for Farren, and I'm saddened for my own loss. I can pretend all I want, but this trip is deadly serious.

Farren catches me swiping at a tear trailing down my cheek, and he takes my hand.

"Hey, hey," he soothes, "we're going to find her. Everything will be okay."

I bite my lip and squeeze his hand. "Promise?"

"I promise," Farren says in the most serious tone I've yet heard him use. "At any cost, Essa, we will get my sister back. I will lay my life down for her if it comes to that."

"I know," I whisper, my voice pained. "I hope it doesn't, though."

"Me too," he says.

I wish I could wrap my arms around Farren. Everything inside me urges me to seek comfort from him. I wonder if he longs to seek the same from me. If he does, he's not showing it.

Releasing my hand and pinching the bridge of his nose, he says, "We should get you settled in your room. I want you to stay inside while I take a look around the property."

I nod. "Sure, okay, of course."

He continues, "There's also some surveillance-camera footage I need to check out."

"How do you plan to access those?" I ask, curious.

With a much-needed air of levity, he glances my way and replies, "Oh, Essa, trust me. I have my ways."

I don't doubt for a minute that he does.

I EXPECT for us to spend only one night in Indianapolis. But when Farren comes up with a lead on more surveillance footage—Haven's card was used at a gas station across town—we stay an extra night. Unfortunately, however, nothing substantial comes from the lead, and we decide to leave early the next day.

In the morning when I wake up, first thing I do is check the time.

8:10.

*Shit.* Farren expects me to meet him at the car by eight thirty.

I jump up and race around the room, gathering clothes, folding, and packing. But before I head to the shower, I check to make sure everything I unpacked is definitely repacked. As I'm lifting and checking under the bedding, which I'm leaving a wreck—*sorry, housekeeping*—I catch a murmur through the thin wall separating my room from Farren's.

I stop and listen. It sounds as if Farren is talking on his new burner phone. His voice is low, though, and, for me, incoherent.

"I hope he's getting news about Haven," I whisper to myself, eternally hopeful. And then, with a sigh, I climb off the bed, close up my suitcase, and head into the bathroom to get ready for the day.

After a quick shower, I stand in front of a small mirror hanging on a wall above the basin. I'm trying to decide if I should pin my hair up into a loose bun or try something different with the long locks. My hair is still damp from showering, so I opt to braid it. I always like the way my hair looks—all wavy and bouncy—when I take a braid out.

"Wonder if Farren likes my hair loose or bound," I say to my reflection as I finish braiding. And then I roll my eyes at myself. "Ugh, Essa, you're becoming one of *those* girls."

However, when I walk out to the car, I don't really care if I am becoming one of *those* girls. Farren Shaw is worth going the extra mile. I thought so before, but when I see him at the car, placing his suitcase in the trunk, I am definitely sure. I stop in my tracks just so I can check out how good he looks. Impeccable, that's what he is, even when casually dressed. I'm practically tiptoeing as I again start walking his way. I'm hoping for extra time to enjoy the view. Unfortunately, Farren hears me, of course. He spins around. Even though he's now facing me he doesn't seem to notice my ogling of his defined pecs and bulging arm muscles, both showcased beautifully in a snug, dark-green T-shirt. He notices nothing, because, to my delight, his eyes are focused on me. Specifically, he's checking out my bare legs, on full display in white Daisy Dukes.

I clear my throat.

Paying me no heed, his eyes rake up and over the tight yellow tee I'm wearing. When he finally meets my questioning gaze, there is absolutely no apology in his burning greens—not for blatantly staring at my legs and not for the hungry, lust-filled look he gives me right now.

It suddenly dawns on me that Farren may be as attracted to me as I am to him. *Thank you, Jesus.* But before I have a chance to think on it more thoroughly, or come up with something witty and flirtatious to say, Farren asks in an even tone, "Are you ready to get back on the road, Essalin?"

Quickly, I reply, "Yeah, sure."

I hand my suitcase to him, and while he's tossing it into the trunk, I venture, "Did you find anything useful at all on the surveillance cameras?"

He turns back to me. "No. If Haven was really here—or at the gas station—then she was kept out of sight. The kid who was working the front desk Saturday night was no help, either."

"You showed him a picture of her?"

"Yes, Essa." he replies dryly.

I feel silly for even asking such a stupid question. Of course Farren covered all the bases.

"So, where do we go next?" I tentatively inquire.

"St. Louis."

"Is that where you think they took Haven?"

"No." Farren starts walking around the car to the driver's side door, and I proceed to the passenger side. He places his hand on the door handle and looks over at me across the roof. "I need to meet up with someone in St. Louis, someone who can help us. He's been helping me track Haven's movements thus far."

"Who is this person?" I want to know. "Do you work with him?" *At your mysterious job*? I silently add in my head.

"Yes," Farren, to my surprise, responds. "His name is Rick Martinez. He's a good guy. You'll like him."

"Will I be meeting him?" I ask, surprised.

"You will. We're meeting him for dinner this evening."

Once we're in the car, I glance over at Farren. "Where is Haven?" I whisper. "Has her credit card been used anywhere new?"

He scrubs his hand down his face. "That's the problem, Essa. I don't know anymore. Activity on her card has ceased."

My chest tightens. "Oh my God."

I know things are bad when Farren has no words to comfort me.

I SOON discover that a funny thing sometimes happens when you find yourself in a dire situation. Well, I discover it's the case for me when I start to realize the only way to stay sane is to think about something—anything—other than the seriousness of the situation I'm in.

So, much like our first day of traveling, I focus on the passing scenery as Farren and I log miles through the state of Indiana. I take a couple of pictures with the disposable camera he bought me. But most of what we're traveling through is farmland, just like back in Pennsylvania and Ohio. With that being the case, finding interesting subjects, ones worthy of photographing, is limited.

That is, until we reach the St. Louis area. As we head into the city, I spot the Gateway Arch. It's the first major US attraction I've ever seen, and within seconds, I am leaning out the car window and snapping photos like crazy.

"Wow, how cool is that?" I remark when I finally settle back in my seat.

"Very cool," Farren replies. He gives me a small smile as he glances over at me. "It's very cool, indeed."

I don't think Farren is as wowed by the arch as I am, but he seems quite pleased with my enthusiasm.

"Want to drive in a little closer?" he asks.

I nod enthusiastically, a grin bubbling at my lips.

Farren remains on the highway, but the route he takes offers several great angles. I get in a bunch of amazing shots, until the arch fades from view.

When I lower the camera to my lap, Farren says, "So, I think you'll like where we're staying. It's in the heart of downtown St. Louis. And, I'm happy to report that this hotel is much nicer than the budget motel we stayed in the past two nights."

I twist toward him, stretching the seat belt out with my hand to accommodate my movement. "Oh yeah?" I say, intrigued. "What's the name of the place?"

"Union Station."

"That's a nice one?"

"Definitely," he replies. "Union Station is a St. Louis landmark, much like the Gateway Arch. It was once a busy railroad station, but it's long since been renovated. There's a hotel there now—the one where we'll be staying—and some restaurants and shops."

"Sounds nice," I say.

Farren nods to the camera I'm holding in my lap. "Bring that in with you when we check in. You can take some pictures of Grand Hall. You'll love it, I'm sure."

"Oh, getting to know me, huh?" I tease.

He slides his gaze my way. "I am getting to know you, Essa," he says in a low, sexy voice. *Oh my.*

I'm thankful for the darkness when we drive into a parking garage. It gives me time to compose myself, lose the redness from my cheeks. When we emerge from the garage, outside of a very cool-looking Union Station, I'm recovered. I snap a pic of a clock tower that looks like it belongs in a quaint European village. And when we step into what Farren told me was once one of the busiest railroad station in the world, I discover he was right about the place being amazing. I stare up at the ceiling, which is majestic, all curved and soaring.

"This is beautiful," I whisper.

I snap a few pics, and then Farren and I walk toward a richly varnished check-in counter.

"I knew you'd like it in here," he says. Then, with a smirk, he says, "A little nicer than the Super Eight, huh?"

"Ha-ha." I laugh. "I'd say it's *much* nicer."

It's amazing that under the circumstances, Farren has taken into consideration what I may or may not like. I think he kind of likes me. Then again, maybe Farren is just naturally attentive to women. Suddenly, the thought of all the many ways in which Farren could be attentive to a woman floods me with a slew of lusty feelings, feelings that warm my body and heat my cheeks.

I start to fan myself, just as Farren finishes checking us in. He turns to me and his brow creases. "Are you okay, Essa?"

"Yes, yes, I'm fine." I wave my hand, which inadvertently attracts a bellhop over to us.

"May I take your bags to your room?" the bellhop asks Farren.

I've been saved by the bellhop, which, for some reason, makes me giggle.

After Farren hands off our bags to the young man, we take an old-time elevator up to our floor. "Our rooms are down this way," he says, pointing to the right when the elevator doors open. We turn and walk down a long corridor to the two rooms he has checked us in to.

When we stop at the second-to-the-last door near the end of the corridor, Farren hands me a key card. "This is your room," he says. He then gestures to the next door down. "I'll be right next door."

"Great, thank you."

I glance around, like our bags might suddenly appear, and

Farren reminds me that it may take a few minutes before the bellhop gets the bags up to our floor.

"Oh yeah, that reminds me," I say. "What time are we meeting your friend?" I glance down at my yellow tee and Daisy Dukes. "I think I should probably change."

Farren chuckles as his eyes move over my body quickly.

"Yeah, that look is definitely cute," he murmurs. "But changing into something different would probably be a good idea."

"What should I wear?" I ask.

I've only been told that we're meeting Farren's friend—work partner, whatever—at a restaurant this evening. I have no idea if we're going to a fancy place or a more casual venue. "I'd like to dress appropriately," I add.

"To answer your first question," Farren replies. "Can you be ready in about an hour and a half?"

I nod. "Yeah, no problem."

"Perfect. As for clothing, wear something nice."

"Uh…" I shift from one sandaled foot to the other. "We may have a problem there."

He raises a questioning eyebrow, and I explain, "I didn't pack any really dressy clothes. A couple of summer dresses, but nothing, like, sophisticated."

"That's not a problem," Farren assures me, the side of his mouth curving up in amusement. "There's a boutique nearby. I'll have them send something up."

"Shoes, too?" I blurt out when I remember I packed nothing but sneakers and casual sandals.

He chuckles. "Yes, Essa, shoes, too."

Farren turns to head to his room, and I watch him walk away. Right when he's about to enter his key card in the slot on the door, I suddenly remember something.

"Hey," I call over to him, "don't you need my sizes?"

Pausing, he says with confidence, "Don't worry, Essa. Whatever I have the boutique send up to you, I guarantee it will fit."

Farren then slips into his room, leaving me insanely curious as to how he can just look at a woman's body—in this case, mine—and know her measurements. He sure seems confident. I guess we'll see.

Thirty minutes later, after I've showered in a bathroom the size of my entire room at the Super 8, my dress and shoes arrive. I quickly discover Farren had every reason to be confident. His assessment of my figure is spot-on.

Smiling, I slip the little black dress over my head and smooth the silky material over my hips. The dress is short and sleeveless, with a cutout that exposes my back. I spin in front of the mirror. This look is good—sexy, yet classy. I dig out a pair of black leather pumps from the box that arrived with the dress and find they, too, are a perfect fit. "That Farren," I murmur to myself.

Once I'm all set to go, I step out into the hall. Farren is coming out of his room at the same time. And…wow! He looks delicious every day, but he's exceptionally yummy right now. I sigh. Farren is male-model beautiful, but his dark, edgy side makes him sinfully hot. I can't stop staring. He's wearing a black suit that fits him to a tee, a white dress shirt, and a deep maroon tie. His raven hair is slicked back, and he's freshly shaven. I want to touch his smooth cheek, trace the line of his strong jaw.

"Essalin?" Farren takes a step toward me, while I continue to stare at him like a deranged fool. "Is something wrong?"

*God, no. Unless wanting you to take me back into my room*

*and take all the clothes you just bought me off of me is wrong.* I can't say something like that, though.

I wave my hand around to give myself a chance to find my bearings. "I'm fine," I reply once I'm back on track.

He takes a step closer, the hallway light glinting off his highly shined shoes. "Are you sure?" he asks softly.

"Don't mind me," I reply. "I was just having a moment there."

*Shit. Did I really just admit that?* I'm not as on track as I thought.

Farren's brows go up, and he inquires, "A moment?"

There's mirth in his deep green eyes, eyes I could get lost in. But now is not the time.

Embarrassed, I mumble, "Stop, please," and avert my gaze from his.

Chuckling, he says, "I'm just giving you a hard time, sweetheart."

Ooh, sweetheart. I like this new term of endearment, even if it is attached to a comment that confirms this gorgeous man knows damn well the effect he's having on me. The only saving grace to my dignity is that when I peek up at him from under my lashes, I notice that he is checking me out, too. And if his suppressed smile is any indication, he appears quite pleased with what the boutique sent my way.

Or maybe—and I'm hoping this is it—he's just pleased with me.

"Shall we?" he asks, following his perusal.

When he gallantly offers his arm, I say, "Such a gentleman."

"Hardly," he scoffs.

I don't press for elaboration, though I wonder what that means. With the hand not in the crook of his arm, I adjust a tendril of hair that slips from my upswept do.

"You look very beautiful tonight, Essalin," Farren says on our way to the parking garage.

I look over at him. "Thank you. So do you."

Farren smiles tenderly at me, and I melt.

The flirtations, mostly in the form of sidelong glances and lips pressed together to keep from smiling too much, continue all the way to the car. But on the way to the restaurant, things turn serious when I say, "So, tell me about your friend, Rick. How long have you two known one another?"

Farren breathes in deeply, exhales slowly. "A long time," he says at last. "Over ten years. Rick and I served in the military together. We met on my first tour of duty. We became friends then." After a lengthy pause, he adds, "That part of our past was a long time ago, though. More recently, we were been deployed to a lot of the same places…before we were discharged, of course."

"So he was special ops, too?" I venture.

Farren glances over at me. "I should have guessed Haven would've told you all about that."

"She did," I confirm. And then I ask, "Is that okay?"

He nods, but when he fails to respond, I try to fill the silence by saying, "I imagine many of your special ops missions were not only secret, but also very…"—I search for a word—"dangerous."

Farren laughs, but it's devoid of humor. "Yes, Essa, all the missions were very, as you put it, 'dangerous.'"

Okay, so obviously dangerous is not nearly a strong enough adjective to describe what Farren has experienced.

He appears to lose himself in thought, so I prompt, "Rick was on your team or whatever all the time, then?"

"Not all the time," he clarifies, sighing. "But often, yes."

"And you still work together in the private sector?"

"Yes."

I want to get back to the special ops stuff, ask Farren what kinds of things he and Rick have had to do. I'm curious about all they've seen, which I imagine is a lot. But I know enough about Special Forces to know Farren probably isn't allowed to divulge too much, particularly regarding the specifics of where he's been or the things he's done. Still, I long to learn more about this man I'm traveling with, especially in regard to the life he's lived thus far. Farren is not just mysterious; he's fascinating. I can't imagine the things he's seen and done...in the distant past and in the not-so-distant past.

And that brings me back to the here and now, with the same damn questions. What is it that Farren currently does for a living that has resulted in Haven's abduction? I'm sure the two are connected. But how is he connected to Eric and Vincent? It's all potentially disturbing, but I comfort myself with the possibility I may learn more when I meet his friend Rick.

A little while later, on the top floor of a downtown St. Louis high-rise, I do, indeed, meet Rick Martinez. He's a very good-looking man, almost as attractive as Farren. When the two men greet each other in the dimly lit, mahogany-paneled lobby of the restaurant we're to eat in, they display an easy camaraderie. It's clear they trust one another quite a bit.

Before Farren introduces us, I take the opportunity to look Rick over. I peg him to be about thirty. His hair is jet black and slightly longish in the back, the strands brushing at the collar of his expensive-looking suit jacket. Rick is exotic looking, with high cheekbones, olive skin, and almond-colored eyes. The dude is smooth, too. He takes my hand and brushes his lips over my knuckles when Farren finally introduces us.

Farren immediately shoots his friend a back-off look that even I pick up on. Rick straightens and drops my hand. An awkward moment ensues, until a young hostess with fiery red hair and very red high heels arrives to seat us.

As she leads us to a booth in a back corner, I hear Rick murmur to Farren, "I'm sorry, friend. I didn't realize she was yours."

*Yours?* I roll my eyes. But, truthfully, a tiny part of me wants to belong to Farren Shaw. Oh, who am I kidding? Pretty much all of me is on board with that idea.

As the food is served and the meal progresses, Rick remains cordial, but there's no more flirting from him. Clearly, Farren is in charge. And Farren has laid down the rules. But, I have to wonder, what exactly is Farren in charge of? What kind of operation are he and Rick involved in nowadays? And how would men like Eric and Vincent fit into the equation, since surely they do. I mean, Farren knew who they were when I first mentioned their names. Even though he has yet to confirm or deny it, I feel sure I'm right. So does that mean Rick is acquainted with Eric and Vincent, too? Did they all work together on something in the past? Maybe they were in the military together? Were Eric and Vincent special ops, too? Did something go wrong somewhere? Was Haven taken in some sort of retaliatory move?

My mind is whirling as I come up with question after question. Farren and Rick, meanwhile, fall into a discussion of the "old days." I take note that though we're supposedly meeting with Rick to discuss Haven, there's not been one mention of her.

*At least, not in front of me*, I think. There was a point when I excused myself to the ladies' room. Perhaps they discussed her then.

The two men continue to reminisce, and I decide to take an active part in the discussion. They're discussing a special-ops mission they were once a part of. Rick mentions something about rebel forces, and Farren says, "Fuck, man, that was some crazy shit."

"Sure was," Rick agrees. "We lit that camp up, Shaw. Remember that?"

Farren nods and takes a drink from his glass of red wine.

Rick continues, "Central Command never expected us to have the balls to destroy every cache of weapons." He laughs, takes a sip of his own red wine, and then adds, "Of course, you take the credit for that. Damn, those were good times."

"The best," Farren agrees, raising his glass.

The two friends toast, and I cut in. "Where did all this happen?"

Not surprisingly, I'm met with stony silence. I stare down at my plate, wishing I had a daring tale of my own to contribute. But what story am I going to tell these two seen-it-all, done-it-all men? Should I share with them how I rebelled and chose five wrong answers on a final last week?

I don't think so.

As I stare down at my barely touched filet mignon, Farren takes notice that I haven't eaten much.

"Are you not hungry, Essa?" he inquires.

Rick glances over at my plate but quickly resumes eating his own meal. In fact, he becomes lost in his meal, allowing Farren to address me semi-privately. The dynamic feels so different here, much more so than when Farren and I are alone. Again, it is crystal clear from the way Rick continues to concede to his friend that Farren is the alpha male.

I'm not immune to Farren's power, either. I'm not all that hungry, yet I find myself responding demurely, "No, I am hungry" as I take a small bite.

I've been attracted to Farren from the start, but now every feminine part of me wants him. He is gorgeous, in command, powerful, and possibly a little dangerous to be around. What's not to like? This is the kind of attraction I've always read about, what I dreamed of and hoped to someday find. And here it is, right in front of me. No wonder college boys always left me cold. All this time I just didn't realize that what I needed was a man like Farren in my life.

Or maybe I knew it all along. After all, I have been crushing on the guy for a long-ass time. So, yeah, Farren Shaw can woo me any day of the week.

But is Farren wooing me?

*Maybe*, I think as his gaze slides to and catches mine. He smiles charmingly, and I smile back. Yeah, maybe Farren wants me as much as I want him. Of course, I'm not dangerous, though *he* may very well turn out to be.

Does that bother me?

Farren shoots me a searing look that makes me feel like prey caught in a lion's sight. Not like Eric's cold look to Haven. This is more about heat and raw lust, something mutual. I go with it, concluding danger associated with Farren doesn't bother me one bit.

In fact, if Farren longs to catch me, I can't wait to be caught.

# CHAPTER SEVEN

WHEN the meal ends, Rick announces that he has to leave. Farren and I are left alone at the table. I have the impression from the pleased look on his handsome face that Farren planned for the evening to go this way.

"Your friend seems very nice," I say, suppressing a smile.

"I'm glad you and Rick hit it off," he replies, a smile of his own barely contained.

I blow out a breath as I lean back in my chair. "So, Farren, what do we do now?"

Scooting his chair a little closer, he purrs, "I don't know, Essa. You tell me."

His words are not just words. Delivered so confidently, in such a masculine voice, his words seduce. Quickly, I gulp down what's left of my red wine. When I'm finished, I murmur, "Oh, I don't know. Whatever you want to do is fine with me."

Farren chuckles, scoots away slightly, and pours what remains in the bottle into my empty glass. He then asks, "What would *you* like to do, Essa? After all, the night is young."

"And so are we," I quip, clinking my glass to his before he has the chance to lift it to his full lips.

Farren chuckles, drinks his wine. I think he's amused I'm more than a tad tipsy and uttering silly quips.

But I suddenly have an idea. "I know," I say excitedly. "We should go to a place where we can dance."

"Like to a club?" he asks.

"I wasn't really thinking that," I reply.

My first thought of a dance with Farren is something romantic, like a slow dance. Not dancing at some rowdy club.

Feeling bold, I say, "I'd prefer to go someplace where it would just be you and me."

Farren is quiet for what feels like forever, and I start to think maybe I've been too bold, assumed too much. Maybe a club is more to his liking. But, to my delight, a sly smile spreads across his face.

He stands. "Come on," he says, offering his hand. "I have an idea."

Walking away from the table with me at his side, Farren flags down our waitress. She hurries over. When she reaches us, he whispers something to her. She nods and points to a darkened stairwell in the corner of the restaurant. Farren slips her a few bills before leading me, his hand cupping my elbow, to the stairwell.

"Where are we going?" I ask as we begin to ascend a dark and narrow set of steps.

Farren is behind me, hands on either side of my waist, keeping me moving. He's also keeping me from tumbling backward since my heels are quite high.

When we reach the top, I come to a halt. "There's a door in our way," I so eloquently observe, nodding to what appears to be a very heavy steel door.

Farren leans into me and, while trying to contain his laugher, whispers, "Why don't you just open it, Essa."

I rock back into his solid chest, shivering in the best way possible. He breathes out heavily, like our closeness affects him, too. Warm breaths caress my neck, sending tendrils of my upswept do into a wispy dance. Slowly, Farren reaches around me, his arm almost brushing my breast. He grasps the handle and swings open the heavy steel door with ease.

And there before us lies sparkling downtown St. Louis in full nighttime glory.

"Oh, this is beautiful, Farren," I gush, enraptured.

I like leaning back against Farren, but the cityscape is calling to me, urging me to step out onto the expansive rooftop and take in all the twinkling downtown lights. It's a lovely summer-like evening, and a warm breeze blows as I walk across the rooftop, stopping at the edge. I'm not great with heights, but thankfully there's a high, sturdy railing to hold on to. Placing my hands on cool metal, I turn my head, expecting to see Farren right there beside me, enjoying the magnificent view.

But he's not anywhere nearby.

"Farren…?"

I glance back to the stairwell. He's still standing by the door. He's not alone. He's speaking to the waitress he flagged down before we started up to the roof. She's nodding and handing Farren a just-uncorked bottle of red, along with two wineglasses. When he catches me watching the exchange, he shoos the waitress away and strides over to me.

Along the inside perimeter of the rooftop, there's a brick ledge. I sit down carefully, straighten my classy black dress, and cross my legs.

Farren stops and stands in front of me. Glancing up at his handsome face, I whisper, "Hey."

"Hey back at you," he says, just as softly.

As he balances the two glasses from the waitress in one hand, he uses his free hand to pour a bit of wine into each glass. When both glasses are half full, he hands me one.

"Thank you," I murmur, taking the glass.

He touches his glass to mine, and I ask, "What are you doing?"

He stills, his wineglass pressed to mine. "I'm in the process of proposing a toast, Essalin."

Laughing, I say, "I figured that part out. But what are we toasting to?"

Emerald eyes, dark in the low light, meet mine. "How about we toast to making wishes come true?"

Before I can ask what that means, he clinks his glass to mine. He takes a drink, as do I. Suddenly, as if on cue, soft music begins to play in the background. When I look up at Farren, he's smiling.

"I wanted to dance," I murmur, amazed that he set something up like this so quickly after hearing how I wished to spend the rest of our night.

"And it's just you and me," he says. "As you requested."

He takes the glass from my hand and, along with his, sets it on the ledge. For the third time in one night, Farren offers me his hand. "Would you like to dance, Essalin?"

"I would," I reply.

My heart is racing. I can't stop smiling. Smiling, smiling, I feel such happiness right now. They say people in dire circumstances grow close quickly. Maybe that is what's been happening between me and Farren. I feel a powerful connection with him. And I can't say it's entirely surprising. Our love for Haven provided us with an immediate reason to bond. And then spending time together, retracing her steps, trying to save her, has only strengthened that connection. Farren and I have a shared goal—we both want Haven back.

But there's no denying there's something more intense developing between us.

The careful way in which Farren holds me as we begin to dance to a slow song—like I'm fragile and he's the only one equipped to care for me—strengthens my suspicion that he's falling for me too, in some way.

I relax into him, trusting him. Our bodies sway to melodic lyrics that speak of the beauty of having someone to lean on when times get tough. How fitting. As the song continues, I feel Farren's gaze on me. Glancing up, I find his emerald eyes burning with strong desire and need, assuring me that I am not the only one feeling this heady attraction.

The side of Farren's mouth curves up slightly when he sees his emotions reflected in my eyes. Quietly, he implores, "Essa, what are you doing to me?"

"I don't know," I answer honestly.

I lower my chin and lean forward to place my cheek against his solid shoulder. Farren's fingers wind through my hair, loosening the strands. Pins fall to the ground haphazardly, but I don't care. When my hair tumbles to my shoulders, I lean back, my gaze questioning.

Farren just smiles and shrugs lightly. "I like it better this way," he says.

I nod once, and our eyes remain locked as Farren continues to comb through my hair with his fingers. He uses one hand at first, then both. His ministrations are gentle. I like it. I like the possessiveness in his touch. I like the familiarity. And I like that Farren seems to intuitively know how to touch me.

It makes me want him more than ever.

I lower my gaze to his lips, full and moist from the wine. With a confidence I never felt before, I stand on my tiptoes and lean closer to him. I tilt my head slightly in what I hope is viewed as an invitation.

Farren responds immediately. His grasp in my hair tightens and he urges my head back. Lowering his lips to my neck, his tongue darts out to taste my skin. "Delicious," he says.

I shudder in the best kind of way and murmur, "Farren."

With his hands remaining in my hair and my head still tilted back, he kisses me everywhere…down my neck, across my shoulder blade, back up to my jaw. "Oh," I gasp.

His lips are everywhere but where I want them most—on mine.

I slide my hands up his solid and wide back. I caress the softness at the nape of his neck. And then my hands are in his hair. So silky and soft, just how I imagined it would be. When I pull at the ends of his hair gingerly, Farren groans huskily.

His lips capture mine, at last, and he kisses me *hard*. This is heaven, a dance of lips and tongues. Farren tastes like red wine and man, and I become drunk of him.

He presses his body into mine when I moan, and I am made fully aware that his kisses aren't the only thing that's hard. As his arousal continues to deliciously press into my abdomen, I kiss him like crazy.

Soon, we're practically bruising one another as our hands and mouths express all of this pent-up want and need.

I let out a light moan, and, between kisses, Farren says, "Tell me what you want. Say it to me."

"I want," I breathe out a stuttered breath. "I want…"

I don't know what I want, not exactly. My body wants Farren, more than I've ever wanted anyone, but my inexperienced self urges me to slow down.

"Essalin?" Farren pulls back slightly, his eyes boring into mine, searching for a go-ahead or a denial.

*What will it be?*

"I'll do anything you want," I blurt out. "I don't know how great I'll be, but I want to be with you. I'll try to please you."

I sound like what I am—a mostly inexperienced young woman who doesn't know what she's getting into. Understanding dawns in Farren's eyes. His hold on my hair loosens, and though one hand remains wrapped loosely in the long tresses, his other hand skims down to the small of my back.

"Essa…" He exhales loudly. "Look, we don't have to do anything you're not ready for."

"But I am ready," I insist. "I want to be with you."

Farren eyes me skeptically. "You really think you're ready for what this is leading to? You really think you're ready for *me*?"

*Holy hell, I don't know.* What I do know is that the starry-eyed girl part of me wants to believe if we become intimate it will lead to something more. But the practical woman side of me knows this might only be about sex. Mind-blowing, amazing sex I'd surely never forget, but sex for sex's sake, nonetheless.

And the problem with that is that I want more. I don't want a sex-only thing with Farren. Even so, I'm torn. I don't know how to proceed.

I try to look away, but Farren's hand goes to my cheek. I have no choice but to meet his gaze when he urges me to.

Quietly, I say, "I'm just not all that experienced, Farren."

His brows shoot up, and I quickly amend, "I don't mean I'm a virgin…if that's what you're thinking."

The look on his face tells me that's precisely what he's thinking.

I want to be forthcoming, so I admit, "I've only had sex one time, though."

"Essa…" Farren says on a sigh.

I close my eyes and say, "I guess I'm just confused. I don't really know how this is supposed to work." *Oh, what am I babbling about?*

Farren says nothing.

When I dare to take a peek up at him, he arches one brow questioningly. "How this is supposed to work?"

"Like," I begin my explanation, taking a step back, "if we were to sleep together. I don't know—"

"Shh…" He touches my mouth tenderly, cutting me off. "You don't have to explain anything, sweetheart." Gently, he urges me back into his arms, and I nestle into his strong hold.

"No sex tonight, then," I joke, my cheek pressed against his smooth-textured suit jacket.

Farren chuckles lightly and says, "No sex tonight, Essa."

Music is still playing in the background, and he starts to move my body with his. "Will you still dance with me, though?" he asks.

I sway with him as I say, "I can do that."

"Good. I like dancing with you," he murmurs into my hair.

"I like dancing with you, too," I whisper back.

All the hard ridges of his body are pressed to my soft parts. He feels so good. As we move together, I relax into him, let him lead. For as much as I want Farren—and, God, I do want him at some point—sleeping together this quickly wouldn't be a good idea. I like him entirely too much, and I don't want to end up crushed.

But if things go in the direction I hope for, I sense a man like Farren would be careful with my heart.

I sigh and hope that someday Farren Shaw might actually want my heart.

THE next day, after we check out of the Union Station Hotel, Farren and I head straight to the parking garage. There's an ease between us as we walk in relative silence. Farren appears lost in thought, but I'm okay with that. I'm busy scanning the area, trying to recall where we parked the white sedan when we returned last night. I swear it was on the second level, third row from the ramp, but I don't see it anywhere.

"Oh my God, Farren," I exclaim, stopping and pivoting left and right. "I think someone stole our car."

Farren doesn't say a thing, and when I glance over at him, he's trying not to crack up.

"What?" I say. "What's so funny?"

"Our car wasn't stolen," he replies as he composes himself.

He motions for me to follow him as he walks to a parking space a few yards away. Stopping in front of a black luxury SUV, he says, "We're switching to this."

My eyes slide from Farren—dressed today in black jeans and

a snug black tee that accentuates his muscular build—to the sleek vehicle he's referring to.

"Oh, wow, nice," I say, nodding approvingly. "This is definitely a step up."

"Better than the family sedan?" he asks lightly, his tone jovial and teasing.

"Much."

Farren grins flirtatiously, making my heart skip a beat. But then he turns away to pop open the back lift gate. He lifts up the cover to the cargo space inside, and I get a good view.

"Holy crap," I blurt out. "That's a lot of weapons you have in there."

The cargo space is filled with automatic rifles, handguns, and other weaponry I've never seen before. I assume the vehicle switch is compliments of Farren's friend Rick, but I also now have a strong suspicion that the arsenal has been with us from the start. No wonder Farren was always making sure he was the one placing our suitcases in the trunk. He's been hiding this cache of weapons all along. Well, I guess we passed some point of no return last night. Farren must trust me now, enough to let me in on his former secret.

"Now you know why we've been driving and not flying," he says, closing the back of the SUV.

"Makes total sense to me now," I concur, nodding.

I guess he's surprised by my easy acceptance. He laughs and motions for me to get in the vehicle. "Come on, Essa. Let's get rolling."

Truthfully, I'm relieved we're armed to the teeth. Not that I have a clue on how to handle any of the firearms. But with his extensive military background, I'm sure Farren does.

We grab a quick breakfast before we leave St. Louis. And then, for the first hour or so on the road, I doze. When I wake from my impromptu nap, I realize I have no idea where we are heading. I never bothered to ask.

"Hey," I say, stretching and yawning, "where are we going?"

Farren glances over at me, his gaze lowering briefly to my snowy-white lace crop top. The bottom hem is curled up higher than it should be, thus exposing a fair amount of skin between the bottom of the shirt and the top of my low-cut jeans.

I straighten my clothes, and Farren turns his focus back to the highway. "New Mexico," he answers at last. "But first we're stopping in Oklahoma City."

"Oh, okay." I pause and then tentatively ask, "Did Rick have news on Haven? Is she in Oklahoma? Or is she in New Mexico?"

After dancing half the night away on the restaurant rooftop, Farren and I returned to the hotel. We were both exhausted, and following a chaste kiss on my cheek, we bid each other goodnights and went to our rooms. I never had the chance to ask him what new things Rick has uncovered.

But I find out now.

"Yeah, Rick had intel," Farren says, frowning. Since I suspect it was not good news, I place my hand on his squared shoulder.

Sighing, he continues, "Haven's car was found abandoned in Oklahoma City."

I gasp, but Farren ignores me and keeps talking, almost like he has to or he may lose it.

"All indications are that Haven is still alive." He pauses, and then says, "Thank God." A beat passes, and he adds, "Despite the stop in Oklahoma, she'll be taken to New Mexico."

"How do you know?" I interject.

"I just know."

"I've sent Rick there ahead of us," he continues. "He's able to fly, since, as you saw,"—he jerks his chin to the back of the SUV—"I'm holding the bulk of the weapons. We'll head to New Mexico soon, Essa, but first I want to make sure it was Haven's car that was dumped."

I have a million questions, and I begin to rattle them off. "Farren, why would Eric and Vincent abandon Haven's car all these days later?"

Silence.

"And how do you and Rick know this stuff?"

Silence.

I falter momentarily, unnerved. I'm sure Farren expects me to be flummoxed by his lack of responses. But, no, I forge on.

"How does all this tie into you, anyway? Like I said before, I know Haven was taken due to something related to your mysterious job. And I know you told me not to ask questions, but, please, please, Farren, tell me something. This is hard for me, too."

I choke up, and he pinches the bridge of his nose. After a beat, he says, "I know, Essa. And I'm sorry. What do you want to know? Ask me, and I'll try to give you what I can."

Finally, some answers.

I take a deep breath and begin with, "Do you know Eric and Vincent?"

"Yes."

My heart stutters. "Are those their real names?" I whisper.

Farren chuckles, but it's not because any of this is funny. "Surprisingly, yes, those are their real names." And then he qualifies, "Actually I should say those are the names I've always known them by. It's anyone's guess as to what their real names are. They've probably been through so many aliases they've forgotten what their given names are."

*Okay, that's disturbing.* "So," I venture, "*how* do you know them?"

"That," he says, shooting me a look of warning, "I can't tell you."

I accept that, since he's otherwise being forthcoming. I quickly move on to something different.

"Okay, what about Haven's car? Why did Eric and Vincent keep it for so many days if they planned on dumping it from the beginning?"

"To keep up appearances, initially," Farren says. "In case the authorities would have taken more of an interest. It's the same reason why they used Haven's credit cards for gas and hotel stays."

"To make it look like she was traveling of her own volition?"

"Yes."

"So," I continue, "they stopped using her cards when it became clear nobody was looking for her?"

Farren shoots me a meaningful sidelong glance. "Except we've been looking for her, haven't we, Essa?"

"Oh-h-h," I say, catching on. "Eric and Vincent have always wanted you to know they took her. That's why they continued to use her credit card. So you would see all the charges."

He responds tightly, "Yes."

"I was right all along then," I exclaim. "You are somehow involved."

No response.

"What about your friend Rick? Is he involved in this, too? He has to be; he knows too much."

No response, which I take as a confirmation.

"Is he definitely someone we can trust?" I ask gently.

That sure gets a response.

"Rick is one of the good guys, Essalin," Farren replies vehemently. "I assure you he can be trusted completely."

I breathe out a sigh of relief. Thank God, since Rick is the one who will reach New Mexico—where Haven might be—first.

When Farren falls silent once again, I ask, "What's wrong? What aren't you telling me?"

"I'm just surprised you're out of questions."

"Why?" I whisper, dread creeping up my spine. "What should I be asking?"

"Aren't you wondering which one I am, Essa?"

"What do you mean?"

"Aren't you wondering if I am one of the good guys or if I'm one of the bad?"

I can't tell if Farren is messing with me or not. I shrug and, with a touch of humor, say lightly, "Guess I'll find out."

But there's not an ounce of humor in Farren's voice when he replies. "Yeah, I guess you will."

# CHAPTER EIGHT

Not surprisingly, there's an odd vibe in the SUV for the next hour. The rain that starts to fall doesn't help lift the mood. Farren remains quiet. Contemplative, I assume. I mostly read, happy that I picked up a paperback at our last stop for gas.

Eventually the rain stops. The sun comes out, and, to my relief, the tension lifts right along with the bad weather. Despite his cryptic words, I just can't think of Farren as a bad guy. From everything Haven has told me, he's always been good. He was a good student, a good son. And he's still an amazing brother to her. Farren was a kid who was forced by circumstances to become a man early—after his father left the family abruptly and especially after his mother died. Since then, from what I've observed, he's done everything possible to take care of the only real family he has left—Haven.

But there's still a question I can't ignore: What has Farren been involved in recently? What is he involved in now? Something illegal, I have to assume, based on how secretive he is whenever the subject comes up. Those huge sums of money he pulls down certainly make things look even more suspicious.

Contemplating all of this, I sigh. Farren looks over, his expression giving away his curiosity. But before he can ask what I'm sighing about, I lower my paperback and say, "I'm tired of reading."

"Okay," he says slowly. "Are you hungry?"

I nod once. "It has been a while since we've eaten."

"Say no more," Farren says brightly.

It's obvious he's trying to make up for the last hour of silence and the uncomfortable vibes in the car. He takes the next exit we come to, and we find a sandwich shop just down the road. Farren orders a massive deli sandwich, roast beef and cheese on pumpernickel bread, with just about every topping and condiment available.

While the lady behind the counter works on Farren's masterpiece, I tell the girl taking orders that I'll have the same. "Just no mustard," I add.

Farren snickers under his breath, and I say, "What? I'm hungry, okay?"

"That's fine, Essa. I'll just be surprised if you can finish it."

Ten minutes later, we're back in the SUV, eating our massive sandwiches. And sure enough, Farren's supposition comes to pass.

I lower my sandwich to the wrapper in my lap and mutter, "Ugh, I'm done. It's delicious, but I can't eat another bite."

Farren glances over at my half-eaten roast beef and cheese. He laughs and offers to finish it for me. *He sure has a hearty appetite*, I think as I hand him the rest of my sandwich. I have to wonder if *all* his appetites are this hearty.

The flush on my face must clue him in as to where my thoughts are drifting, for he asks all too knowingly, "What are you thinking about, Essalin?"

"Oh, nothing," I fib. Clearing my throat, I add, "Let's talk about something, though."

"Okay," he says slowly, hesitantly. "What do you want to talk about?"

I shrug. "Oh, I don't know. Anything, really."

Farren finishes the sandwich I couldn't eat, wipes his mouth with a napkin, and then suggests, "Why don't you tell me how you met my sister?"

"She never told you?" I know Farren and Haven share a lot, so this is a surprise.

"Well, she did tell me she met you at freshman orientation."

I nod. "Yeah, that's right."

Farren gathers our food wrappers and napkins and stuffs them in the bag everything came in. His attention returns to me when he's finished.

"Okay, so you met at freshman orientation," he says. "That doesn't explain one bit how you and she became such good friends."

"Are you asking if there was, like, a defining moment or something?"

I've posed my question slowly, tentatively, because there absolutely was a defining moment in my friendship with Haven. But it's not an easy story to tell.

Farren reads things so well that I can't fool him. He settles back in his seat and says, "There was a defining moment, wasn't there?"

"Yes," I admit, frowning.

Farren has unknowingly touched on an experience from freshman year that I'd rather forget. But, for as much as I try to avoid recalling that fateful Halloween night, I find I now want to share it with this man. And I should. It's a story of how his sister saved my ass.

I take a deep breath, exhale, and begin…

"After Haven and I hit it off at that early orientation, which was held when we were still seniors in high school, we kept in touch. We talked and texted all the time throughout that summer. Fall of freshman year we picked right back up where we'd left off. We'd arranged to share the same dorm room, and we hung out all the time. People sometimes questioned how we could be friends. I mean, after all, Haven was so much more popular than me. But you know how she is. She made sure I never felt left out."

"She's always been like that," Farren says quietly.

I glance over at him. His head is leaned back on the headrest, and he looks sad. A part of me longs to comfort him, but I know he wants to hear this story.

I continue, "Well, anyway, she got invited to a lot of parties, like the very best of the best. She invited me often, and sometimes I tagged along, but other times I chose to stay back in the dorms and study. Halloween that year, though, there was one party everyone wanted to go to. It was an annual event, held every October thirty-first at some rich student's parents' house. It was kind of legendary. You had to go at least once. Anyway, the kid was a senior that year, so it was going to be my first and only chance to go."

"And you wanted to go?" Farren inquires.

"Yeah, to that party, yes. I very much wanted to go to that one."

When I fall silent, lost in the memory for a minute, Farren prompts, "So you and Haven went to the party?"

"We did. And it was a costume party, of course, with it being Halloween and all."

"Costume party, huh?"

Farren appears curious, and I figure he's about to ask about my costume. *Oh no.*

I try to divert him by saying, "So, Haven went as a Sex Kitten—"

"I don't even want to know what that costume entailed," Farren interrupts. He rolls his eyes.

I laugh, and recalling Haven's barely there black bustier, red micro-mini, and five-inch stiletto heels, I agree, "Yeah, you probably don't."

Shaking his head, he says, "So, what did you go as?"

*I knew he was going to ask.* Now it's my turn to roll my eyes. "Something stupid."

"Come on," he says. "It can't be that bad."

"Oh, it is."

"What was it?" he asks, trying again.

"Don't laugh."

"I won't."

"Promise?"

"Essa, just tell me."

I scrunch my eyes shut and blurt out, "I went as *New Moon* Bella."

"Who?" he asks, completely baffled. "What the hell is a *New Moon* Bella?"

I am not about to go into a long, detailed explanation. If he missed *that* phenomenon, there's no sense in trying to explain.

So I just say, "She was a character from a popular series of books that were being made into movies at the time."

"Okay."

Before he starts digging for more detail, I hurry the story along. "The costumes aren't important, anyway." I wave my hand. "So, we went to the party. But somehow Haven and I got separated. I was kind of wandering around when this cute guy asked me if I needed a drink."

I pause, remembering my naïveté back then. "I'd heard of date-rape drugs, of course," I say softly. "But I never thought someone would actually slip me one."

Farren reaches over and touches my jean-clad knee. "Essa…"

"Nothing happened," I say in a rush. "I mean, not really."

I'm visibly shaken, even two and a half years later, and Farren says, "Essa, you don't have to say anything more."

"But I want to. I have to." My eyes find his. "I want you to know."

"Okay." He nods in a way that lets me know he understands that sharing this story—with him—is important to me.

"Sometime later," I go on, "I woke up in a bedroom of the house. I was on a bed. I knew then that I'd been drugged. My head felt so heavy, and everything was out of focus. Anyway, the cute guy was with me. He didn't look so cute anymore, though. He was on the bed next to me, already undressed. And he was in the process of taking *my* clothes off."

I can't look at Farren, so I close my eyes as I recount the foggy, disjointed memory. "I wanted to push him away, and I tried. But I couldn't make my arms move. I remember him getting mad when he started pulling off my skinny jeans and one leg got stuck on a navy Ked he'd left on me. He gave up on getting the jeans off completely. He just pushed the denim material aside, left the one shoe on me, too. He ripped my shirt open, snapped open my bra." I take a stuttered breath and whisper, "And then he spread my legs."

My eyes remain shut. I hear Farren swear softly under his breath. He laces his fingers with mine.

"He was climbing on top of me, Farren, pushing my underwear aside. I knew I was done for, and I started to cry. And that's when Haven busted in."

Farren squeezes my hand, the small action so comforting that I feel safe enough to open my eyes as I finish recounting my story.

"Haven started screaming at him," I continue. "She startled him so much that he jumped off of me before anything happened. And then, with no hesitation, Haven took off one of her stilettos and whacked him right in the balls with the sharp heel." I can't help but chuckle. "She was amazing, Farren. Her move was so smooth, like some ninja-girl thing."

Farren lets out a laugh. "That's my sister," he states proudly.

"Right, and once the guy recovered, he grabbed up his clothes and took off."

"So you were okay?" Farren's voice is back to being concerned.

"I was." I sigh. "But I wouldn't have been if it hadn't been for Haven. She saved me, Farren. She stopped that guy. He could have done anything to either of us. He could have hit her, attacked her, too, anything. But she was fearless." Suddenly, I break down. "I miss her, Farren. I love her. We have to find her. It's my turn to save her."

Farren soothes me with soft words. "I know, sweetheart. I love her, too. And I promise you we'll find her." He leans across the console and wraps his arms around me.

I welcome his embrace, but the console prevents us from getting close. "Damn this thing," I mutter.

And then I climb right over the console and on to Farren's lap until I'm straddling him. He moves his seat back accommodatingly and holds me to him tightly.

"I'm sorry," I whisper. "I shouldn't have asked you so many questions earlier. I trust you. I do." I lean back and stare into green depths. "No matter what you're involved in, Farren, I know you're one of the good guys."

Farren smoothes hair I wore down today—specifically for him—away from my face. He doesn't confirm or deny anything. And his expression remains inscrutable.

Doesn't much matter. This close to Farren, straddling him, memories from the night before rush back to me, stirring up so many feelings. I bite my lip and lower my chin. But when his fingers reach up and caress my cheek, I glance back up.

Farren searches my eyes while cupping the side of my face. His thumb brushes over my bottom lip. "So soft," he murmurs, like he's a little bit amazed by me.

I want so badly for Farren to kiss me again. My hand goes to his chest, and I grip his T-shirt. When I tug—just a touch—he inches closer.

Our eyes close at the same time, and a second later, his lips touch mine, with soft brushes of contained passion. Like last night, after my admission of inexperience, Farren again handles me with care. But all his tender kisses and gentle touches only serve to heighten my desire. Hell with my heart, I long for him to do more than just kiss me.

Today is spring chilly, and both Farren and I have on jeans. But the dark material of the pair he's wearing does little to hide that he is just as aroused as I. With my arms wrapped around his neck, I kiss him back with more and more urgency. And when I scoot forward in his lap, every hard inch of him presses against my core.

I moan into his mouth and circle my hips.

"Essa," he says in a husky voice as he breaks our kiss, "don't." His firm hands on my waist still my movements.

"Is this the part where you tell me you have a girlfriend?" I question.

His fingers flex at my sides. "No, there's no girlfriend."

"A girl in every port, then?"

He arches an eyebrow my way. "Port?" His eyes sparkle amusedly. "I was in the army, Essa, not the navy."

I smack his solid pec. "Ha-ha."

He cocks his head slightly, eyeing me with interest. "Why would you think I have a girlfriend?"

I shrug.

"For the record, Essa," he says, "I wouldn't have been kissing you like that if I had a girlfriend."

I look away. "So, why did you stop?"

"Hey…" He touches my cheek, urging me to look at him. When I do, he says, "I didn't stop because I don't want you."

"Do you think I'm too inexperienced?" I venture in a soft tone.

"Not at all," he replies, smiling. He brushes back a strand of my hair. "I like that you're still mostly innocent. It makes you, well, you." His eyes meet mine. "And, Essa, I like *you*. I like you a lot."

I can't help but smile. But I'm not just smiling. No, it's much more than that. I am beaming. Not only does Farren look particularly gorgeous up close like this, with his full lips a little swollen from kissing me, but, damn, he just admitted that he likes me.

"I like you, too," I whisper.

He pulls me to him and gives me a heartfelt hug. "We should get back on the road," he says into my hair.

I lean back and nod. "Okay."

While I am climbing back over the console to the passenger side, I decide I'm okay with letting Farren set the pace of whatever is happening between us. I just hope he doesn't wait too long to finally decide he wants to do more than just kiss me.


A FEW hours later, we reach Oklahoma City.

"We're stopping here for the night," Farren announces as he pulls into the lot of a modest, circa 1950's motel.

"Aren't we going to check out the place where Haven's car was dumped," I inquire. "I mean, that's the whole reason why we're in Oklahoma City, right?"

He throws me a sidelong glance as he places the SUV in park. "*I* am going to check out where the car was dumped. *You* are going to stay here." He gestures to the single-story motel building.

"Oh, lovely," I murmur as I take in the surroundings.

It's kind of like we've time-warped back to that sixties movie *Psycho*. The motel is a perfect match. There's just no creepy Gothic house up on the hill. In fact, there are no hills. It is mostly flat here. Glancing around, I can see there are no other hotels or motels in the vicinity. It appears we are stuck with the Bates Motel.

"I'd probably be safer with you," I mumble under my breath when a haggard bum hobbles by.

Farren makes a scoffing sound. But after we're checked in to two rooms directly next to one another, he reconsiders. "Maybe you should go with me," he says just as I'm turning the key (no key cards here) to let myself into my room.

I quickly agree, and we make a plan to meet back outside the rooms in half an hour, giving us each time to clean up after all the hours we spent on the road today.

Thankfully, when I step into the room, despite the old-fashioned furnishings, the place appears to be very clean. I take a quick shower, throw on a different pair of jeans, as well as a fresh linen blouse, and then meet Farren outside.

He's still wearing jeans, but he's changed into a black button-down shirt. The sleeves are rolled up, exposing his strong, corded forearms. I can't stop staring, and as we start toward the SUV, I sigh longingly.

Farren is slightly ahead of me. He glances back at me over his shoulder and asks, "Is everything okay?"

"Yep," I reply, my eyes traveling over his wide, commanding shoulders and down to his torso that tapers to a perfect V. "Everything is perfect."

And for the moment, everything is perfect indeed.

# CHAPTER NINE

B UT things don't stay perfect. They so very rarely do.
Reality creeps back in as Farren and I drive away from the motel. We travel to the outskirts of Oklahoma City, to a derelict part of town where abandoned warehouses and old railroad tracks dominate the barren landscape. If I wasn't with Farren, who is more than capable of protecting us, I'd turn tail and run far, far away.

We slow to a stop and park in front of what appears to have once been a train depot, like from a hundred years ago.

"Well, this is creepy," I say, jerking my chin to the boarded-up structure.

"Don't worry. We're not going in there," Farren assures me as we exit the SUV. He points to a dirt path snaking around the side of the building. "The dump is back there. That's where we need to go."

"Oh, that's so much better," I mumble sarcastically.

I stare down at the crisscross of old railroad tracks and the clumps of weeds growing between them that we'll have to walk through to reach the path.

When he sees me frowning, Farren says, "Come on. You'll be fine."

With a resigned sigh, I follow him over the tracks and to the trail.

"All we need now is for a tumbleweed to roll by," I remark.

Farren laughs. "That might happen," he says. "This is an old ghost town, you know."

"No, I didn't know." Cringing, I latch on to Farren's arm. "And that, by the way, does not make me feel any better."

A second later, a rat the size of a small cat scurries by. I scream and squeeze his bicep. "I hate this place," I cry.

"Yeah," Farren mumbles, more somber now. He wraps his arm around me protectively. "I'm not too crazy about it either."

When we reach the back of the building, my hate for the Godforsaken place increases tenfold. There's a giant hole in the ground, like a crater. But this is a crater from hell. It's more like an abyss.

"That's the dump," Farren informs me, his arm dropping from my shoulders.

We both step closer. "You're not really planning on going down there, are you?" I ask.

The abyss is filled with discarded farm equipment, large appliances...and automobiles.

"Yes, I really am planning on going down there," Farren replies.

As I scan the contents of the dump I feel sick, and not just because Farren is going to lower himself into the horrid place. We're here to verify if it was Haven's car that was dumped, but I didn't expect to have such a gut-wrenching, visceral reaction to seeing her navy-blue Jetta. Seeing it now, though, discarded several yards below where I'm standing, and wedged between an old refrigerator and a tractor that has to be at least fifty years old, I can't stop the sob that escapes me.

"We had so much fun in that car," I say, my voice cracking.

I think of all the late-night ice cream and candy runs— provisions for all-night study sessions—Haven and I embarked on. I think of the talks she and I had in that car—worrying about school, worrying about boys. All the good times come rushing back to me. Like how we used to roll down the windows, turn up the radio, and sing along to our favorite songs.

I share all this with Farren and finish with, "God, Haven's voice was so pretty."

"Don't say 'was,'" Farren whispers.

I look his way, and my heart breaks. "Oh, Farren…"

If seeing Haven's car abandoned like trash is upsetting to me, it's devastating for her brother. When he catches me staring at him, though, he schools his features quickly.

"Wait here," he says, clearing his throat. "I'm going down. Whatever you do, *do not* move from this spot."

I nod and assure him, "I'm not going anywhere."

Farren begins to work on securing an old rope that he finds discarded on the ground. He ties it to one of the posts supporting the back portico of the train depot. Within minutes, he's done and lowering himself to where Haven's car rests.

I watch as the rope twists and flips around on the ground. In the dying light of day, it looks like a flailing bone-colored snake.

*Ugh.* I shudder and focus solely on Farren's form disappearing into the shadows as he lowers himself deeper and deeper into the abyss. Soon, I can no longer see him.

After a minute of complete silence, Farren yells up, "Essa," startling me.

Jumping, I tentatively step closer to the edge and yell back, "Are you all right?"

Just as I finish speaking, Farren comes into view. He's a few feet away from Haven's car. The rope is dangling over what appears to be some dangerously sharp and rusty farm equipment. If Farren falls or the rope drops any further, he could be in peril.

"Essa," he says loudly enough to garner my attention. "Steady the rope."

I kneel and grab for the moving rope. I try to keep the rope still, but it ultimately takes me sitting on the damn thing for it to quit twisting around on the ground.

"Perfect, Essa," Farren calls up. "Now, just continue to keep it steady."

I do as he asks, and the rope stays settled long enough for him to jump over to the hood of Haven's car. Farren reaches around the side and pops open the door. Quick as a blink, he's in the car. From my vantage point, I can't see what he's doing. I only detect movement. I remain on the rope so it stays steady for him to jump back over to it when he's done.

A few minutes pass, and when Farren emerges from the Jetta, he jumps over to the rope. He starts to shimmy up, shouting as he goes, "Move, Essa."

I scoot away just in time to avoid a potentially nasty brush burn from the rope twisting and bending, same as it did before. When Farren hoists his body over the edge of the crater, I rise to my knees, crawl over to him, and wrap my arms around him. He hugs me back. There's no explanation needed as to why we both feel a need to be held right now.

Sitting back on my heels, but with my arms still held loosely around Farren, I ask, "Did you find anything? Were there any clues inside the car?"

He shakes his head grimly. "No, nothing helpful. But that is definitely my sister's car down there."

With neither one of us wanting to spend another moment in the place where Haven's car was dumped like random trash, we hurry back to the SUV and return to the motel.

I WAKE at 2:22 on the nose. The LED numbers on the bedside alarm clock glow in the darkness, bathing everything in an eerie, red sheen. I roll over in the lumpy motel bed and breathe in deeply. A vague scent of air sanitizer and stale smoke fill my nose, reminding me that once upon a time there was no such thing as nonsmoking buildings.

Unable to find sleep again, loneliness creeps in. If I were back at school, I'd feel no need to call my parents—we generally only speak once or twice a month—but here on the road, and with Haven missing, I long to hear a familiar voice. However, I know calling my parents, even from the burner phone, could put me (and Farren) in jeopardy. Surely, the men who kidnapped Haven have noted I'm no longer in Pennsylvania. They probably suspect I'm traveling with Farren, which means my parents' phones, landline and cells, could very well be bugged.

Dismissing any further notions of contacting Mom or Dad, I burrow under the scratchy motel blanket. I'm chilled, though, from the inside out. Nothing can warm me. I toss and turn, wondering if Farren is restless, as well. He hides his worry well, but I know his concern for Haven's well-being has ratcheted up a notch after finding her car abandoned in that hell hole-like abyss.

Slipping out from under the covers, I head to the tiny motel bathroom. When I flip the switch for the light, fluorescent illumination floods the tiny room. Wincing at the blinding light, I mutter, "Jeez, that's bright," and wait for my eyes to adjust.

After I relieve my bladder, I wash my face and brush my teeth. I then comb my fingers through my sleep-messy hair. "Where are you going?" I ask my reflection.

I can't help but smile. I'm going to the one place I know I'll find comfort, warmth, and peace. I'm going to Farren's room.

Five minutes after my decision is made, I am outside, my knuckles poised at the door to Farren's motel room. I hesitate, chastising myself for not slipping on something a little more demure. As it is, I'm in nothing but a skimpy lime-green T-shirt and matching boy shorts. Shoes would have been a good idea, too. Who knows what kind of bugs are scurrying around out here? Just as that particular thought crosses my mind, some squiggly thing brushes by my foot. I jump back a step and start to pound on Farren's door.

"Farren," I whisper loudly, "are you awake? It's me."

I knock more insistently. If he is asleep, he won't be for long.

When, predictably, the door swings open, I am graced by the presence of one damn fine-looking man. I forget about bugs; I forget about my skimpy outfit. All I can do is mouth, "Wow," while I peruse Farren from head to toe.

He's sporting just the right amount of sexy scruff, darkening his strong jaw. The top half of his body is bare, his shoulders appearing wider and stronger than when he's clothed. Perhaps it's due to all the muscles. Damn, he's cut. My eyes travel down Farren's smooth chest to his washboard abs, and then to the fine trail of dark hair that disappears just under the band of dark boxer briefs. Black boxers, I take note. I had a feeling.

"Essa?" Farren rasps in a sleep-thick but utterly sexy voice. He crosses his arms, muscles bunching, and leans against the frame of the door.

His green eyes meet mine. And, oh, that look. I know that look; I probably have it, too. I have two choices here: jump the man or make a joke and dispel the almost-combustible sexual tension between us.

I choose to joke.

Gesturing to strands of dark hair that are sticking up at odd angles on his head, I say, "Disheveled much?"

To which he rapidly responds, "Naked much?"

His gaze rakes over my barely clothed body.

"I'm dressed," I protest, my voice raising an octave.

He reaches out and lifts the hem of my tee, exposing the waistband of my lime-green boy shorts. "Barely," he scoffs. "You're basically standing outside in your underwear."

I smack his hand away, albeit in a playful manner, and retort, "These are shorts." He quirks an eyebrow, and I amend, "Well, kind of."

Suppressing a grin, he moves aside and says, "Essa, get in here."

I walk into his room, turn back to him. And then we both bust out laughing. *This* is why I came to Farren's room. He has a way of making everything better. The strong foundation we've been building may be constructed on the back of a tragedy, but it's not without moments of levity…like now.

I'm still smiling when Farren steps around me. He stretches across the bed to turn on a lamp. And that's when my smile falters. With his bare back facing me, and the glow from the just-turned-on lamp brightening the darkness, I'm afforded a perfect view of a long, jagged scar extending across the smooth skin on Farren's lower back.

Before I can stop myself, I reach out and run my fingers along several inches of puckered, silvery-white edges.

Farren spins around, and I pull my hand back swiftly. "I…I'm sorry," I stammer. "I shouldn't have done that."

He steps toward me, narrowing the space between us in seconds. He lifts my left hand and snakes it around his side. Placing my fingers right back on the scar, he says softly, "You never have to apologize for touching me, Essa."

Once again, I trail my fingers along the puckered skin of the scar, whispering, "What happened?"

"Knife fight."

"You lost?"

"If I'd lost, I would be dead."

"Is the other guy…?"

"Dead?" Farren finishes my unfinished question. I nod, and he responds, "Yes, I killed him."

When my hand falls away from his back and I fail to respond, he asks, "Does that bother you?"

I shake my head. "No."

It's the truth, it doesn't bother me. Farren was obviously fighting for his life. And I'm glad he came out the winner. Again, though, I am reminded of how different our lives are. Farren is a warrior. He's seen and done things I can't even begin to fathom.

But I like his worldliness. Just like I know he likes my innocence. We balance each other in that way, like two sides to a coin.

When I glance up at him, Farren is watching me. "What are you thinking?" he asks.

"Nothing, really."

His arms slide around me, while my own hands find purchase on his bare shoulders.

"Nothing, really, huh?" he says, smiling a small smile. He lowers his lips to mine and says, "Why do I not believe you?"

I want to tell him what I'm thinking—like how much I'm starting to like him, *really* like him. I want to tell him that I believe we could be right for one another and how we should give this thing a chance. But how do I say these things? What if it's too much?

I don't say a word regarding my thoughts. Instead, I press my lips to his, and murmur against his mouth, "Should I go back to my room?"

His lips move with mine. He kisses me softly, tenderly.

"Do you want to go back?" he questions when he breaks our kiss.

I shake my head as he walks me backward to the bed. "Okay, then," he remarks, smirking. "Glad that's settled."

"Are we going to do more than kiss?" I bravely inquire.

He raises an eyebrow and stops just when the edge of the bed is pressing against the back of my knees. "Do you want to do more than kiss?'

"Yes," I reply.

And that's the point where I watch him give in. *I'm done fighting this*, his expression says. Farren is then all over me… hands, lips…caressing, kissing. Lowering me gently to the bed, he covers me with his hard body.

I squirm beneath him, purposely creating friction between his bare chest and my almost-bared breasts. "More, more, more," I chant between kisses.

But I don't get more yet. He stops, flattening his palms on the bed so he can prop himself up over me. With his arms caged around me, his emerald eyes find me. His intensity demands I don't dare stray from his gaze.

"I plan to take things slowly with you," he says quietly as he lifts the hem of my T-shirt just an inch.

"Okay." I nod.

Studying me, his knuckles graze my abdomen, and he asks, "Has anyone ever given you an orgasm, Essa?"

"Um…"

Flattening his warm palm on my skin, he says seductively, "Besides you giving one to yourself, of course."

I breathe out a raspy, "Besides myself, no."

His fingers—so gentle, yet so firm—trail up under my tee. When he reaches my breasts, he circles my nipples lightly. Slowly, he cups the weight of one breast, then the other. "Would you like someone to give you one?" he inquires. His breathing quickens along with mine. "Do you want *me* to make you come, Essa?"

"God, yes," I whisper.

My heart pounds with anticipation, and my body quivers with lust. Farren lowers his mouth to mine and kisses me again, sweetly and gently. "Relax," he whispers.

He plies at my nipples, making them erect and ultrasensitive to his touch. "Don't stop," I breathe out.

"I don't plan to," he assures me.

And upon hearing that, I am grasping at the hem of my tee,

lifting and maneuvering to slip out of the lime-green cotton. The only thing on my mind is getting my clothes off as quickly as possible.

# CHAPTER TEN

HASTE, though, is not what Farren has in mind. He stills my hands with my shirt halfway off. I whimper in protest, and he covers my body with his.

Softly, against my lips, he says, "Slow down a little, Essa. There's no rush. I want you to enjoy everything I'm going to do to you tonight."

His mouth is so warm on mine—so good—and I want to know what's coming. "And just what are you planning to do to me?" I ask.

He pulls back so he can look down at me. His emerald eyes sear my already-scorched soul. Doesn't he know I am putty in his hands? I suppose he does and that's why he's keeping things under control.

"You'll find out soon enough," he tells me with a smug grin.

And then there's no more talking. We communicate with

movements, little nudges, glances, and nods. When he gestures that I should lift my back up off the bed, I do so. He gently slips my tee over my head. I lay back, and his hand slides under my ass, nudging me. I compliantly arch my hips, and he tugs my boy shorts down my legs. When I am left naked before him, he sits up and rocks back on his heels. His eyes move over me, taking me in inch by inch. A delicious shiver moves up my spine. And when I take note of his impressive arousal, barely covered by his boxer briefs, needs stronger than I've ever before experienced ignite in me.

I'm not secure with my body, though, so when his eyes continue to soak me in, I feel compelled to say, "I'm not model perfect, Farren."

Suddenly feeling shy, I place one hand over my heavy breasts and the other hand over my bare pubic area. Are my boobs too big? Should I not have waxed down *there*? Apart from those nagging thoughts, I begin to wish I had a third hand to cover my not-completely flat tummy.

Farren, though, seems not one bit bothered by any of those things. In fact, he tells me, "I like everything about your body, Essa."

The look in his eyes backs up his words. His gaze is appreciative, delivered in a distinctly male way—the kind that has the ability to make you feel downright beautiful. And I do feel beautiful. Right now, I feel like I'm the prettiest girl on the planet.

So when Farren nudges my hand away from my breasts, and then moves the hand covering my sex, I don't resist. He takes another sweeping survey of my uncovered body. This time, it's like he's contemplating what to do first to me.

I shiver in anticipation, and he leans down and slowly kisses a heated path from my collarbone to my breasts. "Feel good?" he murmurs.

"Very," I reply.

He nuzzles and lifts a breast to his mouth, his lips covering the nipple. He sucks and licks and drives me flat-out crazy. He then moves to my other breast and does the same thing. After a few minutes of this, I am instinctually lifting my hips, seeking release. My movement doesn't go unnoticed by Farren. His fingers part my folds and glide along my slick core. With his mouth latched on to one breast, and his fingers working me like a finely tuned instrument, my climax builds and builds.

He winds me up till I'm ready to spring, and when he releases my nipple from his mouth and presses a path of wet kisses down to my core, I am at the peak, chanting, "Oh my God, oh my God."

"Not God, Essa," Farren says softly, his hot breaths caressing my pubic bone.

*No, not God.* "Farren," I correct.

He lowers his head and touches my clit with his tongue, and I explode. "Oh, Farren, Farren," I moan, writhing and arching.

I go slack, but Farren is not anywhere close to being finished with me. He moves his fingers in and out of me, hitting my sweet spot in just the right way. At the same time, he sucks on my nub, licking and lapping. I'm overwhelmed, and sweet pressure quickly builds again. I suck in a breath, and when Farren presses his tongue to the underside of my clit, waves of pleasure wash over me. I finally understand what all the fuss is about.

Two orgasms in succession, and I find all sense of propriety is lost. I grind my sex right up into Farren's face. But he doesn't seem to mind. He hoists my ass up higher and shoves his tongue deep inside of me.

"Gah—oh, fuck, Farren." Another intense orgasm renders me incoherent.

When I finally come back down to earth, he sits up. I expect this to be the point where he moves up my body and makes me his. After all, I can see how hard he is. His erection now extends beyond the top edge of his boxer briefs. The tip is moist with pre-cum, and for the first time in my life, I long to put a cock in my mouth—Farren's cock.

He catches me staring at his dick and quirks an eyebrow. "Like what you see, Essa?"

I nod.

He tilts his head slightly. "What are you thinking?" he asks.

I'm quiet, and he prods, "Essalin?"

I whisper the truth. "I'm thinking that I want to know what you taste like."

Smiling, he leans down and kisses the insides of my still-quivering thighs—once, twice—and then he scoots up the bed until he is kneeling next to my head.

When he takes off his boxer briefs, I gush, "Wow. You're, like, really huge."

Farren chuckles and lets me stare in amazement.

"I can't wait to feel you inside of me," I murmur.

And that makes him groan. "Essa…"

But tonight is about taking things slowly. I know he'll make me wait. Still, I can't stop staring…and desiring.

"Essalin," Farren rasps, his voice thick with his own need, "look at me."

He trails a hand down to where I am, frankly, dripping. My eyes meet his, and he slides one finger into me. When he adds a second, my hips, of their own accord, begin to move with him.

"I don't think I can take much more," I gasp.

"You can take a lot more," he tells me.

And so I move with him. I'm so wet that his fingers slide with ease between my swollen lips. "There you go, baby," he says as his thumb works my clit.

When he adds a third finger and pumps more rapidly, I say, "I think I'm going to come again."

"I know you're going to come again," he replies.

I lick my lips and reach for him. "Come with me, then."

He scoots closer, and I take him in my mouth greedily, surprising myself. But the things Farren has made me feel tonight have me feeling fully open to him. I'll do anything he wants me to. And I want to please him as much as he's pleased me.

I imagine how we look right now: Farren kneeling next to me, my head turned to him so I can suck his cock. And me, spread wide on the bed, Farren's fingers deep inside of me. It's erotic; it's hot, and when I feel him start to pulse, I don't pull away. I want all of him...

And I get all of him. The groan he emits as he's coming in my mouth fills me with satisfaction that I've fully pleasured Farren Shaw.

Afterward, I myself am so incredibly satiated that I have no energy to get up and brush my teeth. "Oh my God, I can't move," I murmur.

Farren covers me with a sheet that smells of us. He gets out of the bed. "Wait here," he says.

I watch his gloriously masculine body as he walks to the tiny motel bathroom. "Gorgeous," I mutter to myself.

When he returns, after I hear him peeing and washing off at

the basin, he's carrying a tumbler of water and a toothbrush with a curl of toothpaste atop the bristles.

"Thank you," I say as I pull the sheet higher and sit up.

Farren hands me the toothbrush, and I brush. He glances around the room, finds an empty plastic cup on the table next to the bed, and holds it out to me. "Spit," he commands.

After I do as I'm told, I wipe my mouth with the back of my hand and say again, "Thank you."

He hands me the tumbler of clean water and takes the toothbrush and cup of yucky toothpaste spit back to the bathroom. A few seconds later, I hear him brushing his own teeth. And then he returns.

I'm leaning across the bed, trying to reach the table next to it so I can place the cup of water there. Farren gently slides the cup from my grasp, smiles, and accomplishes the task for me. When he slips back under the covers, he pulls me to him. "How do you feel about what we did tonight?"

I glance up at him from where I'm sprawled across his broad chest. "What do you mean?" I ask.

He brushes back hair that has fallen to my cheek. "I know you're not very experienced, Essa. That's why I kept things, well, limited. I just want to make sure you're comfortable with the things we did do."

"What?" I drag out the *a*. "Are you kidding? I loved everything we did."

I'm sure I sound overly enthusiastic, and my cheeks heat when I realize how my comment, and the way it's been delivered, proves his point regarding my inexperience.

But he doesn't mention any of that. Instead, he asks, "Was that the first time you've been…uh, pleasured orally?"

I'm sure, by his hesitation, he was about to use a much cruder term for what he did to me. But it is sweet that he cleaned it up for my sake.

Still, I feel awkward for being such a newbie in this area of sex. I plant my face in his chest and murmur, "Yes," against hard muscles and smooth skin. "It was my first for the other thing, too." He's quiet, and I glance up. "Did I do okay?"

Farren chuckles and replies, "You were perfect, Essa." He wraps his arms around me. "Now, let's get some sleep."

I sleep the best I have since Haven went missing. Sleeping in Farren's capable arms is pure bliss. Unfortunately, when I wake up the next morning, he's not there. The shower is still dripping, so I assume I must have just missed him. Returning to my own motel room, I take a shower and get dressed. I choose a pair of gray cutoff shorts and a sky-blue top to wear on this fine day.

As I'm pulling my shorts up my legs, I hear Farren returning to his room next door. I finish dressing then hurry and pack up my things. I don't want to be the one to hold us up from getting back out on the road. When I'm done I rush over to Farren's room. As I walk in, after a light knock on the slightly ajar door, I find Farren leaning over a map that he has spread out over the surface of the small table by the bed. He's wearing dark pants and a white button-down, sleeves rolled up.

"Where were you?" I ask, taking a tentative step toward him.

He glances up at me. "Oh, I had to speak with Rick."

"Rick is here in Oklahoma City?" I exclaim. "I thought he was going straight to New Mexico."

"He is in New Mexico," Farren replies distractedly, his eyes back on the map. "I talked with him on the phone."

"But our burner phones are here." I gesture to the bag Farren keeps his in.

"Actually"—he looks over at me—"we needed new ones. That's why I went out." He reaches into his pocket, takes out a small cell, and tosses it my way.

I catch it just as he says, "Give me your old one later today, and I'll dispose of it."

"Oh, okay."

Farren returns to studying the map, and I take another step closer. He seems a little closed off today, and I pray it's not because of what happened between us last night.

"Are we still going to New Mexico?" I quietly ask.

It seems like a fair question, since he's poring over a map of that state. Plus, New Mexico is supposed to be our next destination.

"Yes," Farren replies slowly. "But not today."

"Oh." I'm surprised by the change in plans. "I thought time was of the essence."

Farren gives me a look like my comments are amusing. He smiles, and I feel like he's opening up to me again. Guess he was just distracted.

"Time *is* of the essence," he confirms. "And we'll still be going to New Mexico…just not today."

"Can I ask why?"

He pinches the bridge of his nose. "Rick has a team set up to rescue my sister, and—"

"Whoa, wait." I put up my hand. This is why he seemed distracted. "You know where Haven is? She's definitely in New Mexico?"

I'm filled with renewed hope, but I'm only cautiously

optimistic. We may know Haven's location, but she's not been rescued yet. And the men who have her aren't exactly nice.

"We have a potential location, yes," Farren says. "But it's nothing definite. I don't want to be on the road, however, and not be able to reach Rick. So, for the next few days, we remain where we are."

I can't help it, I'm so excited that this whole Haven-in-danger ordeal may be coming to a close that I race over to Farren and throw my arms around him.

"This is so incredible," I murmur into the crisp, starched cotton of his dress shirt. "I can't wait to see her again." Glancing up, I bite my lip and ask, "You don't think she'll be mad we, uh, sort of hooked up, do you?"

Farren smiles down at me, and, caressing my cheek, he says, "No, she won't be mad. You know Haven's not like that."

"I know, but under the circumstances…"

"Hey." He urges me to meet his gaze. "I think we may be getting way ahead of ourselves here. Let's just see how the rescue attempt goes. If things go well, we'll head down to a safe house that is west of Las Cruces. That's in southern New Mexico. That particular safe house is where I've directed Rick to take Haven once he has her. It's not a perfect location, but it will do for a while. Anyway, if things go as seamlessly as I'm hoping, you can go ahead and ask Haven yourself how she feels about us."

A lump rises in my throat. I've not allowed myself to dwell on how much I've been missing my best friend, but I let go a little now. "I've missed her so much, Farren. I can't wait to see her. But I'm kind of afraid to get too excited. Do you know what I mean?"

I look up at him, and he gives me a small smile. Then he

closes his arms around me.

Holding me in his comforting embrace, he says, "I know exactly what you mean, Essa. I know the feeling all too well."

# CHAPTER ELEVEN

WITH the burden of a missing Haven off both our minds, I get to know Farren in a different way. He becomes a man unburdened by underlying worry for his sister. He kept the level of his concern well hidden, but I'm certain the not knowing part was killing him. So the change is good for many reasons. I'm much more lighthearted as well. And, sure, we're not out of the woods yet when it comes to Haven, but this is the best things have looked since the beginning. And it shows in my and Farren's demeanors.

"You seem different," I say to Farren as we stroll along the sidewalk one afternoon. We're on our way to a cute old-time movie house about a quarter mile from our motel. The plan is to catch the matinee of a low-budget horror movie that's playing.

"Different how?" he asks.

"You just seem"—I shrug—"I don't know. Happy, I guess."

He shoots me a sly smile. "Maybe it's because I *am* happy, Essa."

"Because Haven has been found and will be rescued any day now?"

"Yes, there's that, of course. Among other things…"

We reach the movie house, so I'm not able to question him further. Though I think I know the answer anyway. At least I hope I do.

Inside the retro theater, Farren and I share a tub of buttery popcorn, drink jumbo pops, and laugh about how characters in scary movies always do the most stupid things.

"Why do they always go where nobody in their right mind would *ever* step foot?" I ask Farren, in a whisper, just as the movie begins.

The movie opened with a girl in her late teens creeping down a set of dank, dark basement steps.

"I hate basements," I whisper, leaning into Farren's solid shoulder. "You'd never catch *me* going down those stairs. That's supposed to be a haunted house, right? Who in their right mind would go straight to the basement?"

"Essa, shh," Farren admonishes. But he's grinning as he drapes his arm around me.

I snuggle in close to him. He always smells so intoxicatingly good, and now is no exception. Soon, I'm able to relax a bit. Well, until some shadowy figure jumps out at the girl from under the basement steps. Then, I jump in my seat and scream, "See, I knew it!"

The girl is dragged off, and I grasp the soft cotton of the T-shirt Farren is wearing.

He laughs at me. "Essa, weren't you saying when we first sat down that the special effects in these movies always suck?"

"Not in this movie," I retort, clinging to Farren for dear life.

"Essa…" He kisses the top of my head. "…You are too damn cute."

Good thing he finds me cute, since by the end of the movie I am halfway in his lap.

"That movie was terrifying," I declare a few minutes later when we're leaving the theater.

"Good thing I was with you," Farren replies.

"Good thing you were," I agree, bumping into him.

The days pass with Farren and I spending all our time together. Sure, he takes breaks to speak with Rick on the progress of the rescue attempt. But since the pieces are falling into place as planned—Rick is putting together a rescue team—Farren and I have plenty of time to concentrate on each other.

Oh, and the fun we have…

We go out to dinner every evening, and we play during the day. We discover a nice park for walking down the street from the motel. We take strolls there on sunny afternoons. I get to know Farren better, and he gets to know me. And at night, we get to know each other in ways that don't involve much talking. No matter what we do, though, we have a great time together. Even when we have to pay a visit to a local Laundromat—we're running low on clothes—we make the most of it.

The morning we're at the Laundromat, Farren is teasing and flirting with me while folding his jeans and T-shirts. I'm at the other end of the folding counter, but he keeps edging in closer and closer.

"What are you doing?" I ask, laughing when he's practically on top of me.

"Checking out what you're folding there," he says nonchalantly, nodding to a set of silky red Victoria's Secret bra and panties. "I don't think I've seen those on you yet," he remarks.

"I wore them on one of our first days," I say. "Before we were, uh, messing around."

"Messing around," he mumbles to himself, chuckling. And then he leans in even closer, his breath warm and sweet at my ear. "Hmm, maybe you can wear those tonight for me. You know," he quips, "before we get to the 'messing around' part of things."

"Farren," I admonish, blushing.

Images of him peeling the lingerie off of me and then covering each inch of newly exposed skin with hungry kisses have me feeling hot and horny right in the middle of the Laundromat.

"Maybe I can wear them sooner," I suggest. "Like as soon as we get back to the motel."

Farren leans down and kisses my lips lightly. "I'd like that, Essa," he tells me.

But before we can race back to the motel, Farren has to drop off his nicer clothes—dress pants and button-down shirts—at the dry cleaner next door.

"Have them ready by tomorrow morning," he tells the withered old woman at the counter after she takes his clothes.

She has a hooknose and no-nonsense eyes that flash in irritation when she barks, "Two business days is the best we can do."

Farren hands her a fifty. Quirking an eyebrow, he says, "Now can you have the clothes ready by tomorrow?"

She snatches up the bill. "Yes, sir," she says, her tone suddenly breezy. "Your clothes will be pressed and ready by nine."

"Make it eight."

The counter woman can't meet Farren's hard stare. She acquiesces and says, "Eight it is."

"Do you always get your way, Farren?" I ask on the way to where we parked the SUV.

"Mostly," he replies with a cocky grin. "Throwing some money around always helps."

I just shake my head and smile in return.

Damn, I am falling for Farren. Spending all this time together, continuously, with no breaks, has allowed us to grow close, very close. Just the other evening after eating something that didn't agree with me, I was feeling sick and Farren stayed by my side all night. As he held me in his arms I asked him to tell me something to distract me from my aching belly. He told me dirty jokes the soldiers in his basic-training unit had once shared. I was soon laughing and forgetting all about my upset stomach.

I'm finding Farren is everything guys my own age aren't. He's attentive and exceptionally sweet to me, and he makes me feel good about myself. Not to mention he sure is incredibly nice to look at.

And that's what I'm doing once we're back at the motel. I'm watching a very hot, very handsome Farren lower his head to my breast. I'm not wearing a thing as I lie on the bed. Remember that sexy lingerie? Well, it was put on...and promptly removed—very slowly—by Farren. Farren, with his dark hair currently mussed from my fingers raking through the silky strands again and again.

He latches on to a nipple, and I gasp in response. I watch as thick, corded muscles in his shoulders and arms bunch and contract as he moves his body over mine. So far, Farren has been above me, beside me, behind me, and under me as we've engaged in many sexual acts. The only place he's not yet been is inside of me.

And I. Am. Dying.

"Please, Farren," I plead, the weight of his erection pressing enticingly at my thigh. "Just put it in for a second."

He releases my nipple and looks up at me. "Patience, Essa," he replies.

"How can you be so strong?" I ask.

"How can I not?"

Farren won't articulate it, but I know what he's doing. It's not just a wait-until-Essa-is-ready thing, though there is that. Farren is also molding me—sexually—to be exactly how he wants me to be. He's making me his, teaching me what he likes. He shows me how he wants me to touch him, and he asks me to tell him which of the many things he does to me I like best. Turns out, I like pretty much everything he does. I respond favorably to Farren's every touch, his every grasp. I learn to let myself go. I've become comfortable with Farren. My body craves what he gives me, and I know he enjoys watching me revel in pleasure. And I certainly enjoy pleasing him in whichever way he desires.

The man is infinitely creative, too. Like the next morning in the shower…

We're not actually showering. No, not yet. Farren isn't even in the shower. He's seated, naked, on the edge of the tub. I'm in the shower, but I'm not washing. I am getting myself off for Farren's pleasure…and for my own, of course.

Hot water pours down my back, adding to all the heady sensations. One foot is up on Farren's bare thigh. He wants to see everything I do to myself, and he wants to see it all up close. We've left the shower curtain half-open and water is shooting everywhere.

But neither of us cares. Farren is too busy watching me. And he's jerking off.

He finds a rhythm that matches the one I have going as I slide my fingers over my clit and into my pussy again and again.

I gasp, he groans. My toes curl and his quad beneath my foot tightens. "I'm close," I rasp.

In response, he aims his cock at my folds, and when I start to pulse, so does he. Hot spurts of his essence hit my pussy, as well as my moving fingers. My orgasm is prolonged when I think of how erotic and dirty this act is…and how much I love it.

"Did you like that?" Farren asks a minute later as he's getting into the shower behind me.

I lean back against his hard chest. "Yes," I reply, "very much."

Farren picks up the soap and gently lathers my shoulders. His strong hands ply at muscles that are sore from him working me in so many sexual ways. His hands skim down my back, and he murmurs, "My Essa."

"I am your Essa," I whisper.

And it's true. I am becoming his in every way. Farren molds me. He shapes me. He's making me ready to become his in the only way he hasn't had me yet.

And, boy, am I ever ready.


WHEN we get word from Rick that the rescue attempt has been a success—Haven is safe and at the house near Las Cruces—Farren and I head back out on the road. The weather is perfect, and I'm in a fine mood, so I take loads of pictures with the disposable camera Farren bought me on day one.

When I reach the last shot and utter a curse, he looks over.

"Ready for another?" he asks.

"I think so," I reply.

At our next stop, Farren buys me an entire bagful of cameras.

Two hundred miles into our travels, though, I'm kind of done with snapping photos of passing scenery. I do, however, sneak in a few great profile shots of Farren. Strong jaw, light stubble, sunglasses…Yeah, those pics promise to be keepers.

When my photographer-moment passes, I'm awash in guilt. I haven't asked much about Haven and the rescue mission.

Glancing down at my lap, I do so now. "So, Haven is definitely safe?"

Farren keeps his eyes on the road ahead. Not that I can see his greens anyway, due to the sunglasses. "She's safe," he replies levelly.

But something feels amiss.

"How'd it go so smoothly?" I inquire. "Did Rick just waltz in to wherever she was and take her."

Farren snorts. "It wasn't quite that simple, Essa."

"Were Eric and Vincent there?"

"No," he states.

That leaves me chilled—the thought that Eric and Vincent are still out there.

"Then who was watching Haven?" I ask.

"Guards."

"How many?"

"A few."

"What happened to them?" I press.

Farren looks over at me. I wish I had the nerve to reach over and snatch off his sunglasses so I could see what's really in his eyes. But I wouldn't dare.

When his gaze returns to the road, he says, "What do you think happened to them?"

"They were incapacitated?" I venture.

He laughs. "You could say that."

"I don't want to talk about the guards anymore," I suddenly snap.

"Good," Farren says dryly.

"So," I begin anew, "what's the plan for when we reach New Mexico?"

Farren exhales audibly, and I know he's glad the subject has veered away from the rescue-mission recap.

"We'll meet up with Rick and Haven," he says. "He's driving her up to Albuquerque after she's seen by a doctor."

"A doctor?" My brow creases. "I thought she was okay?"

"She is," Farren says carefully, "more or less. Still, I want one of our people to check her over."

"You have doctors that work with you?"

"You'd be surprised at the people I work with," Farren replies.

This is the most open Farren has ever been. I sense he wants to talk, and that he may even be finally ready to share some things with me. It's not entirely surprising. After all the time we've been spending together, there's no way he's not feeling as close to me as I am to him. He is only human, after all.

Confirming my suspicion that he wants to talk, he continues. "We're just lucky we have Haven back with us. A few more days and she would have been somewhere in Mexico…where it'd take us God knows how long to find her." He sighs disgustedly. "The things that would've happened to her down there…"

When he trails off, I carefully ask, "What would've happened?"

There is still so much I don't know. But Farren knows. He's

obviously deeply involved, as is his friend Rick. How else would they have all this inside information? Besides the time they spent working together on special-ops missions, Farren and Rick obviously still work as a team for someone now. But who employs them? And why? What's the real endgame here?

Farren glances over at me. He's painfully beautiful as the sun shines on him through the windshield. *God, you're stunning*, I think. But I can't afford distraction right now. I want an answer.

I again ask, "What would've happened to your sister in Mexico, Farren?"

A muscle twitches in his jaw. "Let's just say bad things, Essa. Very bad things."

I'm exasperated. "Please, Farren, you have to give me something more. Like, how do you know all this stuff? Don't I deserve some answers? I mean, even after..." My voice cracks.

I feel close to him. How could he not feel close to me as well? But if that were true, he'd give me more, right?

"I just don't know," I mumble.

"Don't know what?" he asks, his patience growing thin.

"I thought we were getting close." I stare out the side window. "That's all."

His hand goes to my knee. "We are getting close, sweetheart."

I misunderstand him and snap defensively, "I meant beyond the physical stuff."

He swiftly withdraws his hand from my knee and says sharply, "I was referring to things beyond the physical stuff, Essalin."

"Oh." Now, I feel like an ass.

A long moment passes. Farren sighs and takes off his sunglasses. He says, "Look, I'm sorry. I didn't mean to get angry with you."

"I'm sorry, too," I reply, my tone truly apologetic. "I made an assumption."

"That's okay," he says.

"Yeah, but you know what they say when you go and 'assume' something."

Farren makes a chuffing sound. He knows I'm trying to lighten things up. Smiling, he says, "Yeah, best not to assume. It makes an *ass* out of *u* and *me*."

We both start laughing, and when things settle, he sighs and says, "You've been very patient, Essa. And I know I should be more forthcoming with y—"

"Farren," I interrupt, my eyes lowering to my lap. "You don't have to tell me anything. I'm good."

His hand returns to my knee, and he says, "But I want to tell you, Essa. I really do."

And that is how, somewhere near Amarillo, Texas, I find out what it is that Farren really does.

"After I was discharged from the military," he begins, "I was approached by a man named Barnes, Mr. Quinton Barnes."

Farren quiets after he reveals his employer's name. I'm also silent, contemplating. I know I've heard that name before. In a business context, I'm sure of it. But I can't think of where.

It comes to me, though, when Farren says, "Mr. Barnes is a very wealthy man, very powerful, with connections all over the world."

"I've heard of him," I tell Farren excitedly. "I read about Quinton Barnes in Business Studies, freshman year."

"I'm not surprised you've heard of him," Farren replies. "He's a very successful businessman."

"He's private, though, right?" I say. "I think I remember

reading that he made his fortune later in life and that he's always been somewhat of a recluse."

Farren appears surprised that I recall such detail. Suddenly, and inexplicably devoid of emotion, he states, "Yeah, that's right."

*Weird.*

"So," I say brightly, trying to lighten the mood. "Mr. Barnes is super powerful and wealthy. What did he want from you?"

"It's something he still wants, Essa," Farren says flatly.

"And that is…" I prompt.

"He wants something all the power and wealth in the world can never give him."

"What does that mean?" I softly inquire.

Farren hesitates, and for a moment I think he's going to say something pertaining to himself. But then he simply says, "It means he wants justice for his daughter."

"And *you* can give it to him?"

"Yes"—he levels me with an intense stare—"I can."

His eyes return to the road, and I ask, "Why does he want justice for his daughter?" *Justice only you can give*, I add in my head. "What happened to her?"

Farren shoots me a sidelong glance. "Are you sure you want to know?"

I take a breath then exhale. "Yeah, I want to know."

"His daughter was kidnapped, abused, tortured, sold into sexual slavery, and, eventually, murdered."

*Holy hell.* "Good God."

"The men who kidnapped her are part of the same organization that took Haven. It's all part of something big, Essa, something very big. Eric and Vincent work for that organization. Their job is to kidnap women, girls even. They generally prey on runaways, people with no ties to anyone. But that's not always the case."

"Is this like something mob related?" I question.

"I wish it were that simple," Farren says, scrubbing his hand down his face. "The criminal organization that engages in those practices does have mob ties. But it's also part of a larger conglomerate, a conglomerate with many legitimate businesses, businesses it can hide behind."

"So," I ask, "it's just the one arm of the conglomerate that's bad?"

"Yes," Farren confirms. "That's why Mr. Barnes's daughter was taken. He refused to sell one of his companies to a very powerful man within the corrupt part of the organization, a man known simply as Dawson."

"Dawson," I whisper. The name alone turns my stomach.

"He stays behind the scenes, this Dawson. I've met with him a few times, and on first glance he gives the impression that he's just another older, conservative-looking businessman. But, really, he's a very sick and twisted man." Farren's voice grows grim. "He delights in the humiliation and pain of others."

I cringe, and Farren hurriedly finishes up with, "Bottom line, Dawson lost a lot of money when Barnes wouldn't play ball. Taking Mr. Barnes's daughter was retribution."

"But to take his *daughter.*" I'm aghast. "Good Lord, what was her name? And how old was she?"

Farren looks stricken when he says, "Her name was Annemarie." He composes himself almost instantly, though, and adds, "She was sixteen."

I feel sick. "Poor Annemarie," I utter.

Sixteen and captured by a sick, twisted man, a man who has

the power to make people disappear with no questions asked. I lower the window an inch for some fresh air.

"Are you okay?" Farren asks.

"I think so." I wave my hand. "Yeah, I'm fine. Go on."

Farren breathes in deeply, like he's calming himself. "Anyway, Mr. Barnes presented a compelling case when he spoke to me. He said I could bring on whomever I needed to make things happen. And then he made me an offer…a very lucrative offer."

"An offer to do what exactly?" I inquire.

"Infiltrate the organization. Bring it down, for good."

"Bring down the entire conglomerate of businesses?" I exclaim, flabbergasted that such an endeavor could even be possible.

"Not the entire conglomerate," Farren confirms. "But he wants the human trafficking stopped. He wants the sex-slave trade incapacitated. That means the criminal organization must be brought to its knees, including Dawson."

"And you and Rick have made progress in that direction?"

"Yes, but it's not always the two of us working together. We sometimes work alone, and we sometimes work with teams we've assembled, men we've worked with before, men who can be trusted."

"Special Forces guys?" I venture.

"Often, yes," Farren replies.

Softly, I inquire, "Is that why Haven was targeted?"

Farren nods, running his hand through raven hair that's gotten longer since we first set out on this trip. "Rick and I have caused some major damage, as have our teams. We've disrupted their operation."

"This was why you were spending time in Thailand and

then in South America?" No wonder Farren said the places he'd traveled to were far from pretty. God, the things he must have seen.

"Yes," he replies. "Most of the human trafficking passes through places where corruption runs rampant. It's easier that way to pay people off, to get away with things. Last month I was in Venezuela. I was alone down there. The operation was too sensitive for more than one man." He takes a deep breath. "Even so, I was able to save eight women. It was pretty rough for a while, though. I wasn't sure if I'd be able to get them out, especially since I had no backup. But knowing I was helping those girls get away from that life kept me focused, and I was ultimately successful."

"That's amazing, Farren," I say in a low voice. "What you've done, how you've put yourself on the line."

I want to add that I'm in awe right now, but I don't.

Farren glances over at me, and then back to the road. "Anyway, in Venezuela, I infiltrated the drug cartel that was holding the girls captive, and that's where I met Eric and Vincent. They thought I was on their side. Naturally, their opinions changed once I escaped with the women. Kidnapping Haven is retaliation, a warning to stop." He pauses and then says quietly, "So now you know, Essa."

"Now I know," I echo.

We're both quiet for several minutes, and then I reach over and touch his arm. "I knew all along you were one of the good guys."

Farren gives me a sad smile. "That's debatable. I've had to do some bad things along the way, things that have been less than honorable."

"I'm sure," I murmur.

Drug cartels, human trafficking, duping a corrupt organization into thinking you're on their side…

I hasten to add, "I don't think I want to know any specific details."

Farren replies dryly, "No, Essalin. I assure you that you don't want more detail."

Silence descends. But, after a while, there's comfort in the quiet. All this honesty has torn down any remaining barriers between us. There are no secrets anymore, none that matter, and I am left with the knowledge that despite things he's had to do, Farren Shaw is ultimately a good man.

We continue on our journey, closing in on the New Mexico border, and it soon becomes apparent from the relaxed set of Farren's shoulders that confiding in me has been a relief for him, too.

We talk and listen to music. Farren smiles more frequently as we log mile after mile, and God is his smile beautiful. At one point a sleek sports car passes, and I make a joke about our SUV.

Farren laughs. "Is that a hint that you're ready for a different car?"

"Um"—I hem and haw—"you want the truth?"

This earns me another sidelong glance, one filled with mock impatience. "Yes, the truth would be good."

Scrunching up my face, I admit, "Yes, I kind of am ready for something different."

Farren makes a quick call on his burner phone, listing a series of numbers (latitude and longitude?) to whoever's on the receiving end.

"What was that all about?" I ask, just as we're entering the state of New Mexico. We exit the interstate almost immediately and turn off onto some lonely desert road.

"That was about a surprise for you," Farren says cryptically.

Ten minutes later we're at an abandoned warehouse, not a soul in sight. Farren stops the SUV, gets out, and slides open a large metal door on the front of the building. When he gets back in the SUV, he drives straight into the warehouse. A motion-activated light illuminates the empty interior.

But the warehouse isn't completely empty.

When I see what is in there, I promptly gush, "Oh...my...God..."

Farren places the SUV in park, leans over, and whispers in my ear, "Do you like your surprise?"

"Do I ever," I remark.

In front of me is the car I was expecting Farren to have from the start of this adventure—a sleek red sports car.

"What is it?" I ask.

"It's a car, Essa," he deadpans.

Since he's still close to me, I push him away, albeit playfully. "Ha-ha. I mean what *kind* of car is it?"

"I know what you meant," he tells me, opening the driver's side door. "Come on. We'll go check it out together."

Farren knows exactly what kind of car it is. After all, I soon come to learn, it's his.

"Not a rental?" I ask, just to be sure I've heard him correctly.

"It's all mine, baby," he says, smirking.

He then informs me that the shiny red car is a Ferrari 458 Italia. That doesn't mean a whole hell of a lot to me, but I suspect it's fast as hell.

Farren begins to fidget with the removable hardtop, saying as he works at it nimbly, "This is only the first part of your surprise."

I circle the perimeter of the car, admiring its sleekness. "What's the second part?" I distractedly trace my index finger along the smooth hood.

I look up when I get no response. Wow. And if I thought Farren's smiles earlier were amazing, I was sadly mistaken. The smile he gives me now blows all the others away.

He fishes a key from his pocket and hands it to me. "Let's go have some fun," he says.

I whisper, "No way."

"It's your turn to drive, right?"

I take the key hesitantly. "So," I say slowly, "it's finally my turn to drive, and you want me to drive *this* car?"

"Yes." Farren chuckles and takes my hand. With his other hand at the small of my back, he guides me to the driver's side door. "You're going to be driving a Ferrari, Miss Brant, one of the fastest cars in production. This news should make you happy."

My response?

I level him with an are-you-kidding look.

And then we get into the car.

There's no need for words, since I can't begin to convey to Farren how excited I am. Nor can I express how incredibly happy he's made me feel in this moment. But it's not just the Ferrari that's brought me joy. It's Farren. Farren in my life is good for me. He's entered my life at the perfect time, even if the circumstances have been far from ideal. And maybe I've come into his life at the right time, too. It sure seems that way when I look over at him and take note that he seems pretty damn contented himself.

And that is the point when I realize I want this relationship we're building to continue. I don't want things to end after Haven is rescued and we return home. My life, the life I want, well it feels like that life just beginning. One inevitable detour has led me here, but now I need another to keep us together. I've had a taste of Farren, and I'm hungry for more.

I glance over at Farren as I place the key in the ignition. He smiles back at me. There's something more in his expression, though. Something that makes me entertain the notion that maybe, just maybe, Farren Shaw wants this to continue, too.

# CHAPTER TWELVE

A HUNDRED and twenty miles per hour—that's what the speedometer reads when I glance down at it.

I hit the gas.

With me in the driver's seat of a car I never dreamed I'd ever even sit in—let alone *drive*—I barrel down a long stretch of blacktop desert road that's as straight as an arrow.

"I can't remember ever feeling this free," I shout to Farren over the loud engine noise and wind.

He smiles. "You're doing great," he shouts back.

"Damn, Farren"—wind whirs through the open top, blowing my hair everywhere—"this thing is fast."

He chuckles, nods. But at 150 mph, he urges me to "ease up a little, baby."

My cheeks warm, and it's not from the blazing sun beating down on us. No, I'm heated by the recollection of how Farren uttered those same words to me an hour ago, before we left the warehouse, and after he'd loaded our luggage and his cache of weapons into the Ferrari. His hand trailed up my skirt when he was back in the car. I was seated in the driver's seat, and within minutes, I was grinding down hard on his fingers.

Now, just like then, I don't listen.

I don't ease up, and when we hit a patch of gravel, the wheel jerks in my hand. I lose control—again, just like earlier. But instead of coming hard, like I did clenched around Farren's fingers, my whole body now tenses in a different way.

"Essa," Farren warns.

Finally, I ease up on the gas and hit the brakes. The car fishtails but remains on the road. When we come to a full stop, I let out a held-in breath. "Oh my God, that was awesome."

Farren twists in his seat, placing his hand at the back of my head. He twines his fingers in my hair and closes the gap between us. His lips crash to mine, hungry and greedy. We can't get enough of each other these days. I lose myself in Farren as he urges my mouth open. He touches his tongue to mine. He tastes delicious, even as he consumes me.

The ache between my legs that never really completely goes away when I'm with him—no matter how many orgasms he gives me—pulses now. I drop my knees apart, and since I have on a dress and the panties I put on this morning were lost somewhere in the car during our earlier encounter, Farren's fingers are on my clit immediately.

"That feels so good," I murmur as he works his magic.

We're in the middle of the road, but there's not a soul in sight. It's all brown desert landscape everywhere you look. And when I lean my head back, the only thing above us is a clear and vibrant blue sky.

Farren's lips touch my neck, and he kisses up to my ear. "Come for me, sweetheart," he urges. "Come all over my hand, just like you did before." He twists his fingers inside of me, hitting just the right spot, and he gets what he wants.

While I am pulsing, hard, he whispers in my ear, "I can't wait to fuck you, Essa."

I buck against the seat, my orgasm prolonged by his words. And then I'm over-the-top, time-stops coming when he huskily adds, "Show me how much your pussy wants my cock."

I explode, implode. Time stops. When I recover enough to once again move, my hand goes to Farren. I unzip his jeans, lower his boxers, and grasp his swollen length. He's more than ready, so I jack him how I know he likes—hard and fast.

"Shit, Essa," he groans. He raises his hips, lowers his pants and boxers a bit more. "Keep doing it just like that, baby."

When I sense he's close, I lower my head and take him in my mouth. If there's one thing I've learned about myself, it's that I love the taste of Farren. He knows I'm into it, so he releases in my mouth. And after I've swallowed and pulled back slightly, he taps his dick to my lips. "Lick the last of it," he commands.

I like demanding Farren; it suits his alpha-style. There's a tiny drop of fluid at the tip, and I make short work of it, licking and cleaning him off with long strokes of my tongue.

I can't believe this is me—the girl who thought she hated all things sex. But everything Farren has shown me, or had me do, I've enjoyed. The dirty stuff, the sweet and loving things—it is all perfection as far as I'm concerned. But truthfully, when it comes right down to it, it's the man I do these things with—and who does them to me—that makes everything so good.

I think Farren knows this, as well. He hesitates to fuck me, because he knows how much everything means to me. He knows how I feel about him. And he knows he'll have me completely when he makes us one.

And he's right—once I am with him in that most intimate way, I will forever be his.

W̲E find a place to stay for the night. It's in the middle of nowhere, somewhere west of Santa Rosa. The tiny motel is adobe stucco. I like it, it's cute.

Farren, who took over driving duties after my near spinout in the desert, pulls into a tiny gravel-and-sand parking lot. Dusk has descended and a blue neon cactus sign, suspended on a pole, flickers to life. The letters under the cactus spell out "Blue Cactus Inn."

"This place is so quaint," I muse. "It feels kind of special."

Farren parks the Ferrari outside the motel office, and when he cuts the ignition, he turns to me and says, "I'm glad you like it." He opens the driver's-side door. "I'm going to run in and get us a room, okay?"

There's a small store with a café attached across from the motel—the only other establishments in sight. Pointing to the tiny wooden structure, I say, "Do you want me to grab us something to drink?"

"Sure," he replies, "that'd be great."

I'm sure Farren is expecting me to buy soft drinks, but when I step into the store, I decide this night calls for a bottle of tequila. I grab some salt and a few limes, too.

"Having a party tonight, young lady?" the grizzled old man

behind the counter asks when I place everything on the counter.

I'm not sure how to respond, until I see in his faded but sparkling blue eyes that he's teasing. Smiling, I say, "Kind of."

I don't plan to get annihilated tonight, but I sort of long to cut loose. This whole day has been about pushing boundaries and feeling free. I want to keep that vibe going.

When I return to the room and start taking things out of the bag, Farren raises an eyebrow. "Tequila, Essa?" he chides playfully.

"I figured we needed to loosen you up," I tease back.

"Be careful what you wish for," he retorts.

A couple of hours later, we're seated in the middle of the king-sized bed that takes up most of the space in our small motel room. I am cross-legged. I've showered and changed into a pair of running shorts and a racer-back tank.

Farren is facing me. He leans back against the headboard, his long legs stretched out in front of him. He's wearing faded jeans and nothing else. I'm trying not to stare at his smooth chest, ripped abs, and the fine trail of dark hair that disappears into his unbuttoned jeans. Oh, but not staring is tough.

Sighing, I force myself to look away. I'll get some of that later.

Raising the bottle of tequila, I declare, "Time for another shot."

"Go for it, killer," Farren replies.

"I meant for you," I say.

I'm a little tipsy, but Farren appears to be barely affected by the alcohol he's consumed. Plying him with more might make him open up. Sure, he's been forthcoming, far more so than at the beginning of the trip, but I sense he's holding something back, something big.

I pour him a shot, and then hand him the glass along with the saltshaker and a wedge of the lime we cut up earlier.

Eyeing me mischievously, he grasps my ankles and straightens my legs from their cross-legged position. I tumble back slightly, giggling. That doesn't deter Farren. He sits up, leans down, and licks the inside of my right thigh. He then sprinkles a little salt on my now-wet skin and licks it off slowly.

I can barely breathe.

When he straightens up, he raises his shot glass. "Cheers," he says, smirking before downing the contents in two seconds flat.

While he sucks on his lime wedge, he pours me a shot. He pops the lime out of his mouth and says, "Your turn."

"Okay." I eye him seductively. "But I get to do a body shot, too."

Laughing and lying back, he says, "You'll get no argument from me."

I contemplate whether to take my shot from his wide chest or his hard abs. "Decisions, decisions," I murmur.

The abs ultimately win. And after licking, salting, and licking again, I throw back my shot.

I then sit up straight and say to Farren, "Tell me something about you that I don't know."

He laughs as he hands me a lime wedge. "Where would I begin?" he says.

I suck on the lime and smack his leg. "See," I mumble around the lime. I take the wedge from my mouth and toss it onto the nightstand. "That just proves there's still so much you haven't told me."

His expression turns grim. "What do you want to know, Essa?"

This is my chance to dig for more info, to possibly uncover more secrets. But do I really want to turn our fun, cut-loose night into something serious? It will turn to exactly that if I keep pressing Farren to divulge more regarding his line of employment. I decide I'd rather keep things light. So I focus on something more benign.

"Tell me about when you were a kid," I say.

"Hasn't Haven filled you in on all of this?" he asks tiredly.

"Sure, she's told me some things. But those are *her* stories. I want to hear yours."

"Okay, fine." He crosses his arms across his smooth chest and leans back against the headboard again. "Do you want to hear a happy story or a sad story? I have plenty of both."

"Happy," I tell him.

"Hmm…" He appears lost in thought. "How about if I tell you a story from when my mother was still alive?"

"Sounds good." I scoot a little closer to him. "All right, I'm ready."

"One day," he begins, "back when Haven was about seven, and I was around fourteen, we found this tiny stray kitten in the backyard of the rented house we were living in."

"Was this in Buffalo?" I interject. "Haven told me you moved around a lot after your father left. But I think I remember her saying you and she spent a few years there when you were kids."

"Yes, we were living in Buffalo at the time," he confirms. "Anyway, the kitten was probably only a few weeks old. It was still at an age where it needed to nurse. But Haven and I couldn't find his mother anywhere. We assumed something must have happened to her."

"Aw," I say, "that's sad."

"It was, but we gave the little guy a home."

I smile, and he chuckles. "Shit, Essa, that kitten was such a raggedly little thing. He later turned into a pretty gray tabby, with dark stripes, but at the time he was this scrappy little puff of fur."

"He sounds super cute," I say softly.

Farren nods. "He was. So, since he was so young, we had to feed him with a dropper until he was old enough to eat solid food."

Smiling, I say, "How sweet. I bet Haven loved feeding him. She's such a softy."

"That's for sure," Farren replies, laughing. "Haven was ecstatic. She even made up a feeding schedule for him. Not that Mom and I ever had a chance to take a turn. She took over all the kitten-parenting duties." Quietly, he adds, "Haven sure loved that little guy."

I sense the "little guy" was not only special to Haven but to Farren as well.

"What was his name?" I ask.

The side of his mouth curves up into a grin. "Wadsworth."

"Wadsworth?" I start giggling.

Shaking his head, he's sure to inform me, "That was Haven's doing, not mine."

I laugh once again, and Farren shimmies down from the headboard. When he's lying flat on the bed, he pats the spot next to him. I lie down on my side and rest my head on his chest.

Farren, while he plays with my hair, continues his story…

"Once Wadsworth was a little bigger and stronger, he was nothing but trouble. Cute trouble, though. He got stuck in the ductwork, climbed up the chimney. Haven wanted to make him a house cat—we even had him neutered—but he was having none of that."

Farren takes a deep breath, my head rising and falling in tandem. There's a short period of quiet, and I think it's spent with Farren and I just enjoying this closeness. He wraps his arms around me and holds me for a minute before continuing his story.

"Anyway, when Wadsworth started going outdoors, that's when the real trouble began. One day, when he was about six months old, he disappeared. We couldn't find him anywhere."

"Oh no," I gasp. I raise my head and look up at Farren. "Did you ever find him?"

Farren smiles down at me. "Yeah, we found him. Here, he'd climbed up a tree in the woods behind our house, an old oak that must have been around seventy-five feet high. He was almost to the top and couldn't get down."

"Did you call the fire department?"

That remark earns me a level stare. "Essa, you do know they don't do that kind of shit anymore, right?"

"I know it now," I cheerfully retort. And then, in a more serious tone, I inquire, "So, how'd you rescue Wadsworth?"

Farren pauses. His gaze, though directed my way, appears faraway, like he's remembering, reminiscing.

At last, he says, "I climbed up and got him."

"What? You climbed a seventy-five-foot tree without any safety precautions?" I'm wide-eyed and, though it's many years later, scared for Farren. I'm also impressed.

He nods. "It wasn't that big of a deal. I just did what needed to be done."

I'm flooded with a rush of emotions. Farren is fearless. He's a man who does whatever needs to be done to protect the vulnerable. Long ago it was a little kitten that needed rescuing.

And nowadays Farren helps with something far bigger—rescuing and saving young women in dire trouble.

I suddenly want to hug Farren, kiss him, love him…

Did I just say love?

Before I have a chance to unwind that statement and analyze it, Farren scoots over, keeping me in place until he's completely under me, our faces inches apart. He slides his hand under the back of my tank top and says, "Do you want me to tell you more stories, or do you want me to touch you?"

I can feel him hardening beneath me, which makes me rasp, "I want you to touch me."

His eyes hold mine as he begins to touch me everywhere. He peels my clothes off one by one, and when there is nothing left to remove Farren touches me with his mouth.

His lips skim over my shoulder, down to my breasts. I arch, and he sucks, licks, and nips at one nipple, then the other. Soon, he's moving down my body, showering kisses across my abdomen. He moves lower still, till he reaches where I'm hot and wet.

"Farren," I gasp, his tongue teasing at my clit.

I swell under his touch, come undone under his mouth.

Farren discards his jeans and his boxer briefs. He moves back up my body.

I feel him—all of him—pressing at my core. And I want this. I want him, in this most intimate way.

"Please," I whisper, so afraid he'll stop.

But he doesn't stop. Not this time. He settles his body more solidly between my legs. I open wider, and the tip of him goes in. "God," I gasp.

Just that tiny bit feels so good. But I want more. I want all of what Farren has to give me.

"Look at me, Essalin." His hand is at my chin, thumb brushing over my cheek. My eyes meet his, and he says, "You sure you want this? There's no going back."

The tip of him is still inside of me, and I try to move my hips to take in more, but his weight on me holds me in place.

"I want this," I assure him. "I want all of you."

"I don't come with promises," he says softly. "I'm not some college boy you can wrap around your finger."

I hold his gaze, searing green, darkened by the lust he is feeling. "I know," I respond. "I don't want that anyway. I never wanted that." And then I admit, "I've always wanted you, Farren. It's always been you."

He stills. He's inside me, but not. His eyes search mine. "Essalin…"

He sighs. His gaze is raw, and I know he can't hold off any longer.

And then it finally happens. Farren shifts his hips and fills me. And nothing has ever felt so right.

He doesn't move. No one does. He leans his forehead to mine and closes his eyes. And maybe Farren doesn't come with promises, but I do. I belong to him. Whether it was intentional or not, he's molded me to be his and his alone.

We breathe together, joined as one. And then he begins to move…just a slow in and out. He's still molding me, just in a different way. He's teaching me what to expect from him. He picks up the pace at some points, goes slow at others. He shifts me this way and that, drives into me from various angles. He's trying me out. And as I learn how Farren likes to fuck, I respond to him accordingly.

Wrapping my legs around him tightly, I dig my nails into his back. "You feel so fucking good, Essalin," he tells me.

I want to tell him he feels amazing, too, but hell if I can talk. It's just moans and incoherent sweet nothings that escape my mouth. That is, when Farren's mouth isn't on mine, kissing me insistently, making me accept his tongue as willingly as I accept his cock. And accept it, I do. Farren fucks like the alpha he is. He's amazing, and before long I'm at the threshold of unparalleled ecstasy.

When he feels me tensing, he quickens the pace. "Let go, Essa," he commands.

His words push me over the edge. I close my eyes and grip his shoulders as I come and come. He pumps into me, a final succession of hard thrusts that don't stop until he empties into me. He knows I'm on the pill, and we both know we're clean, so I revel in the fact that even when he withdraws, he's still in me in some way.

Farren gets up to go to the bathroom, and I watch, in awe that his amazing body was just on me, *in* me.

He returns with a warm washcloth and starts to clean me up. "Are you all right, sweetheart?" he asks.

He appears concerned, so I make sure to respond in a cheerful, satisfied voice. "Are you kidding? I feel great."

He chuckles, kisses me lightly, then continues to dote on me. I stretch languorously as he finishes with his gentle ministrations with the washcloth. He eyes my body lustily, and when I look down I see he's starting to get hard again. It makes me feel good that I can turn him on so quickly after he's just climaxed.

I pull my knees up, and he places a hand on one. "Want to do it again?" I ask, brow rising.

With a suppressed smile, Farren spreads my legs and climbs

in between. "Essalin." He says. "What have I created?"

While he's smoothing away hair from my face, I say to him, "You've created someone who wants you again, and again, all the time, a lot—"

He silences me with his mouth and gives me what I want— him.

# CHAPTER THIRTEEN

THE plan is to leave bright and early so we can meet up with Rick and Haven in Albuquerque by noon. But then Farren gets word that there's been a delay.

"The doctor couldn't be reached until yesterday evening," he explains.

We're in the little café attached to the side of the store across the street from the motel, the one where I bought the tequila.

"He's seeing Haven today," Farren continues. "Once we get the all clear for her to travel, Rick will notify us."

I haven't spoken to Haven, but I suspect Farren has, so I set down my fork—I've barely touched my pancakes anyway—and ask, "Have you talked to Haven?"

He lifts his coffee to his lips and murmurs from behind the ceramic cup, "Yeah, I talked to her briefly, once."

While Farren sips his cup of joe, I ask if I can talk to her.

"Essa," he responds with a sigh as he lowers his cup to the table. "Even the burner phones aren't one hundred percent secure. They can be tapped into and traced. I think it's best if we wait." He offers a stunning smile, one surely meant to placate me. "You'll see her soon enough."

I'm placated, for now, but I still have another question. "Are we still heading to Albuquerque today to wait for Rick and Haven there?"

"No," Farren replies, "we're staying here until I get word that they're heading up there."

"I'm fine with staying here," I say quietly.

I'm speaking more to myself than to Farren. And it's the truth. I like this little piece of serenity out in the middle of nowhere. I like our tiny motel room, where we laughed and loved last night. I liked how afterward the neon glow from the motel sign kept the night illuminated, even when all the lights were out. Farren's body was cast in shades of blue as I watched him sleep. He appeared as contented as I felt.

I sigh now, and Farren looks over at me across the table. "What are you thinking about, Essa." He smiles coyly. He knows.

But I still reply. "I was thinking about last night."

He reaches out and takes my hand in his. "It was pretty amazing," he murmurs.

"It was," I agree.

After our moment has passed, we finish our breakfast and head back across the street to the motel. Much later in the day, we hear from Rick. The doctor, though, we discover has advised Haven not to travel for another day or two. Rick informs Farren that his sister is suffering from a respiratory infection—the result of having been kept locked up in "cold, damp" places.

When I'm told this, by Farren, I shudder at the thought of what Haven must have endured. Cold, damp places? Ugh. Where were Eric and Vincent keeping my friend as they traveled from state to state with her? I ask Farren that exact question but get no answer.

I don't press, and as we stay on at the Blue Cactus Inn, Farren begins to grow quieter and quieter. He withdraws into himself. I know he has a lot on his mind, so I try to be understanding. And even though he's not as talkative as usual, I enjoy being around him nonetheless. Farren comforts me in a way no one else ever has, and, as a consequence, I've grown quite reliant on his presence.

*Best not to dwell on exactly what that might mean.*

The afternoon that we hear from Rick that Haven will soon be well enough to travel, Farren says to me, "How do you feel about driving out to the desert today?"

"Aren't we already in the middle of the desert?" I deadpan as I gesture to the window in our motel room.

Farren, standing near the bathroom door, levels me with a not-amused expression. "What I meant was I think we should drive to someplace more desolate. An area with less people."

Hey, we're in almost desolation here at the Blue Cactus Inn, but it's true there are still people around. Not many, but enough.

I don't know what Farren has planned, but since we've remained local up to this point, I nod once and say, "Sure, sounds good to me." I'm on the bed, lying on my stomach and casually flipping through a magazine I found in a drawer.

I rise to a seated position and ask, "What exactly are we going to do out in the middle of the desert, Farren?"

He steps over to the bed and sits on the edge. He reaches out

168

and trails a finger along my jaw. "It's a surprise, sweetheart," is all he says.

Farren's surprises have, thus far, proven to be rather amazing, so I'm eager to leave.

"Let's go, then," I say as I toss the magazine aside and stand.

Farren turns to grab the car keys from the dresser, and I take a moment to straighten my shorts. I also make a quick adjustment to the bra I'm wearing under a tank top. My bra is black, but my tank is vibrant blue.

When Farren and I step outside the room, he says, "Your shirt matches the sky, Essa."

"It does," I reply, laughing as I glance up, down, and then back up. With my eyes still on the clear sky, I add, "I don't think I'll ever get used to how pretty it is here in New Mexico. Does it ever rain?"

"It does," he tells me, "but not much."

As we stroll to the car, Farren takes my hand.

Minutes later, we are driving down the road—fast—with hot wind whipping through my hair. On a whim, I ask Farren, "Can I drive on the way back from wherever it is we're going?"

Farren's car is beyond sweet, and though he let me drive it the day we picked it up at the warehouse near the state line, I've not been behind the wheel since.

"Maybe," Farren replies, a ghost of a smile curving his lips. "I'll have to think about it."

He's totally giving me a hard time. I know I'll get to drive the car back to the motel.

"You're so mean," I playfully retort. "First, you won't tell me where we're going, and now you have to 'think' about whether or not I can drive. It's just cruel, I tell you."

He laughs and places his hand on my knee. Giving it a light squeeze, he says, "I see your point. I'll be sure to make it up to you later. How's that sound?"

His low voice and now-wandering fingers hold promise, leading me to breathe out, "Mmm, that works for me."

I like that after the past couple of days of sullenness, my flirtatious, fun Farren is reemerging. I tilt my head back and enjoy Farren's hand on the inside of my thigh, caressing softly as the blazing sun warms me further. And it's in that exact second I finally admit to myself what I've known for a while—*I'm starting to fall in love with Farren Shaw.*

There's no point in denying it any longer. Admitting it silently, to my own self only, doesn't mean I'm ready to share the news with the object of my affection. Farren doesn't strike me as a man with time for relationships and love. Hell, he already told me he doesn't come with promises.

I cover his hand with mine, halting any further progression up my leg. That motion earns me a sidelong glance.

"Everything okay?" Farren wants to know.

"Yep, everything is great," I say. I don't add what I'm thinking: *for now.*

We travel a dozen dusty desert roads, making turn after turn. Finally, we slow to an almost-stop and drive—very slowly—off onto a large, flat area of sand and sparse desert vegetation. We stop a few hundred yards in, at a wide clearing where several tall saguaro cacti are lined up in a perfectly straight row. It looks as if someone planted them that way on purpose. But I doubt that was the case. Nature often has a way of giving order to the most random of things.

When I'm out of the car, I take note that many of the cacti are riddled with bullet holes.

"Aha," I say to Farren, who is leaning into the storage space behind the seats. "We're here to shoot stuff, aren't we?"

I've been bugging Farren to teach me how to shoot, and it seems a shooting lesson is, indeed, what's in store for today.

When Farren straightens, there's a gun in his hand. He's loading it. "That's exactly why we're here," he replies.

Pointing over at a badly shot-up cactus, I say, "We're not going to shoot at that poor thing, are we?"

"One, among many," Farren quips.

"Oh," I reply.

He glances over at me from where he's loading a cartridge into another gun—a .45. "Trust me, Essa, they won't feel a thing."

"But they look so wounded already," I protest.

Farren chuckles amusedly. "Babe, we're a little limited on targets out here. Do you have a better suggestion?"

I shield my eyes from the blazing sun with my hand and scan the area. There's nothing but cacti and rocks. "Nope, I guess they'll have to do," I conclude.

Farren hands me the .45 and says, "Let's go see what kind of damage you can do, Essa."

Minutes later, Farren is behind me, his hard body pressed to mine as he steadies my grip on the gun. "Pick out a spot," he says softly into my ear. "Then squeeze the trigger gently."

It's a little hard to concentrate with Farren so close. It makes me think of the many times over the past few days when we've been this close. Closer even, and gloriously naked, joined as one. A delightful shiver runs through me at my recollection.

I smile and lean back into Farren. I know he's smiling, too. He's probably thinking the same thing as me.

Still, ever focused on my lesson, he urges me to pay attention. "Concentrate, Essalin," he says.

"I am," I reply, and then I pull the trigger.

I hit my target—a tall saguaro—dead center, at the exact point I was aiming for. "Wow," I mouth.

"Shit," Farren mutters under his breath. "I think you may be a natural."

I nestle back into him and close my eyes. He feels so good. "I did okay, then?"

His mouth at my ear, he whispers, "You did better than okay, sweetheart."

His low, sexy voice and his masculine scent distract me. I lower the gun and turn to him. "Can I tell you something, Farren?"

He nods once.

"It's kind of bad," I warn as I lower my chin and look up at him through my lashes.

"All the more reason to tell me," he replies huskily.

In a husky voice of my own, I say, "I am so turned on right now I can barely concentrate."

He sighs, lowers his lips to mine, and kisses me gently. When he pulls back, he says softly, "Later, Essa." I groan, but he holds resolute. Turning my body so I'm once again facing the target, he says in a serious voice, "Right now, I need for you to learn how to protect yourself. I don't know what we may encounter before this is all over. I want you to be ready for anything."

Now, I'm *certain* things aren't going as smoothly as planned. There must be some kind of trouble with Rick and Haven. That is why Farren has been so quiet the past few days.

I take the rest of my shooting lesson seriously, listening to and putting into action every single thing he suggests. And, like with my first shot, I remain surprisingly accurate.

"Maybe I am a natural," I say to Farren when the shooting lesson is over and we're packing up the car. "I think you were right."

"I usually am," he replies lightly.

I roll my eyes and mutter, "You are so cocky."

With a chuckle, he finishes placing the guns in the car.

When he hands me the keys, I say, "Are you sure? I was only teasing earlier. I don't have to drive."

"But you want to, right?"

"I do," I admit.

"Then it's settled," he says.

As we drive back in the direction of the Blue Cactus Inn, I pay no heed to any posted speed limits. I'm too busy enjoying Farren's amazing car.

Farren says, "Turn here," when we're a few miles from the motel.

"We're not going directly back?" I question.

"Nah," he says lightly, "let's play a little; see what this thing can do."

With that decided, we have a blast with the Ferrari. Each of us takes a turn opening it up on various empty stretches of pavement. By the time we pull into the motel parking lot, Farren and I are exhausted from our fun in the sun.

It's twilight, and as Farren and I walk to our room—hands touching—under a muted blue-and-orange-streaked sky, it feels as if we're the only two souls on earth. We're sort of in a Farren-Essa zone, but the minute we step into the room, Farren's burner phone rings.

Farren takes the phone into the bathroom for more privacy, and I flop down on the bed. Through the closed door, I hear enough to discern he is speaking with Rick.

When the call ends, Farren remains in the bathroom. The water starts up, and I hear him stepping into the shower. I could use a shower myself—I'm sweaty and dusty from our time in the desert—but I hold off on joining him. I know if I'm in the shower with Farren, we'll get distracted.

I'm still smiling at *that* thought when Farren emerges from the bathroom, a white towel perched dangerously low on his waist.

I take a few minutes to admire him. He's all damp skin, lightly tanned from the hot desert sun, and sharply defined muscles. God, he is unfairly gorgeous. And he's mine...at least for now.

Oblivious to my perusal, Farren turns away and drops his towel.

"God, you have a great ass," I blurt out.

While I continue to admire his taut behind, Farren chuckles, making it clear he's all too aware I've been checking him out.

I go to him.

Gently, I touch the scar on his lower back, and he turns to me, magnificent in his nakedness. He raises a questioning eyebrow.

"This isn't over, is it?" I whisper.

"Not by a long shot," he admits flatly.

"That was Rick you were talking to, right?"

He nods, and I swallow the lump that rises in my throat. "Whatever you end up having to do, Farren, please, please be careful."

He cups my cheek. "I'll be fine, babe. I always am."

My hand is still wrapped around him, touching his scar. I tap it lightly. "Not always," I remind him.

He smiles sadly. "Take your shower, Essa. We need to leave tonight."

"Tonight?" I take a step back. "Why? What's happening now?"

"Albuquerque is off. We're heading straight down to Las Cruces, and I'd like to get there before morning."

My insides are flipping and flopping at what this sudden change in plans might mean. I softly inquire, "Is Haven all right?"

"For now she is." Farren closes his eyes, pained. When he opens them, there's true concern in his emerald gaze. "I need to get down there, though. Something was off with the doctor. It wasn't the original guy I sent. Rick thinks their location may have been divulged."

"To the bad guys?" I ask shakily.

"Yes," he replies.

I gasp, and Farren soothes me by placing his hand on my arm. Caressing me gently, he says, "Haven's been moved to another safe house. She should be fine there, but I can't take another chance. Not when Rick is the only man there to protect her."

"What about the team he had assembled?" I ask. "The ones who helped him rescue her."

"They've been dispersed," Farren explains. "It's not as if the team hangs out together for a few days after the mission is complete."

"Oh…" I trail off. And then I say brightly, "Well, at least Rick is still there."

Farren sighs. "That's true. And he's good. But not as good as me."

His words aren't uttered in a cocky tone. It just is what it is.

When it comes to things like this—protecting people, engaging in ongoing dangerous missions—I've already figured out that Farren is the best.

He wraps his arms around me and holds me for a minute, until I say quietly, "I better get cleaned up so we can get going."

He nods once, and I slip out of his grasp and into the bathroom. It's still humid and misty in the small space, but the mirror is mostly clear. As I start to undress, I assess my reflection.

*Wow.* I am almost unrecognizable. Not just that, but I also feel as different as I look. I'm no longer the timid, afraid-to-take chances college student I was the day I left Oakwood. And it shows in my confident expression.

But that's just the start.

I slip the blue tank that Farren thought matched today's sky over my head. My skin is lightly bronzed from the sun, just like his. My hair is lighter, blonder than usual. Dark blonde has turned to a light golden shade, complete with coppery highlights.

My body is different, too. I'm thinner than I was and firmer in places I wasn't so very firm before. "It's all the great sex," I murmur to my reflection in the mirror.

But there's something more. There's a sparkle in my eyes that wasn't there before.

I feel alive, *really* alive. And I know why. The reason for that not-so-minor change is the man in the next room.

# CHAPTER FOURTEEN

A s we travel through the night, under a velvet blanket of black that appears covered with a million stars, the temperatures plummet. Relieved that I grabbed a light jacket from my suitcase before I packed everything, I tug the denim fabric tightly around my body. The flimsy tangerine top I'm wearing is no match for the cool nighttime desert air.

Farren, ever observant of my movements and ever-thoughtful of my needs, turns on the heat. "Cold?" he inquires.

"Just a little," I confirm. I nod to the vents, where warm air is starting to pour out, and add, "Thanks, though."

"Of course," he says.

I appreciate that he's thinking of me, as I know there are far more important things weighing on his mind. Things like getting our butts down to the southern part of the state as quickly as possible. So far, we've stuck solely to the interstates, but Farren now hits the turn signal and moves over to the exit lane.

"Are we stopping somewhere?" I inquire.

"No," he says. "I just think we can make better time on the back roads since it's so late."

"Okay," I say, yawning. It is late, very late, and I can barely keep my eyes open.

Farren pats my knee, his hand sliding up under the black material of my maxi skirt so he can feel my skin. He likes my skin, he likes touching me.

"Get some sleep, sweetheart," he whispers.

A few minutes later, with Farren's comforting hand on me, I fall asleep.

Sometime around dawn, I wake with a start. Farren's hand is gone, as is Farren. I sit up quickly, blinking. I'm still in the Ferrari, which is pulled off, askew, in a gully on the side of a desolate stretch of road. There's not a soul in sight, just wilderness everywhere I glance.

Staring out at the stretch of black asphalt directly in front of me, the bright yellow line in the center blurs in the dim early morning light. The rising sun blankets the vast desert, the distant mountains, and the sparse vegetation.

"Where are we?" I mutter, even though I'm all by myself.

*Where is Farren?*

For a second, I panic. And then I spot him out in the desert. Farren is a dark silhouette, standing quietly, shoulders squared. He's staring out at the mountains in the distance as the rising sun turns the peaks from silt brown to blood red.

I don't know what's wrong with Farren, but I sense from his tense stance that something is nagging him.

I get out of the car and go to him. My skirt and top billow

wildly, stirred by breezes not yet warmed by the sun. Glad that I tied the jean jacket around my waist last night after the car finally warmed up, I loosen the knot at my middle and work the denim fabric up my arms.

Warmed, I continue walking.

But when I reach Farren, he doesn't acknowledge me. He just continues to stare pensively at the blood-red mountains.

I touch his forearm. "Farren?"

Snapping out of whatever trance he was in, he turns to me. Smiling sadly, he says my name. And then he reaches out and trails his index finger from my cheek to my lips.

I kiss the tip of his finger, but he drops his hand. "What's wrong?" I ask.

Sighing, he says, "Remember when I told you about the man named Dawson?"

"Yes, the elderly businessman who's secretly evil."

"He's not elderly, Essa," Farren says, smiling slightly at my mistaken assumption. But his smile fades quickly when he continues. "Dawson is an older man, yes, but never let his age fool you. He's not to be underestimated." He pauses. "You are right about one thing, though."

"What is that?"

"Dawson is absolutely evil."

I involuntarily shudder, and not from the chill still hanging in the air. "So, what do you need to tell me about him?" I whisper.

"I have to go meet him."

My chest tightens. "Why?"

"Many reasons," Farren says cryptically.

"Oh," I murmur.

He goes on. "Ideally, I'd prefer to meet him alone"—his gaze goes to me—"but I can't."

"Why can't you meet him alone?"

"He knows I'm in New Mexico, Essa. And, unfortunately, he's been made aware that I'm not alone. He knows you're traveling with me."

*Okay, this is not good,* I think.

"So"—my voice cracks—"you're taking me *with* you to meet him."

After an audible, frustrated exhale, he says, "I've thought about it a lot, and I think it's best if I do. You'll be safer with me than if you waited somewhere alone."

I know Farren means there's a chance I'll be abducted—like Haven was—if he leaves me alone in some motel somewhere.

"Why do we need to meet him?" I press.

Farren runs his hand down his perfect features, always beautiful, but especially so in this early red-dawn light. "Dawson is under the impression I've gone rogue. Contrary to what I first believed, he has no idea I've been working for the man I told you about. The man named Mr. Barnes."

"The man who lost his daughter?"

"Yes, that man." Farren takes a breath, and then continues. "I was so convinced Dawson must have figured out my true motives for infiltrating his organization. I was sure that was why he abducted my sister. But though he did take Haven as retaliation, it was for a different reason. He thinks I rescued those girls in Venezuela so I could sell them in my own trafficking ring. He thinks I stole what he views as his property."

"Property?" I scrunch up my face. "God, he really is sick."

"He's also very dangerous," Farren says grimly. "But having him believe I've gone rogue is the best-case scenario."

"For who?"

"For everyone involved," Farren replies, though that tells me nothing.

"So, what do we do?" I ask.

"We meet with Dawson. I let him think I *was* planning to start my own sex-slave ring."

I cringe, and Farren reminds me, "It's just a cover story, Essa."

"I know. But still…"

Farren ignores my commentary and continues. "I need for him to think I changed my mind. I need him to think that his taking Haven made me reconsider. Let him believe he sent the message not to mess with his business, let him think it was received. He'll think his plan worked, and he'll leave Haven alone." His expression softens as he adds, "It will also ensure that you'll be safe from here on out, too."

Farren's words, though comforting, remind me that my time with him will come to an end, and soon. In response, my heart clenches and a lump forms in my throat. I have all these feelings for Farren. If I just poured my heart out to him here and now, then maybe…

But, no, I can't say anything. Not when we have this important—and potentially dangerous—meeting to contend with.

Resolving that I'll talk with Farren later, I lift my chin, my focus renewed on what needs to be done first. "What do you need me to do?" I inquire.

Farren explains the logistics of the meeting. We're to meet Dawson at a home he owns near the Mexican border. "It's a point of operations," Farren says somberly.

"Did he hold Haven there?" I ask.

He shakes his head. "No. Rick has spoken with her concerning all that went down. He reported back to me that Haven was almost always with Eric and Vincent. If not, then she was with guards." He scrubs a hand down his face. "And for as bad as all those men are, they are nothing compared to Dawson. Thankfully, Rick extricated her before she was moved to the house that we're going to. It's the last stop before the captured women are sent to Mexico."

"Where do they go from there?"

He shrugs one shoulder. "Central America, South America, all over, Essa."

"That's sick," I say, disgusted.

"That's why I've been trying to help stop it from happening," he says quietly.

"Have you ever been to this house we're going to?"

"I have," Farren replies curtly.

Recalling how Farren told me he's had to do things he's not proud of—bad things—I decide not to delve for details.

And he doesn't volunteer any.

Instead, he says, "I can't give you any weapons prior to the meeting. Dawson will know if you're armed. But I can't leave you completely unprotected, either. I'll tuck a .38 under the passenger seat. It's easier to handle than the .45."

"Um, okay… But you'll be with me, right?" I shakily inquire.

"Yes, but I'll need to talk with Dawson privately at some point."

Confused, I say, "Yeah, but if we're in his house, how will a gun in the car help me?"

"We're not going into that house," Farren states, his voice firm. "We're meeting Dawson at a specified point along the driveway.

The damn thing is about a mile long; we'll rendezvous there. I plan to talk to him in his car. If things start to go badly when I'm with him, I need you to retrieve the gun." His eyes meet mine. "Don't be afraid to use it, Essa."

"Okay," I croak out.

Farren gently brushes my hair over my shoulder. When it won't stay put, due to the breeze, he tucks the wayward strands behind my ear. "There's one more thing," he says.

"Yeah?"

"When we meet Dawson, I need for you to be completely submissive to me."

Clarity rushes over me. "Oh my God, he thinks I'm some girl you abducted. Like, for this fake operation of yours."

"That's what he thinks," Farren confirms. "And it's important that he continues to believe I took you against your will. If we can pull this off, he'll believe the rogue story."

"Yeah, but," I say slowly, "if you tell him you've reconsidered, he's going to question why I'm still with you."

Farren smiles, and this time it's genuine. "I'll make him think that you got to me. That I'm keeping you for myself."

*Have I gotten to you? Are you keeping me for yourself?* I long to ask these questions, but things are complicated when it comes to this burgeoning relationship. I'm not even sure Farren will remain in the country after all this is over. He could be off to anywhere—to Asia, South America, Central America. Who knows?

"What about Mr. Barnes?" I query. "Does he expect you to continue working for him?"

"I'm not sure, Essa. There may be another angle in the operation where I can be of help."

"You'll keep doing this, then?" I whisper. "You'll continue to go after these guys?"

He sighs. "I have to, Essa. It's important to me."

"It is a lot of money," I mumble.

Farren hears me and says, "It's not about the money. I'm committed to helping Barnes, especially since Haven's been caught up in this mess."

I want to question why he's *so* committed. This is about more than Haven. This is more than seeing things through. And it's more than a cause of some sort.

But what is it? What could be driving Farren to this level of commitment?

Unfortunately, I don't have the nerve to interrogate him, so I just softly say, "Does that mean you'll be in some other country, like, indefinitely?"

I stifle a sob and close his eyes. When I open them, he touches the side of my face. "Essalin…"

I grab up his hand. "I'm sorry." My voice cracks. "I know you said no promises, or whatever, but I just…I just don't want this"—I wave a hand between us—"to end."

"I care for you, Essa," he tells me. "I do."

"Okay, how much?" I blurt out. His brows go up, and I amend, "I mean, I know we haven't known each other all that long. But spending every day and night together like we have kind of throws the rule book right out the window, you know?"

He nods, and, encouraged, I continue. "Farren, all I know is that I feel something for you, something I've never felt before." I take a much-needed breath. "I'm not saying it needs to be defined, not yet. But I also don't want to continue on without at least declaring something."

Farren's response isn't some sudden declaration of love, but it's a pretty strong reaction when he pulls me to him roughly. His lips crash down to mine, and he kisses me, firmly at first, but then more gently. "Essalin Brant, you're going to be the death of me," he murmurs against my lips.

I run my fingers through his silky hair and down to the nape of his neck. Clutching the back of his shirt, I say, "Never. It will never come to that."

His lips return to mine, and soon I am so turned on that I begin shaking. Farren, knowing my needs and wants almost better than I do, lifts my skirt and makes short work of my panties. He allows me to tug his shirt over his head, but he has me keep my own shirt and jacket on. When he backs me up to a large boulder and leans me back against it, I understand why. Though the boulder is smooth, the clothes left on my top half will keep my back from getting torn up.

And torn up is what would happen, as there's urgency to Farren's actions when he hoists my legs up around him. Within seconds he's undoing his pants, lowering them, and freeing his erection.

I sense he needs to be inside me—feeling me—as much as I need to feel him. Still, he meets my gaze, his eyes questioning if this is all right.

I nod and say, "Yes, yes."

Very slowly, and never looking away, he lowers my body onto his, burying himself deep inside me.

I gasp. He groans. But he doesn't move, not at first. He just holds my gaze. And when he says my name, with us joined as we are, I know in the deepest recesses of my being that Farren feels as strongly about me as I do for him.

And today, right now, for where we're at and what we still face, that's enough for me.

# CHAPTER FIFTEEN

D AWSON'S estate is close to the border, so close that if you threw a stone from the edge of his vast property, you'd be almost guaranteed it'd land in Mexico. Not that you'd know where one country ended and the other began. It all just looks like desert to me.

However, as we close in on the elaborate entrance to Dawson's property, it becomes clear this particular oasis is vastly different from the barren desert land surrounding it. Dawson's estate is a gem in desolation. There are huge gates at the entrance, and a wrought iron fence encloses the meticulously landscaped greenery. Shrubs, flowers, and grass as lush as it would be back in Pennsylvania this time of year grow in abundance.

Farren pulls up to the entrance gates and stops at a control box on a pole. He enters a code, and the gates open slowly. I know he's been here before, so his knowing the code is no real surprise.

Still, it's a bit unsettling.

Off in the distance—about a mile away, like Farren mentioned—a huge house looms. Even from this far away, I have a bad feeling about the place. Just to be sure neither one of us is stepping one foot in Dawson's residence, I say to Farren, "We're not driving all the way up to the house, right?"

"No," he assures me with a comforting pat to my knee.

"Well, at least this part is pretty," I remark as I gesture to all the exotic flowers and greenery growing along the sides of the driveway.

"Don't be fooled by appearances," Farren replies dryly.

"What happens here?" I carefully ask. "You said this is where girls are brought before being sent over the border."

"Yes, this is where they're brought." Farren blows out a long breath. I can tell he doesn't want to talk about this. Sure enough, he says, "As for your first question, I think it's best if we don't talk about the things that happen here."

I know then that Farren has had to take part in at least some of the bad things that have occurred on these grounds. Suddenly, the flowers don't seem so pretty anymore; the greenery, not so bright. It's all a farce. The young women who are brought here probably think this is a sanctuary after the things they've experienced up to that point—like how Haven was kept in "cold, damp" places.

They have no idea the worst is yet to come.

Farren slows to a stop. We're not quite to the house, but we're close enough that I can see it's as opulent as the grounds. Turrets, a limestone exterior with intricate detail work, the house is magnificent. But for as stately as the huge home appears, there's still that cold, sinister vibe lingering in the air.

"Maybe we should leave," I murmur.

Just then a black stretch limo appears. It travels slowly to where we're stopped.

"Too late now," Farren murmurs.

The limo parks a few yards away from us.

Farren places his hand on my knee again. "Essa, remember what I told you."

I bite my lip and glance his way. His green eyes bore into me, demanding and making it not such a stretch to say, "I'm supposed to be yours, all yours. I obey everything you say."

He nods slowly. "That's right. I own you."

"You own me," I echo.

The limo door opens, and the man I assume is Dawson steps out. He appears to be in his early sixties. He runs his hand through gray hair that is thinning. His face is heavily lined from the desert sun. His physique—he's clad in a dark brown suit despite the hot weather—is trim, compact, and tight. He's not a particularly tall man, but he holds himself confidently. When he catches me observing him from behind the windshield, he scowls, making his sharp features harden.

"I'm kind of afraid," I whisper to Farren as I avert my eyes.

"Good." He places his hand on the door handle and opens the door. *There's no going back now.* "Fear will keep you alive, Essalin."

Farren steps away from the car, and I watch as he strides toward Dawson. Farren is much taller than the older man, far broader in the shoulders. Now that I take a better look it appears Dawson's suit has some sort of shoulder pads attached to make him look bigger. Even so, Farren dwarfs him. And despite Farren's casual attire of a fitted black tee and faded jeans, he's far more suave and put together than squirrely Dawson.

I sit dutifully in the passenger seat, watching and waiting for a sign from Farren to join the men. The air conditioning is off, and though the windows are down, it's stifling in the car. Even so, I begin to shiver. I rub my arms, trying to generate heat. I wish I'd worn something less revealing. My too-short white shorts and skimpy red camisole have me feeling far too exposed. But this outfit is what Farren directed me to put on.

*I'm playing a role*, I remind myself.

When Farren reaches Dawson, the two men shake hands. I hear Dawson say, "I see you brought your young, pretty thing with you. Does this mean we'll be playing with her today?"

Farren tenses, only a bit, but it's enough that I notice. Dawson, however, pays no heed. His cold, obsidian eyes bore through the windshield glass, focused on me like there's nothing between us. He says a few words to Farren that I can't make out.

Farren then startles me when his voice rings out, gruff and commanding, "Essalin, come here."

Warning bells go off in my head, urging me to stay put. But since I trust Farren implicitly, I obey his command.

When I've just about reached the men, Farren grabs my arm roughly. He yanks me to him. He wraps his arm around me and moves his hand to my chin, his thumb digging into my jaw. "Say hello to Mr. Dawson," Farren growls in my ear.

I know this isn't Farren. He's also playing a role. But his rough handling has me whimpering instead of doing what he's requested of me.

The pressure of Farren's hold increases and he tilts back my head. "Essalin, do as you've been told," he hisses.

Dawson chuckles, and I reluctantly squeak, "Hello, Mr. Dawson."

"I see you have a strong-willed one here, Mr. Shaw." Dawson says, smiling coldly. He steps closer to me, and Farren pulls me into his body protectively. "Those are always the most fun to break," Dawson remarks.

This gross man is so close to me that his fetid breath fills my nose. I long to turn away, but Farren's hand stays put on my jaw, holding me in place. His grasp tightens, like he knows what I'm thinking. I have a feeling turning away would be a very bad idea.

Thankfully, after one extremely long minute, Dawson steps back. Farren loosens his hold, and his fingers stop digging into my skin.

I breathe a sigh of relief.

My relief is short-lived, though, when Dawson says, "Let's have a look at her." His tongue darts out and he licks his lips in a reptile-like fashion. "Lift up her shirt."

Fear turns to outright terror. Farren knew something like this was in store. That's why he couldn't arm me. A sob escapes me as Farren's hand slips under the hem of my camisole, lifting… and revealing.

I start to cry, and he whispers in my ear, "Shh, trust me."

He continues to lift my shirt higher.

The dry desert air would normally feel like a warm caress, but with my camisole bunched up all around my neck, all I feel is icy and exposed. But my humiliation is not enough for Dawson. He rubs at his crotch and rasps, "Unclasp her bra. I want to see more."

I start to shake and press myself as far back into Farren's chest as I can. Despite Farren's calm movements and demeanor, his heart is pumping faster than normal. I know then that we have to pull this off...or Dawson will kill us. And though I suspect Farren is armed, killing Dawson must be a last resort, due to the potential fallout. This insidious man has influential connections. His reach is long. And though Haven is supposedly safe, Farren won't take any chances.

Resigning myself that this is how things are going to roll, I go lax in Farren's arms. He unclasps the front closure of my bra and peels away black lace, exposing my breasts.

"Very nice," Dawson grunts. "Do you mind if I touch?"

Tears roll down my cheeks. Is this what Haven endured? If so, this kind of shit was probably just the tip of the iceberg.

"This one's not for sharing," Farren—to my relief—replies.

I'm momentarily calmed, until Dawson growls, "I've shared plenty with you, Shaw."

I don't know if Dawson means women who were brought here have been shared with Farren, or if he's referencing the fact that Farren has "stolen" girls from him. My only solace is in knowing that the young women Farren "stole" from Dawson—and maybe slept with in order to keep up his cover story—were ultimately rescued and returned home.

"I said no sharing," Farren states firmly.

Dawson shifts his weight and grumbles, "Fine." And then he adds with a sinister grin, "Do you want to come into the house and fuck her in front of me? I'd be happy with that."

*What? No, no, no...*

For as much as I enjoy Farren fucking me, I have no desire to have this disgusting man watch. I sense these sick requests are angering Farren, too. His body tenses as he says to Dawson, "We're not going into your house. And enough with the girl; she's not important. However, I believe we still have some business to discuss."

I think it's all over, and so, apparently, does Farren. He begins to lower my top. But that's when Dawson states, "Not so fast. I want to see the rest of her before talking any business."

Bile rises in my throat. We can't keep saying no. Farren *has* to talk business with this man. He needs to make a deal with Dawson. A deal that will result in keeping Haven—and me—safe.

That is why when Farren swiftly turns me around and bends me over the hood of Dawson's limo, I don't resist. I put up no fight when he yanks down my shorts and panties, and I don't struggle when he places his hand on my lower back and urges me to arch my ass up high so Dawson can see all of me.

It's all so humiliating, like I'm some object to display and apprise. But the worst part of all is that, because Farren is doing these things to me, my body starts to respond. And it doesn't go unnoticed by Dawson.

"You've trained her well," he comments lecherously. "She's fucking soaked."

I press the side of my face to the hood, tears hot as they stream down my cheeks. It's true; my body is aroused. My camisole was never lowered enough to cover my breasts, and the heated steel my chest is pressed against feels surprisingly good against my sensitive nipples.

"Get her off," Dawson says offhandedly, "and then we'll talk business."

I am so turned on that I'm not as repulsed as I should be by his request. I only crave relief. Still, I hate that this wicked old pervert will watch me come undone. I close my eyes and try to pretend it's just me and Farren. When he slips his fingers into me,

I tighten around him and let out a moan.

"She likes it already." Dawson laughs.

*Shut up*, I think, *shut up*. I wish I could kill Dawson. I think Farren wishes he could kill him, too, as his movements become rougher and harsher. But Farren is still skilled enough with his fingers that I'm soon rocking my hips with the pace he sets.

I forget we're not alone. I writhe on the hood of the limo as Farren works my clit with his thumb. When he twists his fingers, two of which are inside of me, in just the right way, I come.

Once my orgasm subsides and I am no longer aroused, I start to cry.

Farren lifts my limp body off the hood and slips my panties and shorts back up my legs. Quickly, he reclasps my bra and lowers my camisole completely.

The whole time he's whispering in my ear, "I'm sorry, Essa. I am so sorry."

When I turn around, I see Dawson is gone. "Where'd he go?" I whisper while I wipe away my tears.

Farren jerks his head toward the limo. "He's in there, waiting to talk business. He said it was getting too hot to stand around out here."

"I bet," I scoff bitterly. "He's probably in there jerking off after what he just saw."

Farren cups my cheek, so much more gently than before. "Essalin, I'm so sorry I had to do that to you in front of him."

"It's okay," I tell him. "It's not like we had much of a choice. I'm just glad he was satisfied with just you touching me."

Farren's eyes narrow. "I wasn't about to let him touch you. I'd kill him first."

"What about the fallout?"

"Fuck the fallout, Essa."

Somehow, I know Farren is not kidding around. And the fact that he would rather kill than share me makes any humiliation I've endured today a little less horrible.

Still, I can't wait to leave.

Farren sees my discomfort in my eyes and says, "We won't be here much longer. Go back to the car, okay? Wait for me there. And, Essa…remember what I told you."

I nod. I know Farren is referring to the gun he stashed under the seat. "Use it if it comes to that," his expression says, before I turn and walk slowly back to the Ferrari.

I glance back when I'm almost to the car. Farren is getting into the limo to speak with the most disgusting man I've ever met.

This day can't end soon enough.

# CHAPTER SIXTEEN

TWELVE minutes, that's how long Farren is in the limo with Dawson when I start to panic.

"Shit," I mutter.

Slowly, I adjust my hands around the .38 that's resting in my lap. I'm not sure how much longer I should wait. Farren said to use the gun if things go badly. Is this too much time? Should I get out of the car and go rap on the limo window? I don't know. I mean, how long should a meeting like this take?

I glance down at the weapon in my hands. I found the gun easily enough. It was right where Farren promised it would be— under the passenger seat. I retrieved it the second I was back in the car, right after I closed the door. I'll use this gun if I need to. In fact, shooting Dawson would probably bring me a special kind of joy.

But my thoughts are just fantasies. Truthfully, I'm scared.

Scared for me, scared for Farren, and scared this thing Farren is involved in is much more complex than I ever imagined.

Four more minutes pass, and, to my relief, Farren emerges from the limo. He appears to be fine, so my hold on the gun loosens. When he opens the driver's-side door and slides in, I ask, "How'd it go?"

"It went well," he replies as he puts on his seat belt. "Dawson is still hung up on the rogue story, which is a positive for us. I think I was able to convince him that I'm no longer a threat." Farren lowers his gaze to the gun in my lap. "I'm glad you didn't have to use that, Essa. But I'm happy you listened to me and had it available. Just in case."

He takes the gun from me and slips it under his own seat.

I say softly, "I would've used it, Farren, if it meant saving you. I'd have been scared, yeah, but I would've done it."

Farren places the Ferrari in reverse and slowly backs away from the limo, keeping his eyes on the unmoving car until we reach the gates.

"I don't doubt it, sweetheart," he murmurs.

Soon enough we're back on the road, on our way to where Rick has Haven.

"Will Haven be safe from here on out?" I inquire.

Farren nods. "She should be."

"And me?" I say, voice shaky. "Will I be okay when I get back to school?"

Emerald eyes slide my way. "Are you thinking about taking summer classes, after all?"

"No," I reply. "I still plan on spending the summer in New York City with you and Haven."

"Good," he says, sounding relieved.

That prompts me to divulge more. "I'm not really sure what I want anymore."

This time with Farren is changing me...in the best kind of way. I'm learning who I am and what I want to do with my life, and, as I've known all along, it sure as hell isn't something business-related.

"What are you saying?" he asks softly.

I take a breath. "I've been thinking about transferring somewhere different. Oakwood's program is good, but there are far better schools out there for journalism."

"Do you think your parents will go for that?" Farren wants to know.

I hear in his voice that he's trying to gauge just how serious I am about changing schools.

"There's always financial aid." I laugh.

Farren chuckles as he places his hand on mine. "The colleges in New York have good financial-aid packages." He pauses, then adds with a grin, "Plenty of good journalism programs to choose from, too."

I interlock our fingers. "Are you suggesting I move to New York City?"

*Please say yes. Please say yes.*

My heart beats hopeful beats, and then it soars when he responds, "If that's what you really want to do, Essalin, you won't get any argument from me."

It's not an out-and-out request for me to move, but it means something coming from Farren. If there's one thing I'm learning, it's that Farren Shaw is careful with his words.

He smiles over at me, and I whisper, "I'll give it some serious thought, then."

I squeeze his hand, and he squeezes back. Our eyes meet briefly before his gaze returns to the road.

In that fleeting glance, though, there is something in Farren's eyes that belies his earlier words, his declaration of "I don't come with promises."

In his eyes is a promise of sorts—a promise of more.

As we travel the interstate, I watch as the mile markers whiz by. It's mesmerizing, and before long I start to doze off. I sleep fitfully, though, curled up on the leather seat. When I wake at one point, bleary-eyed, we are driving through a thunderstorm. Sheets of rain pelt the car. Lulled by the sound, I fall back asleep. And by the next time I wake, it's getting dark. Or maybe the sky is slate-colored due to the storm.

"Where are we?" I ask sleepily.

Farren reaches over and rubs my shoulder. "Go back to sleep, sweetheart. I'll wake you when we get to the safe house."

I close my eyes. I rest.

I'm awakened sometime later, when one of the burner phones rings. It's not mine, of course, so I resume sleeping.

And that is when I have the strangest dream.

Or is it real?

I dream that it's Rick who is calling. Farren is asking him about Haven.

After a beat, Farren says, "Good, I'm glad she's doing better." And then, "I estimate we'll be there in another hour."

Earlier, when I was sleeping soundly, Farren must have talked to Rick and told him of his meeting with Dawson. I assume this because, after a long pause, Farren says into the phone, "Yeah,

Dawson is a potential problem. I sense he knows I'm more than just some guy who went rogue."

*Wait, what? Farren told me Dawson still believed the rogue story and bought that Farren was giving it up.*

Confusing me even more, Farren then says, "No, no, he made no mention of Barnes. But I think he suspects he's involved. Dawson is starting to put two and two together."

Rick says something, to which Farren murmurs, "No, not at all. She still has no clue who Barnes really is...and I intend to keep it that way."

What? Does Farren mean me or Haven? Maybe Farren is referring to us both? So what does Haven not know? Or, more importantly, what do *I* not know?

One thing is for sure; I am fully awake now. This is no dream. I continue to feign sleep, though, so I can listen.

Farren chuckles humorlessly. "Rick, there's no way Dawson knows who Quinton Barnes *really* is. He has no clue of my connection to him in general, let alone..." His voice trails off, and I feel Farren's eyes on me, assessing if I'm really asleep like I'm pretending to be.

"Hey," he says softly to Rick, "we'll discuss this in more detail when I arrive." He then ends the call.

Damn. This man is too attuned. He knows I'm just pretending to sleep.

Sure enough, he says my name. And when I don't answer, he says a little louder, "Essalin, I know you're awake."

Sighing, I roll from one shoulder to the other until I'm facing him. "Sorry," I whisper, my eyes downcast. When I receive no response, I rub my eyes and sit up straight. "Why did you tell me things went well with Dawson?" I bravely ask.

"Because they did," Farren replies flatly.

"But you originally said Dawson knew nothing of the man you really work for, this Barnes guy."

"That's correct."

"Well, I heard what you said to Rick." I take a deep breath, exhaling slowly. "So, who is this Quinton Barnes? What's your real connection to him?"

Wow, I am really overstepping my boundaries, and it's never been clearer than when Farren levels me with a look that shouts that I've asked way more than I should have.

Still, he gives me an answer. But, unfortunately, it's the same crap he's maintained from the day he first told me about Barnes. "I work for Mr. Barnes, Essalin. There's nothing more to tell."

I accept his answer. But I don't believe it for a minute. And in the spirit of my future journalism—*investigative* journalism—career, I resolve to find out just how Farren Shaw is connected to a mysterious, exorbitantly wealthy man who lost a daughter to human trafficking.

# CHAPTER SEVENTEEN

I'M surprised when Farren exits the highway just outside of Las Cruces and drives straight to a middle-class, suburban subdivision.

"I thought we were going to where Rick has Haven hidden?" I say.

"We are," he informs me. "The safe house is within this subdivision."

I glance around and say, "This neighborhood looks too ordinary, Farren. Like where Walter White lived before he *really* broke bad."

Farren laughs. "So you're a *Breaking Bad* fan, too?"

"Yep." I nod. "I'm sad it ended."

"It was pretty awesome," he agrees. Then, in a more serious tone, he says, "As for this neighborhood, it is ordinary, Essa. That was the appeal when I first found the house we're going to. It's one of the reasons why it's now a safe house."

"What was the other reason?" I ask.

He slows to a stop in front of a very nice white stucco house with black shutters. He says, "Take a look around, Essa. Not everything is as it appears."

*Isn't that the truth!*

I refrain from voicing what I'm really thinking and instead look around as directed. Farren is correct. Though we are in the middle of a neighborhood that, on first glance, appears to be an archetype of typical suburbia, most of the houses in the vicinity are empty, the vacant lots dotted with foreclosure signs.

"This area was hit hard when the recession began." Farren turns off the ignition and leans back in his seat. "It's just now starting to recover. I directed Rick to buy this house a while ago. It's an ideal location, and it's turned out to be safer than expected."

"Kind of like hiding in plain sight," I muse, releasing my seat belt.

"You got it," Farren confirms.

We exit the Ferrari and walk up the driveway to the front of the house. There's no one around anywhere, and everything is quiet. The solitude feels bizarre on a nice evening like this. Uneasiness creeps over me. But when I think on it further, I realize my feelings have nothing to do with the vacant neighborhood. My bad feelings stem from an unsettled notion that things are clipping along much too smoothly. Despite Rick needing to move Haven once—and Farren's detour to meet with disgusting Dawson—this search-and-rescue mission has gone off without a hitch. Now it just feels as if something big might be looming. But for the life of me, I have no idea what that something could turn out to be.

Luckily, I'm quickly relieved of my feelings of doom when Farren knocks on the front door and Rick opens it.

Standing directly next to Rick is Haven.

"Oh my God! Oh my God!" I cry out.

I throw my arms around the girl I haven't seen in weeks. Haven is also a girl I thought I might never see again. "Haven," I say, my voice hitching, "I was so scared for you. I'm so glad you're okay."

We both start crying as she hugs me back, her much-thinner-than-before frame shaking like a leaf.

"Essa," she whispers. "I can't believe you're really here. Rick told me you were traveling with Farren, but it didn't feel possible. I thought it wasn't real."

"It's real," I assure her, stepping back. "And I'm really here."

I glance over and smile at the man who made that happen. I don't voice to his sister that this journey has changed my life in so many ways. But when Farren gives me a small smile, I know he sees in my eyes that I've changed, and that he is a big reason why.

In characteristic Haven fashion, Haven then makes a joke. "Jeez, Essa, I knew it was going to take something drastic to get you off of the Oakwood campus this summer, but letting myself get kidnapped wasn't really the plan."

"God, I hope not," I say, and then I softly add, "New York City would have been better."

"Yeah, it would have," she quietly agrees.

"You almost had me talked into it," I tell her.

"I knew it!" She laughs. "A couple more days and I would have prevailed."

"For sure," I whisper.

A tear rolls down her cheek—over a faded bruise. I reach out and gently wipe the wetness away, carefully so as not to hurt her. I start to tell Haven that I'm going back with her and Farren and that I'll be staying in New York City, after all. But right as I open my mouth, Farren clears his throat.

He's anxious to reunite with Haven, as well. I step away from Haven, and Farren's eyes meet his sister's. A lump rises in my throat. I've known all along that these two siblings love each other dearly, but Haven's softened gaze and Farren's smile show me just how tight their bond is.

Stepping forward, Farren engulfs his sister in a huge embrace, an embrace that is sweet and genuine.

Rick moves away from the doorway and, in doing so, steps backward into the house. He beckons for me to follow. Discreetly, so as not to disturb their moment, I slip past Farren and Haven, leaving them to their reunion.

In the spacious, high-ceilinged entry hall, Rick reaches over and gently closes the door. "Let's give them some time to talk privately," he says.

"Absolutely"—I nod—"sure."

The safe house is very modern, with Spanish-influenced décor like exposed wooden ceiling beams, stucco walls, and wrought iron accents. The shades and tones are neutral, with pops of color here and there. The coordinating furnishings make me think the house was once a model home. I can't imagine Rick or Farren decorating. And employing an outside person to do so would have been too risky.

I cross my arms across my chest, while Rick, looking as good and put together as the evening I met him, takes out his phone and types in a quick text.

*He's probably giving Mr. Barnes an update*, I think to myself.

*Letting him know Farren is here.*

As Rick is slipping the phone back into the pocket of his dark slacks, Farren and Haven join us in the hall. With the initial blush of reunion fading away, I take a better look at Haven. She's thinner than before she was abducted. In fact, she's practically swimming in the black yoga pants and purple V-neck top she's wearing. In addition to the fading bruise on her cheek, there are several more contusions running up and down her arms. Even more disturbing are two fading red hand marks on the sides of her neck.

I shudder, suddenly chilled, and not by the house's superior air conditioning. I glance over at Farren to see how he's taking all of this.

*Uh, not good*, I note. His eyes burn fiery green as his gaze moves over Haven. He shakes his head slowly, his strong jaw clenching. I've learned this man well enough to know he wants to throttle the men—Eric and Vincent—who have caused this harm to his sister.

When a muscle in Farren's jaw twitches, I move closer to him and place my hand on his arm in an attempt to calm him. I want to show him that I'm here if he needs to lean on me.

Both Haven and Rick follow my movement. There's no surprise in Rick's expression, but there sure is surprise in Haven's big aquamarine eyes. Eyeing me and Farren accusingly, she flat-out asks, "Are you two, like…together?"

Shit, I don't know how to answer that question.

But Farren apparently does. "We are," he says. Damn, from his tone there's no mistaking that he doesn't mean we've just been traveling together.

"Are you okay with that?" I quietly interject.

It matters to me what Haven thinks. I certainly don't want her being misled into thinking I'm only here because I hooked up with her brother. True, Farren has made this journey bearable, fun at times even, but I've never lost sight of the fact that finding Haven was the sole reason we embarked on this journey.

I need not worry, though. Farren told me once before that his sister would be fine with what has developed between us, and, thankfully, he appears to be right.

Haven smiles at Farren, then at me. She says, "Of course I'm okay with my two favorite people finding love with each other."

*What? Love? Oh, shit.*

My cheeks flame.

Rick's eyebrows go up.

And Farren clears his throat.

Sure, there's something strong developing between me and Farren, but there's been no mention of freaking love. Not on his part, that's for certain. Haven's a romantic at heart though—like me—so I shouldn't be surprised. Still, I can't bring myself to look at Farren. Not at this stage in the game.

Rick, thankfully, redirects the conversation away from the subject of love when he says loudly, "So, is anyone hungry?"

Rapid murmurs of assent follow, and he adds, "Good. I finished with dinner just a few minutes before you arrived. Haven and I were about to sit down at the dining-room table when we heard your car pulling up to the house."

We make our way to the dining room, and Farren, Haven, and I sit down at the table. Rick excuses himself to the kitchen. I stifle a laugh at the thought of him as a chef. But, not ten minutes later, I come to the conclusion that though Rick Martinez may indeed be ex-Special Forces and a man not to be trifled with, he sure can cook. His homemade pork tamales, chicken enchiladas, and cheesy chili rellenos are to die for.

"Everything is so delicious," I say between bites.

Rick is at Haven's side. He's leaning toward her, encouraging her to have seconds. He looks my way and says, "Thank you, Essa."

"It is very good," Farren, at the head of the table, chimes in.

When I glance over at him, I notice he's intently observing the interaction between his friend and his sister.

Not noticing that she's being watched, Haven smiles at Rick and accepts his offer of another helping. He places more food on her plate, his movements careful around her, and his brown eyes kind. Farren glances at me, and I raise a brow. He shrugs, and then continues eating.

Guess he's fine with the prospect of something developing between Haven and Rick. Same as she was fine with us. The Shaws are like that. Once they accept you, you're in. Rick must truly be someone who can be trusted. Otherwise, Farren would have him on his ass.

After dinner is finished and the plates are cleared, Haven yawns and says she's tired. She stands and stretches, then says to me in a hopeful voice, "Come upstairs with me, Essa?"

I push back my chair. "Yes, of course," I say, standing.

Farren, meanwhile, is preoccupied. He's asking Rick if there's anything to drink in the house. "Like something stronger than soda," he says, nodding to his glass of cola.

"There's aged Scotch in the den," Rick offers.

Farren raises a brow. "Cigars, too?"

"The best," Rick tells him. "Cuban, of course."

"Perfect," Farren says, leaning back and relaxing.

"You boys have fun," Haven remarks lightly, her carefree tone reminding me of how she usually is. "We girls have some catching up to get to." She grabs my arm and starts to pull me out of the room. "Isn't that right, Essa?"

"Yep," I reply as I allow her to tug me along. "We sure do."

Farren, though, stops my progress when he snatches up my wrist. "Hold up," he says.

Haven releases her hold on me and rolls her eyes. Farren ignores her. His thumb caresses where my pulse is picking up. "I'll see you in bed?" he asks, raising a brow.

I nod. Apparently, I'll be sleeping in the same room as Farren. Not that I expected anything different. Rick must have been in charge of setting the rooms up, surely at Farren's bequest.

Farren adds, "Don't be too late," and Haven makes a gagging noise. I can't help but laugh. It's all in good fun. And it's great to see Haven is still Haven.

As we make our way back out to the entry hall and to the stairs, she says, "I can't believe you're sleeping with my brother."

"I thought you were okay with it," I carefully remark.

"I am," she says, slowing as we reach the base of a beautiful, curved staircase. She turns to me. "I'm not entirely surprised. I always knew you thought Farren was hot."

"How'd you know that?" I inquire.

"Duh," she says, snorting. "That time you were downloading pictures of him from my computer was a huge tip-off."

"Oh, God." I cover my face with my hands. "I still can't believe you caught me doing that."

"It's okay, Essa." She tugs at my hands, still covering my face, until I drop them. "I can see how it would happen. He is a nice-looking guy."

I cough. "Uh, Haven, hate to break it to you, but Farren is *way* more than just nice-looking."

She shrugs. "Yeah, I guess. Whatever." After a thoughtful pause, she adds, "Some parts of you being with him are going to suck, though."

"Oh." I raise my brows, curious. "Why do you say that?"

"Well, I sure as hell won't be asking you for any bedroom performance reports. That's for sure."

She grimaces, her face as beautiful as ever, and I laugh. "You mean you don't want to know how big Farren's c—"

She smacks my arm. "Ugh, God, no. Stop!"

But I don't stop. I continue, undeterred since we're both laughing. Well, particularly because Haven is laughing. She needs to laugh after what she's endured.

So I say with a straight face, "Are you absolutely sure you don't want to hear about the things Farren can do in bed? Let me tell you, that big dick of his is—"

She covers my mouth with her hand, but she is still cracking up.

"Seriously, Essa," she says when she calms down, "that is just gross. Brothers do not have penises, okay?"

"What do they have?" I mumble, my words muffled by her hand.

"Nothing," she says. She moves her hand from my mouth. "They have nothing. They just…are."

"Again, I hate to break it to you, Hav, but brothers, even yours, absolutely do have dicks. In fact, some people's brothers' dicks are—"

I don't get any further. Her hand is back on my mouth, muffling my words to gibberish. We're caught up in fits of laughter again. All this silliness is a much-needed stress reliever for us both.

When Haven finally allows me to talk again—albeit with a stern "be good"—we head up to her bedroom.

Haven's room is at the end of the hall, and as we pass the other bedrooms, she points out which one has been fixed up for me and Farren. She also makes a point to tell me which bedroom Rick sleeps in. She looks in a little longingly as we pass.

When we reach the room she's been staying in, I say, "Is there a little something going on with you and Rick? He really is gorg, Haven. I wouldn't blame you."

Haven drops her gaze to the carpeted floor. "Rick is a really good guy, Essa," she says slowly. "And he is super cute. That's true." She sighs. "But I'm not ready for anything, ah, physical just yet. Not with him or anyone else."

"Oh my God, I am such an idiot." I'm rapidly reminded of the events that have brought us here. "I'm so sorry, Haven." I touch her arm, the bruises further reminders of what she's been through. "I should know better than to ask something like that after all that's happened to you."

"It's all right," she says. "And *I'm* all right." She takes a breath. "I mean, I will be all right. I'm sure I'll be back to my old self soon enough."

I smile, tell her she's right. "You're almost there now," I say reassuringly.

But, damn, I'm not sure how Haven will ever get completely back to her old self. Not when, a short while later, she and I are sitting cross-legged on her bed, facing each other, and she's sharing with me the things that happened to her—things that include Eric forcing himself on her, like, multiple times.

"Vincent pretty much left me alone," she says, as if that was a huge consolation.

Softly, I reply, "Haven, I am so sorry you had to go through all that."

She picks up a throw pillow on the bed and squeezes the edges. "It wasn't so bad when we stayed at the motels in the beginning. I mean, sure, I thought it was bad. Eric forced me to do things right away, even when I tried to be willing. He liked when I fought, though. So, I played along and fought him. But then he started hurting me for real…"

She trails off, and I tell her, "You don't have to talk about this, Haven."

"It helps, though," she insists. "I need to get it out. Keeping it inside just makes it all fester. I have nightmares most nights. When Rick hears me screaming, he comes in and holds me. And he listens, Es. He's a good listener." She looks up at me. "So, if you're okay with hearing it, I'd like to tell you more."

Her eyes beseech mine, and I pat her knee. "Of course," I say as soothingly as I can. "Just like always, you can tell me anything."

I sit quietly and listen. And Haven tells her tale. It's nothing short of horrific. Not that I expected anything less. She starts at the beginning, first telling me how Eric and Vincent dragged her away from the apartment at gunpoint while I was out cold.

"First, they made me pack," she says. "So it would look like I left the apartment willingly."

"I knew it!" I silently curse the policemen who didn't believe me.

She tells me how Eric took her with him in his car and Vincent drove hers. "I was kept in the trunk," she states matter-of-factly.

"Oh, Haven."

"In Indianapolis, Eric had us stay at a place where he knew how to get me past the cameras without being seen."

"The Super Eight," I say. "Farren and I stayed there. He checked out the surveillance videos. And, yeah, you weren't on them."

In a quiet voice, she says, "That's where Eric first forced himself on me. I told him I'd do whatever he wanted, that he didn't have to be so rough with me, but he liked being brutal."

"He's sick," I hiss, angered and wishing I had the power to hurt the man who hurt this girl I love like a sister.

I ask where Vincent was during all this, and she says, "I don't know. I guess in another room."

"That's strange," I comment.

She shrugs and continues her story. "We traveled to Oklahoma City next. Eric had Vincent ditch my car there." She pauses and then says somberly, "It went from bad to worse after that."

"What happened?" I inquire timidly. *How much worse can I get?* I think.

A lot worse, I learn when Haven says, "In Texas and New Mexico, Eric started taking me to the homes of his associates. I was kept in the basements."

"Did Eric still…"

"Yeah, of course. All the time." She grimaces. "He and his *friends* would take turns with me. And when I resisted, Eric would hurt me."

My eyes are drawn to the bruises on her body, the red marks on her neck. She looks away and whispers, "Thank God I was rescued when I was."

I shudder, as does she. Our eyes meet, and I see in her aquamarines that a few more days and she may have been unreachable. Not just geographically, but in other ways as well. I look away, wondering how much she knows of Farren's involvement with the men who kidnapped her, the men who hurt her. I wonder if she knows what Farren has been up to these past several months.

Carefully, I say offhandedly, "Yeah, good thing Rick was able to get you out."

She's quiet, and I venture a glance in her direction.

"Essa, I know what you're thinking," she says.

"Do you?"

"Yes," she says softly. "I know more than you think."

"So, you know Farren and Rick work together? You know Farren has been after the organization Eric and Vincent work for?"

"Yes," she says. "I know everything. Rick told me I was taken because of the things Farren has done to stop that organization."

"Rick told you *everything*?" I ask, amazed and kind of shocked that he divulged so much.

"He never would have said a word on his own," Haven replies. "But Farren gave him the go-ahead to tell me everything."

Aha, I didn't think Rick would divulge all that confidential information on his own.

I say to Haven, "So, you know Farren and Rick help other girls who've been abducted?"

"Yes, I know." She nods and then reiterates, "I told you, Essa, I know everything. I know about the organization that Eric and Vincent work for. I know how it's tied to legit businesses. I know about that rich man who approached Farren. I know that Farren hired Rick to assemble teams. And I know that they've been trying to infiltrate the human-trafficking arm of the corporation.

Rick said they've had some success in rescuing a few of the girls who've been kidnapped."

"I guess you do know everything," I say when she's finished.

Everything is quiet, until she says, "Just between us, Essa, Eric is definitely involved in the worst of the worst, but I'm not so sure about Vincent."

I make a face. "Uh, Haven, he kidnapped you along with Eric. Plus, he drugged me that night. I didn't wake up until late the next day."

"I know, but something is different about him."

"Like what?" I want to know.

"For one, he never touched me. Not once. And he certainly could have; Eric offered me to him all the time. And, he was just…I don't know. He seemed concerned with keeping Eric from getting too crazy with me. I don't think he wanted me harmed."

"You were harmed, Haven," I remind her, my eyes fixed on her neck.

"I mean *really* harmed." Her hand goes to her bruised skin. "These marks will heal," she says. "Eric could have done things that were permanent."

I shudder as I take into consideration what Haven is saying. True, Vincent did display some kindness to me the night Haven was taken. He didn't take advantage of me, for one. Hell, he even brought me a bucket when I was feeling sick. And now to learn he never had sex with Haven, even when many of Eric's associates did. Maybe Vincent is not as horrible as I originally thought. But why would he hold back? Why not behave as terribly as the rest of the men? What's his angle in all of this?

"Do you think Vincent works with Rick and Farren?" I throw out.

"I thought that," she replies. "But when I flat-out asked Rick, he said no."

"Yeah," I say, thoughtful. "I didn't get that impression from Farren, either."

We're well and truly stumped on how the mysterious Vincent fits into the scheme of things. But clearly he's not as bad as Eric and Dawson. As I recall horrible Dawson, with a disgusted shudder, I consider sharing with Haven my encounter with the old pervert. But I decide to hold off. It would feel too weird to detail how her brother had to finger me to orgasm in front of another man. If Farren wasn't related to her, I could share. But since he is her brother, I choose to skip the sordid tale.

"What are you thinking about, Essa?" Haven asks. Her tone is suspicious. She knows I'm holding back.

Without going into the specifics of what happened with Dawson, I say, "I was just thinking about someone Farren and I met up with before we came here."

"One of them?" she quietly asks.

"Yeah," I say sourly. And then I ask, "Did you ever meet a man named Dawson during your time with Eric?"

I give her a description, but she shakes her head. "No, he doesn't fit the description of any of the guys I, uh…saw. All of them were younger."

"I think he's the boss," I remark, and then, out of pure curiosity, I add, "What about this Mr. Barnes that Farren and Rick work for? What's the deal with him?"

"I don't know. Rick didn't say too much about him. Just that he approached Farren right after he was discharged from the military."

"Do you know about his daughter?" I whisper.

She nods and replies quietly, "Yes, I know."

Haven and I spend the next thirty minutes trying to figure out what, besides the huge amounts of money, could have lured Farren to work for Quinton Barnes. What was so convincing that he chose to bring on his closest associate and friend, Rick? What could be so compelling that Farren would even put together teams to fight this fight?

"Was human trafficking a cause near and dear to Farren in the past?" I ask Haven.

"Not that I know of," she says, frowning. She is as stumped as I am. "I mean, I'm sure he thought it was awful and all. But, I don't know… I think we're missing something."

"Yeah," I agree, "we have to be missing something. I mean, something made Farren say yes to Barnes. And it wasn't the money. He's said as much." I sigh. "He's just so thoroughly committed. There has to be a reason."

"I agree," Haven says. "And from what Rick has been saying the past few days, it sounds like they're staying in it."

"They are," I say dourly. "Farren told me the same thing."

She shakes her head. "I'm telling you, Essa, there's something more, some missing component."

"It's something to do with Barnes," I declare. "I'm sure of it."

"Why do you think that?" Haven asks.

"I don't know. I wish I could put my finger on it, but I just have a feeling."

Haven bites her lip, contemplating. "Hmm, maybe you are onto something, Essa."

"I think so," I mumble.

And then Haven says the one thing I've been repeatedly

asking myself: "What the hell kind of hold could this Quinton Barnes possibly have on Farren?"

"I don't know, Haven. But I think we should find out."

# CHAPTER EIGHTEEN

HAVEN and I talk well into the night. We put the serious chats on the back burner and focus on nicer things. Like what's ahead of us. She's thrilled when I tell her of my plans to spend the rest of the summer in New York City with her and Farren.

"Your parents are going to freak out," she says, laughing and shaking her head.

I snort. "Ha, you should have heard Mom when I told her I was skipping out on taking summer classes."

"Oh, shit, Essa," Haven says, stricken. "You didn't tell her I was missing, did you?"

"Are you kidding?" I make a face. "Of course not."

Haven is quiet, and her eyes meet mine. She asks, "So, what did your mom say about you not staying on campus this summer?"

I sigh. "She said there'd be 'repercussions' in the fall."

"Guess that means you're getting cut off?"

"Not for tuition, but probably for living expenses."

Haven is having none of that. "No way," she says. "I'll pay your share of the apartment if it comes to that."

"It's probably not going to come to that," I assure her as I glance around the unfamiliar bedroom we're in. The room is neutrally decorated; it's nothing like our homey-feeling apartment back east. This is a just a house Farren directed Rick to buy, a safe house. Talking with Haven tonight has felt like old times. But things have very much changed. Haven is the same yet different. Thing is, I've changed, too. I've come into my own.

Haven is observing me carefully. "What's going on, Essa?" she asks.

I say softly, "I'm switching my major."

Her eyes widen. "Really? What are you switching to?"

"Journalism," I state proudly.

Haven knows I like to write, particularly news pieces. She knows I've written articles for the school paper and that I've contributed to a monthly business review.

Smiling, she says, "I think that's a great idea." And then she adds, "I'm proud of you, Essa."

We spend the next few minutes fleshing out how I can still graduate on time. But in the end, I conclude, "Maybe summer classes are in my future, after all."

Damn, so much for my plans. If I'm serious about switching majors, I may *have* to return to school and skip New York. Something I absolutely do not want to do. Unless... I could always move to New York City permanently, like I discussed with Farren. I could re-set my time table, and start anew.

Before I have the chance to share my thoughts, Haven pipes

up with, "Why don't you take summer classes in New York City?"

"It's a little late to be registering for summer classes at a school I don't even attend," I say.

"Farren has connections at Columbia," she replies matter-of-factly. "I'm sure he can pull some strings."

"Connections at Columbia…" I laugh. "Should I even be surprised?"

Haven shrugs nonchalantly, taking her brother's power and influence in stride. This might be a good time to tell her I may actually transfer to a New York school.

"No way," Haven says after I tell her what I'm thinking of doing.

"I'm considering it," I confirm.

"Hmm"—she eyes me knowingly—"things must really be getting serious with my brother."

I'm not ready for *that* conversation, especially since I'm not even sure where exactly Farren and I stand. But I need not worry, as Haven doesn't press. Instead, she muses, "Well, if you're transferring, then maybe I should, too. After what I've been through, I could go for a change."

"I didn't say I was definitely transferring."

Presciently, she says, "Oh, you will."

I hit her knee. "Shut up, Hav."

We burst into laughter, and now it really does feel like old times. But when things calm, I softly ask, "Did you know all along Farren would find you?"

She sighs. "I hoped he would, Es. I mean, I knew he had the capabilities…and the resources."

"Because of Mr. Barnes?"

"I didn't know about Barnes at the time," she says. "But I

knew someone very wealthy was funding Farren."

Again, the mysterious man's name has come up. But Haven appears too exhausted to get into another who-is-this-Barnes-guy discussion. So we wrap things up. After giving each other huge hugs, I leave Haven's bedroom and go to the room she pointed out as mine and Farren's bedroom.

When I step across the threshold, it's into near darkness. All the lights are out, but there are slim streams of moonlight coming through the blinds. Farren is asleep, so I step around the room carefully, trying to get ready for bed as quietly as possible so as not to wake him. I throw on an old tee and strip down to my undies. After a quick pit stop in the en suite bathroom to brush my teeth and wash my face, I return to the bedroom. Gently, I start to climb into bed, but Farren wakes up immediately.

"Hey," he says drowsily as he rolls onto his back. "What time is it?"

The sheet has slipped down, and it's clear he has on no clothes.

"Um," I reply. I hate to tear my eyes away from his buff, beautiful body, but I do when I quickly check the time on the clock by the bed. "It's after three."

Despite the late hour, a wave of lust washes over me. I slip off my tee, tug my undies down my legs, and lie down next to Farren, completely nude.

Farren slips his arm under me, while I lean over and drop tiny kisses across his wide, smooth chest. When I weave my hand under the sheet, I wrap my hand around his hardening length.

He sucks in a breath. "Essa…"

I start to stroke him. "Do you want me to stop?" I ask coyly. "It is awfully late," I add, my tone light and teasing. "And you were sleeping so soundly."

"Don't you dare stop," he warns.

Farren suddenly flips me onto my back and settles between my legs. I'm so ready for him already. I shift my hips so he can feel just how much I want him.

"What do you want, Essa?" he asks as he holds off on entering me. I look into his eyes. This is no longer about lust only.

I say, with emotion choking my voice, "You." *One loaded word.*

"You have me," he replies, slowly slipping inside of me. *Three loaded words.*

*Do I?* I think to myself.

Farren moves in and out of me so slowly, so sweetly. Our eyes never leave one another. He smiles, pulls out, plunges back in. And I know then and there that I've gone and fallen *completely* in love with Farren Shaw. There's no going back now. This is no longer a fantasy. This is no longer *maybes* and *perhapses*—this is for real.

The intensity of my realization chokes me up, and when I release a stuttered cry, Farren places his palm on my cheek. Stilling inside of me, he asks, "Are you okay, Essa? Do you want to stop?"

"No, no, no." A tear slides down my cheek. He wipes it away. "Don't stop, Farren," I beg.

"Okay," he whispers.

"Please, don't leave me," I add. *Four loaded words.*

He starts to move again, but now he cups both sides of my face. "I'll never leave you, Essalin," he says tenderly. He takes my hand and touches it to his chest where his heart is. "You're in here," he tells me. *Three more loaded words.*

All these words, all these emotions, I am blown apart at the seams. I come. And I cry. And though nobody utters the words, I know Farren loves me, just as I love him.

Yeah, the mighty, strong Farren Shaw can fight most anything. But he can't fight what is destined. He can't fight his own inevitable detour—me.

# CHAPTER NINETEEN

THE next morning, we wake early. Farren holds me in his arms, stroking my hair. We don't speak for the longest time. Instead, we allow ourselves to enjoy the feel of each other's bodies pressed close, *held* close, held tight. We linger, holding on to each other like this might be the last time we're together.

Thing is, I know in my heart that something is about to happen. Maybe Farren knows it, too.

Like a precursor to this unknown *something*, he says, "I have to leave later today, Essa."

I sit up, the sheet tumbling to my waist. "What? Why? Where are you going?"

He looks up at me, his face angelically beautiful. "You saw what they did to my sister."

I nod, and he says, "Well, that will absolutely not go unpunished."

"You're going to search out Eric?" My shaky voice betrays my rising panic.

"Yes. And anyone else who hurt her."

I don't know why, but I feel compelled to make sure Farren knows Vincent didn't do all the awful things Eric did to Haven. I guess I don't want Farren killing the wrong guy.

"For the record," I say, "Haven claimed Vincent never touched her."

"Is that so?" Farren replies, his expression thoughtful.

I bite my lip and bravely inquire, "Is he, by chance, with you guys?"

"No."

"Well, in any case, he left Haven alone. She said he even tried to protect her when Eric got too…out of hand."

I feel Farren's hand, at my lower back, clench into a fist. "I'll keep all that in mind," he says tightly.

I trace circles on his chest. "Promise me you'll be careful."

He pulls me down to him and kisses me softly. "I'll be careful, Essalin. I promise."

"It seems we're always making promises," I say.

"It's the nature of the beast, babe."

"I suppose." I lower my body so that my head is resting on his chest. I listen to his strong heartbeats and ask, "Will you be gone long?"

I feel him breathe in deeply and then exhale. "I don't know," he says. "If things go well, I'll be back in a couple of days."

"Where will you be going, exactly? Where is Eric?"

"Mexico."

A shiver runs through me. Farren won't even be in the same country as me.

Misunderstanding the source of my uneasiness, he says, "Don't worry. You and Haven will be safe with Rick here at the house."

"That's not what I'm concerned about, Farren. I'm worried for you." I scoot up and bury my face in his neck. He smells so good, so Farren.

His hand moves to my hair, stroking, soothing. "I told you, sweetheart, I'll be fine."

"I know you're, like, lethal," I state, making him chuckle. "But you're still just one man."

"I'm one man that can do a lot of damage, Essa."

I know Farren is fully capable of taking care of himself, as well as wreaking havoc on anyone who crosses him, but, at this point, I just want all of this to be over. "Haven is safe. I guess I just want to go home," I say quietly, sharing my thoughts.

"We'll be out of here soon," he assures me. Farren seals his words with a sweet kiss, like another promise.

I just hope this is one he can definitely keep.


By evening, Farren is gone. As a result, Rick, Haven, and I eat a subdued dinner. Rick doesn't talk much, and Haven retires to her bedroom immediately after she's done eating. Her food is barely touched.

I push my own food around on my plate. I'm not hungry, either.

Rick stands and excuses himself, saying distractedly to me, "I'll be in the den if you need me."

Nodding, I proceed to clear dishes from the dining-room table. Afterward, I load the dishwasher and then head to the den myself. I have a few things to ask Mr. Martinez.

The door is open, and when I peek in I see Rick is seated in a plush leather chair. He's facing a gas fireplace, but there's no fire. He has a rocks glass in his hand, filled with amber liquor and a single ice cube.

I start to knock, but he senses my presence and turns. He invites me in.

"I'm sorry," I say as I walk over to where he's seated. "I didn't mean to interrupt."

Gesturing to a chair across from his, he says, "Have a seat, Essa. And for the record, you're not interrupting anything. I was just having a drink."

As I take a seat, he asks me if I'd like something to drink, too.

"No, I'm fine, thank you," I reply.

*I'm not here to drink; I'm here for answers.* This is my thought, but I don't dare make such a bold statement to Farren's friend. Instead, I say, "I was wondering if I could ask you a couple of questions about Farren."

Chuckling, he stares down into his rocks glass. After a minute, he looks over at me and says, "Sure, but I can't promise you any answers."

"You've known each other a long time, right?"

"Over a decade," he says casually, before taking a drink.

I continue, "When Farren asked you to work with him for this Mr. Barnes, did you have a chance to meet the guy first?"

Now, I've got Rick's full attention. His deep brown eyes assess me. "What has Farren told you of Mr. Barnes?"

"Not much," I admit, frowning.

He nods, like this is to be expected. He takes another drink, and I again ask the question he evaded. "So, have you ever met

Mr. Barnes?"

"I have," is Rick's clipped response.

I have so many questions, and I'm not really getting anywhere. Forgoing my careful approach, I blurt out, "Does Barnes have some connection to Farren?"

Rick's brows shoot up. "Such as…?"

"I don't know." I shift uncomfortably. "That's what I'm asking."

Rick leans forward in his chair, narrowing the gap between us. "Why?" he asks.

"Why what?" I squeak out, like I don't know what he's asking.

He shakes his head and makes a scornful noise. "Why are you so curious about a connection between Farren and Mr. Barnes?"

I shrug. "I guess it just seems like Farren is so committed to helping Mr. Barnes. But I can't figure out why. I know it's more than just the money."

"Do you?" Rick says. "Do you really know that?" He throws back his drink and sits back. "Maybe it is just about the money, Essa. Have you considered that? You obviously know Mr. Barnes pays very, very well."

Farren doesn't strike me as being all about the money. Hell, he's said as much himself.

I bristle and counter with, "No, it's more than the money. I'm sure there's something else, something tying Farren to this cause."

Rick looks less than happy, but, still, I press. "Did Farren know Mr. Barnes's daughter or something?"

Shaking his head, he states dryly, "I don't know what you're asking. But she was sixteen years old, for fuck's sake."

"I know." I backpedal quickly. "I didn't mean, like, in any bad way. I just thought"—I swish my hand in the air—"oh, never mind."

And that's when Rick leans forward. His eyes hold mine. He's deadly serious.

Deadly serious when he utters words packing a very big impact: "Essa, leave it alone."

# CHAPTER TWENTY

I AM intrigued, yes. But I do, in fact, heed Rick's words. I leave things alone.

But then something changes two days following our little talk in the den

It is afternoon and Farren has yet to return. A couple of days have passed, but he's not yet home. Consequently, I'm feeling antsy as hell. Shortly before one, I start to rummage around through a small black bag Farren has left behind. I'm not snooping; I'm just hoping to find something of his that I can wear. Like a shirt, or anything. I miss Farren, and wearing something of his—especially if it still smells of him—might make it feel as if he's close by.

But instead of finding an article of clothing to slip into, I find a file. I pull it from the bag and flip through the first couple of pages.

It's a file with information on Barnes.

*Finally*, I think, *information on Farren's mysterious employer.*

Holding the thick folder aloft with a slightly trembling hand, I pause. I know I should put this packet of documents away and forget I ever came across it. But how can I do that? I want answers and having them here in my hand is just too tempting.

The edge of a black-and-white 8 x 10 photo protrudes from the folder, mashed in among all the pages. Quickly, before I have time to reconsider, I pull the picture all the way out. It's a glossy photo of Mr. Barnes. The first thing I notice is that Farren's employer is tall with a lean frame. In the photo, he's standing next to a large desk, one hand resting on the edge of an ornately trimmed piece of furniture. He's wearing a black three-piece suit. His hair appears dark, streaked with gray. There's no denying, though, that Mr. Barnes is a nice-looking older man, classically handsome.

*Okay, so far, so good. The file probably just contains general information. Like public knowledge stuff.*

I place the photo off to the side and continue going through the file. I find a sheet of data that informs me that Quinton Barnes was born on January 5. He's currently fifty-eight years old. He appeared on the business scene, seemingly out of nowhere, nineteen years ago. However, he had a nose for business and made a name for himself rather quickly, with several lucrative real-estate investments. Shortly after he turned forty, he married a woman from an old-money-type family. She was fifteen years his junior. To say her parents were less than pleased would have been an understatement. But over time they grew to accept Mr. Barnes.

"Guess he was pretty charming," I mumble to myself.

The couple remained together up until about a year ago. That's when they separated. As of a couple of months ago, they are officially divorced.

I come across a picture that gives me a probable cause for the disintegration of a two-decade-long marriage. It's a photo of the only child they ever had—their daughter, Annemarie. I know from what Farren has told me that this is the girl who was abducted and murdered. Annemarie is the reason Mr. Barnes is seeking vengeance.

At first, I can barely look at the photo, knowing what the girl went through. This would have been Haven, had she not been rescued.

Finally I gather the courage to stare down at the photo of a girl whose life was snuffed out way too early. The footnote in the margin indicates Annemarie is sixteen in the picture. There's also a notation that the photo was taken the day before her abduction.

I can't take my eyes off the girl. She appears so vibrant, so full of life. How could she really be dead? The picture is a close-up. Her face is angled to the left. To me, the picture looks like a selfie. Probably the last one she ever took.

*Wow, she sure was beautiful*, I think as I take in her flawless skin, her soft features, and her wide grin. Was she happy? It sure appears so. I also get the impression Annemarie was quirky and fun—much like Haven. Her long, dark hair is streaked with vivid blue, and her eyes are sparkling. Although I can't tell if they are green or blue, since she's wearing a lot of heavy, dark eye makeup.

The next few pages I pull from the folder are extremely difficult to view.

Pages and pages filled with specifics of what happened to Annemarie, all in gory detail. Farren has already told me the overview—Annemarie was abducted from her home, sold into sexual slavery, abused, tortured, and eventually murdered—but these pages tell the story in much more graphic detail.

I scan through the pages quickly...

Police reports—abducted at 2:00 a.m., no alarms were tripped. Conclusion: It was a job conducted by professionals.

Medical reports—bruises, burn marks, ligature marks on her neck, and evidence of repeated sexual assault.

God, I'm disgusted. My stomach is churning. Feeling more and more ill, I move through the pages so quickly they become a blur of images and words.

Just as well. I can't read the more explicit passages. That shit is way too disturbing. When I come across the autopsy photos—images of Annemarie's battered, broken body—I can't take it any longer. I stuff the papers back into the file and jam the entire folder deep into the bag.

I'm about to be sick, for real. I make it to the en suite bathroom just in time. As the contents of my stomach empty into the commode, I think of how close Haven came to sharing the same fate as Annemarie. But the creepiest part is that the more I think on it, the more I realize how much the two girls look alike. Maybe there's a certain in-demand look for the girls this insidious organization goes after. Maybe young, beautiful girls with dark hair and light eyes are a hot commodity.

I throw up again, and when there is nothing left in my stomach, I make a vow to ignore any more stumbled-upon files.

Sometimes ignorance is bliss.

THAT evening Haven and I are upstairs in her bedroom talking. I don't mention the file I found. I prefer to forget what I saw, as well as the things I read. Besides, Haven is happy today. She's talking about acting. And, frankly, I'm thrilled she still has the desire to pursue her dream, despite everything that's happened to her.

"If I do decide to return to Oakwood," she says out of the blue, "I plan to avoid Professor Walsh."

"Oh, him…" I roll my eyes. "Yes, please do."

I'm worried Haven might still like the jackass professor, until she says, "Hey, I'm done with him, Essa. No joke."

"Please, Haven," I say in a pleading tone. "Promise me you are."

"I promise," she assures me, and then she quietly adds, "I'm into someone else now, anyway."

I raise a brow. "Rick?"

Smiling surreptitiously, she says, "What do you think?"

"Ooh," I squeal, "I knew it." And then I add, "I'm happy for you, Hav."

Just then, coincidentally, Rick hollers up the stairs. He says he wants us to meet him in the den as soon as possible. He's been in and out a lot today, doing Lord knows what. The one time I did run into him, shortly before dinner—which he skipped—he appeared to be greatly concerned about something.

*Crap, I hope he didn't figure out that I stumbled upon the Quinton Barnes file.* That's my concern as Haven and I leave her room and start down the stairs.

"If he hadn't skipped dinner," Haven snips on our way, "he could have told us then whatever it is that's so urgent now."

I glance over at her. She may be crushing on Rick, yes, but

she is royally ticked that he missed the dinner she made earlier.

"I wonder what he wants to talk about," I muse.

She shrugs. "I have no idea."

When we reach the den, the door is closed. I raise my hand to knock, but Haven pushes the door open and walks right in. "Guess we're about to find out," she tosses flippantly over her shoulder.

Damn, she's really pissed at him. I can't help but smile. I'm glad to see she's showing some fire.

My smile quickly fades, though, when Rick peers up from where he's pecking away at a keyboard behind the desk. He appears to be far from amused at our barging in. "Girls," he says in greeting, nodding his head once.

"Rick," Haven replies curtly.

He ignores Haven's attitude and gestures to two chairs in front of the desk. "Have a seat," he says.

"What's going on?" Haven asks as she's sitting down. Her flippant attitude suddenly turns to concern when she sees Rick's grim expression.

As I sit down in the chair next to her, I add worriedly, "Is everything all right?"

Rick sighs and says, "Maybe."

"Wait"—my heart races—"Farren is okay, right?"

Haven pales but remains silent. I don't think she can even fathom a world without her brother.

But, thankfully, Rick assures us, "Yes, ladies, Farren is fine."

Haven and I breathe out simultaneous sighs of relief. When we glance at each other, our expressions say, "Thank God."

"Actually," Rick continues, "Farren is not only fine. He's on his way back to the safe house."

"Did he, uh…" I stammer, not quite knowing how to phrase the question on my mind. "Is Eric, um…?"

Rick raises an eyebrow. "Dead, Essa?"

I nod, and he replies, "No, Farren was unable to locate him. And there's no more time to search. Farren needs to return to the safe house as soon as possible."

Haven chimes in. "Why? What's going on?"

I see the panic in her face. She doesn't want to end up back in the hands of Eric or his minions. Rick, noticing her discomfort, gently says to her, "Haven, I'll make sure you're safe, no matter what happens, okay?"

Nodding, she whispers, "Okay. Thank you."

She's really come to rely on Rick, and that's good and all. But we still don't know what's happening. Whatever it is, it's something big enough to compel Farren to return without accomplishing his task of killing Eric.

Instead of giving us any answers, however, Rick rolls his chair back and slides open the top desk drawer. He takes out two .38s. Pushing one across the desk to me, he says, "Farren told me you can handle one of these. Is that true?"

"Yes."

"Good. Then, take it. Keep it with you at all times."

I tentatively pick up the gun. "Even in the house?"

"Yes," he replies, "even in the house. Outside, as well. Keep it with you everywhere you go."

He slides the other .38 in Haven's direction. "I don't know how to shoot this thing," she says, eyeing the firearm like it's a snake about to spring at her.

"That's okay. I'm going to give you a quick lesson tomorrow morning," Rick informs her.

"Where?" she asks, frowning.

He motions to a window to his left. There's a clear view of the back of the house. "Out there," he says.

The backyard is not unlike the area where Farren taught me to shoot—all desert for as far as the eye can see. Nothing was ever built behind the houses in this section of the subdivision.

Haven is still frowning, and Rick swiftly provides her with more details of his plan. I guess he's hoping to give her confidence that she can do this. "I'll set up some targets away from the house. The .38 is easy to use." He smiles at Haven. "You'll do fine. We'll make it fun."

I give Haven a reassuring glance, hoping to bolster her confidence. I remind her, "It's not like you have to worry about accidentally shooting any neighbors. We don't have any, since all the houses around us are vacant."

Haven chuckles a little and says, "That's certainly true."

Rick nudges the gun toward her once more, and this time she takes it. Holding it gingerly, she says sadly, "Wish I would've had one of these the night I was abducted."

"I think we all wish that," Rick replies.

*Amen*, I think.

THE next morning, Rick is setting up targets in the backyard. Not close to the house, I notice when I glance out my upstairs-bedroom window. He and Haven are several hundred yards away.

When the shooting lesson gets underway, I step into the bathroom so I can take a long shower. Afterward, I slip a navy V-neck tee over my head and then tug a pair of bright white cotton shorts up my very tan legs. I twist my hair into a bun and pin it to the top of my head. I haven't worn my hair up in a while, but the weather warrants it today. It's exceptionally hot. Even the air-conditioned house is not nearly as cool as usual.

A few minutes later finds me down in the kitchen. I'm throwing together a quick breakfast of toast and scrambled eggs. With a piece of toast hanging out of my mouth, a plate of eggs in one hand, and a juice glass in the other, I kick out a chair and plop down at the table. I eat my breakfast listening to the echo of shots being fired in the distance. All the while, my .38 rests next to my juice glass.

Rick never divulged why Farren was coming back early, and I now wonder what could be the problem. Farren seemed pretty set on finding Eric so he could make him pay for the things he did to Haven. What would pull Farren away from a job unfinished? And what kind of problem could have arisen so quickly?

Without more info I can't come up with any answers. But by the time I'm finished eating, I'm quite distracted anyway, by, of all things, the heat. It's stifling hot in the house. Beads of sweat are beginning to roll down my back.

"Jeez," I mumble, "why is the air conditioning not coming on?"

The air hasn't come on since it last cycled over an hour ago. On such a scorching-hot day, the air should be running almost continuously. Fully aware that a fuse could have blown, I get up from the table and search for a flashlight. In a drawer by the sink I locate one. It's not in the best condition, but it will do. I head to where the fuse box is located…in the basement. Actually, I reluctantly walk in the direction of the narrow door in the corner of the kitchen.

*Ugh, I hate basements.*

Most homes in the Southwest don't have basements, but since this one does, when I finally reach the door, I send up a prayer that this particular basement won't be dark and creepy like the ones in the eastern half of the country usually are.

Unfortunately, when I swing the door open as wide as it goes, I can't determine much on the state of affairs. "Shit," I mumble, "it's awfully dark down there."

I flip the switch on the wall, but, just like in a horror movie, nothing happens.

*Great.*

I turn on my flashlight and aim it down the steps. The batteries are almost dead, so the anemic beam doesn't illuminate much.

After some deep breathing to calm my frazzled nerves, I close the door and start down the stairs. With every step I take, I can't help but recall the movie Farren and I went to see in Oklahoma City. Shuddering, I hope and pray no dark, shadowy figures grab me from under the steps like they did to the lead character.

Taking the final few steps gingerly, I breathe a sigh of relief. "You've made it down the stairs without incident," I say, congratulating myself.

Turning, I direct the flashlight beam to the heart of the basement.

And when I see what—or rather, *who*—is in the center of the room, I gasp and reach for my gun.

But, shit, I don't have it on me. I left it up in the kitchen on the table. *Stupid, stupid, stupid.*

I have three options: scream, use the flashlight as a weapon, or run.

I do all three, in that order.

Unfortunately for me, my scream dies in my throat, the flashlight falls short of the man I've flung it at, and, when I try to run back up the stairs, I am violently grabbed.

Violently grabbed and pulled to the one person I have no doubt is here to hurt me—Eric.

# CHAPTER TWENTY-ONE

STRUGGLE. I try to scream. I scratch and bite. But nothing I do makes a bit of difference.

Eric holds me in place, hand over my mouth.

I am so screwed. But I decide I'm not going down without more fighting. Farren would expect nothing less from me. Same with Haven. Most importantly, I will never again be a helpless victim like I was freshman year at that Halloween party.

So I fight.

I bite Eric's hand, hard, and he jerks it away from my mouth. "Little bitch," he barks.

While he's distracted, I wiggle and twist around, my pinned-up hair tumbling to my shoulders. Seconds later I am facing Eric. With everything I've got, I wind my arm back and punch him in the face.

*Bad idea.* Eric hits me back, three times and three times

as hard. My only saving grace is that they are open-hand hits. Punches would have knocked me out. He obviously wants me conscious for whatever he has planned.

With my head ringing, and still seeing stars, I start to crumple to the cement floor. But Eric is having none of that. He yanks me back up and hisses in my ear, "I should have gotten rid of you back in Pennsylvania."

My head lolls to the side, and I can feel there's a nasty lump forming on my throbbing cheek. Still, I gather the strength to whisper, "Let me go, you sick fuck."

My back is pressed to Eric's chest. He snickers and trails his free hand down to my breasts. Through my tee and bra, he pinches one of my nipples. I wince but try to remain stoic. When he continues to squeeze and twist, however, I can't hold back. It hurts like hell, and I cry out.

He lets go, laughing. My nipple is left sore and burning. Eric says in my ear, "I'll let you go, little Essa Brant. But before this day is over just know I plan to break you."

A tear runs down my cheek. I don't want to show any weakness to this cruel man—that's what he wants—but I can't stop myself. "Please," I cry. "I don't have anything you want."

"On the contrary, you have everything I *need*. You're the perfect bait."

Bait for what? Or rather, who? Is he here to recapture Haven? Does he know Rick is with her? Or—and I suspect this is the accurate presumption—is Eric planning on using me to hurt Farren? If so, he must know Farren is after him. Sneaky fucker, he's doubled back. That's why Farren is returning. Eric is the reason Rick gave me and Haven guns. Farren and Rick are onto Eric. But, still, he has somehow eluded them and arrived earlier than they anticipated.

Eric drags me to the center of the basement. Some light streams in from a single high-set window that is at ground level outside. Looking around, I see there's not much in the basement, some wooden folding chairs stacked against a cement-block wall, a washer and dryer in a corner nook, and a water heater. Oh, and the fuse box Eric obviously tampered with to lure me down here.

"Don't move," Eric says.

He leaves me alone for three seconds, just long enough to grab one of the folding chairs. Not long enough for me to run.

He pushes me down on the chair and binds me with rope he has tucked under the stairs. He gags me with a piece of cloth he finds on the floor. He takes a small roll of duct tape from his pants pocket. With his teeth, he rips off a long strip and presses it to my lips.

"There," he says, patting my sore cheek. "I think we've heard enough out of you for one day."

My breaths come faster and faster. I can barely breathe. The heat, the fear, it's all consuming. Sweat beads on my forehead, but Eric, no surprise, ignores my distress. He's too preoccupied with pacing the cement floor, waiting. Haven and Rick are still out in the back. I hear the discharge of the guns in the distance as the shooting lesson continues.

Eric hears the noise, too. "Haven learning to shoot," he scoffs. "That's some funny shit."

Okay, he knows Haven is here. I'm sure he's aware, as well, that Rick is out there with her. I mentally kick myself again for leaving my gun up on the kitchen table. I should have never set it down, not even for a minute. Now look where I am. No weapons are visible on Eric—he has on dark pants and a thin gray pullover—but that doesn't mean he doesn't have a gun hidden somewhere on his tall body.

Eric suddenly stops pacing. He grabs up another wooden folding chair, opens it, and places it in front of me. He sits down, scoots closer, and stares at me. "You don't even know what kind of mess you're caught up in, do you?"

I can't answer besides a single shake of my head, so he continues. "Do you even know who Farren Shaw is? Do you know why his sister was taken?"

I shake my head again. Even if my mouth wasn't taped, I wouldn't tell him what I know—that Dawson thought Farren was releasing girls so they could work for him. I wouldn't tell him about the whole phony "rogue" story. Maybe he knows, though, and that's what he thinks he's going to enlighten me with.

But Eric makes me think differently when he says, "Do you know who Quinton Barnes really is?"

*I know he's a successful businessman who hired Farren to avenge his daughter's death*, I think as I stare Eric down.

"You have no idea," he snarls. Leaning back, he places his ankle up on his knee and smirks. "Don't worry. I didn't know either. That is, I didn't know until recently. Farren is one smart motherfucker. I'll give him that. He played our organization from the beginning, even duped that sick scumbag Dawson." He snickers and adds, "Rogue, my ass. It was a good story, though, a clever diversion from the truth."

Truth? What is he talking about? Eric clearly knows Dawson. And he's fully aware that the Farren-gone-rogue story is bogus. He has to be onto Barnes, since he mentioned his name. But something in his too-smug expression tells me there's far more to this complicated mess than a wealthy man seeking justice for his daughter.

If the situation wasn't so dire, maybe I could think more clearly. But as it is, I have no more theories. I am officially lost.

Suddenly, I hear voices ring out from upstairs. Rick and Haven are returning from shooting. Damn, they have no idea Eric is in the house. And I have no way to warm them.

Eric hears the activity above us, his head jerking upward.

With her voice muffled through the closed door at the top of the stairs, my captor and I listen as Haven says to Rick, "Wonder where Essa wandered off to? You don't think Farren returned while we were out back, do you?"

"No," Rick replies, "he's not due back for another hour or two."

An evil grin spreads across Eric's face. I have to warn Haven and Rick. But when I try to yell, all that comes out of my covered mouth is a low whimper. Even though there is no way I could have been heard, Eric grabs me by the neck and squeezes so hard that he ends up pulling me partway out of the chair, despite being roped down like an animal.

"Stay the fuck quiet," he warns. His steely eyes bore into my own tear-filled ones. I nod rapidly, and he lets go. If I wasn't tied, I'd be doubling over from the pain. But as it is, only a muffled choking noise escapes me as I try to catch my breath through my nose.

Haven speaks again, and I hear Rick saying something about how hot it is in the house. It's cooler in the basement, but I'm still roasting. I can only imagine what it feels like upstairs.

Suddenly, someone starts to turn the doorknob on the basement door. Eric lifts his pant leg and pulls a pistol from a holster on his ankle.

I knew he was armed.

He makes a shushing noise to me, even though I can't talk. *Asshole*. I am bound and helpless. And that fact is never more apparent than when events begin to occur. Events I find I have no control over.

I whimper and struggle, but there's nothing I can do when Eric races up the basement steps. There is no warning I can shout out when the door swings open. I catch a glimpse of Rick in silhouette, before Eric slams his pistol into Rick's temple. Haven screams as Rick tumbles down the basement steps.

Rick's body settles at the base of the stairs, unmoving. Haven is still screaming, and Eric warns her to "shut the fuck up."

He starts to drag Haven down the stairs as she tries to get herself under control. When she has to step over Rick to move forward, she begs, "Let me make sure he's okay. Please, Eric, just let me check on him."

Eric has her in his grasp. "No," is his one-word response. Thankfully, I can see Rick's chest is rising and falling. He's alive, at least.

When Haven catches sight of me tied up in the center of the basement, she gasps, "Oh, no, Essa." She turns to Eric and says, "Just let her go, please. Take me. Leave her alone."

"Haven," he chides. "Always trying to be the hero, just like your brother."

"Eric," Haven pleads, "please just untie her."

He laughs. "Oh, I will"—Eric's cold blue eyes slide to me—"when I'm ready to fuck her."

I squeeze my eyes shut and pray he's not serious.

Haven starts to squirm in Eric's grasp. "Shut up," she yells. "You're disgusting. Get the hell off of me." She struggles valiantly, but Eric grabs her cheek where there's still a remnant of a bruise—surely one from him—and squeezes hard.

That stops her. She cries out and goes slack. With Haven subdued, Eric swings around the chair he was sitting in. He shoves Haven down on it and ties her up next to me. Her teary eyes meet mine as he tightens her ropes. "I'm so sorry," she whispers.

I give her a look that I hope conveys that this is absolutely not her fault.

Thankfully, despite his disgusting threat, Eric makes no move to sexually assault me. He leaves Haven alone, too. He doesn't even bother to tape her mouth shut. My duct tape, however, remains in place.

Eric waits for Farren. His chips are in place; he has me and Haven. And now he's biding his time, waiting to strike.

I watch as he methodically drags Rick's limp body from the base of the stairs to the laundry nook. Rick is still unconscious. Eric ties him to a pipe, peers down at him. After studying his handiwork of knots, he returns to where Haven and I are bound to the chairs.

He takes his gun out again, makes sure it's loaded, and then says in a tone that chills me to the bone, "Now, we wait for Farren."

# CHAPTER TWENTY-TWO

An hour later, someone arrives at the house. But it's not Farren who starts down the basement steps. When I take in the tall man with the dark hair, a man who slightly resembles Farren, I gasp.

"Vincent?" I mumble through my duct-taped mouth.

Haven's left hand, though tied, is close enough to my tied-up right hand that she's able to stretch her fingers out and reach me. It's a move meant to comfort us both, but when I feel her trembling, my own fear ratchets up a few notches. Vincent may not have assaulted her, but he never attempted to free her either. Nor did he stop the things Eric—and the others—did to her. Plus, I can't forget that Vincent had no qualms about drugging me the night he and Eric abducted Haven.

My body shakes as I wonder what could have brought him here.

Haven, who's clearly the stronger of the two of us, squeezes my hand. "It'll be okay, Essa," she mutters quietly.

There's no need for such a low voice, though. Eric is busy greeting his friend and cohort. "Man, where have you been?" he says to Vincent, his tone betraying his agitation. "I asked Dawson if I could get you in on this"—he motions to us with a sick grin— "but he said you'd gone off the grid."

"Yeah," Vincent replies coolly, glancing nonchalantly at Haven and me, "a family matter arose. But everything is good now."

Eric raises a blond eyebrow. "You sure?"

Vincent laughs and claps Eric on the back, the move both placating and somewhat condescending. *Interesting.* Here I've been, thinking all along that Eric is the man in charge. But it appears Vincent may outrank him in some way.

What way, though…?

As Vincent redirects his focus to a still-unconscious Rick, he asks Eric, "What happened there?"

Eric shrugs. "Ah, just some collateral damage, nothing to worry about. We'll take him out later." His icy blue eyes slide to Haven. "He was with my girl, Haven, out in the back. Bastard probably had his hands all over her. And though I like to share, I prefer to choose who gets to touch her." He steps close and nudges Haven's chin. "Isn't that right, baby doll."

Haven's fingers are still wrapped around mine, and she's squeezing so damn hard I have to grit my teeth to keep from making a sound. Her iron-tight grip is the only indication Haven is fazed. She schools her features so Eric doesn't catch on that he's affecting her so.

"Say yes," he prompts, like he's speaking to a three-year-old.

In that moment, I hate him more than ever.

"Yes," Haven replies compliantly.

Haven is wearing a V-neck top that exposes the swell of her breasts. Eric lowers his hand. He cups Haven's breast. As he squeezes lightly, the cruel, hard look in his eyes betrays his true intent—his soft touch is a farce. And just then, as if to drive that point home, he raises his hand and backhands Haven across the face. Raven hair covers her cheek as her head whips to the side. Eric brushes it back, smiling when he sees there's now a fresh welt on top of her faded bruise.

"Hey, hey…" Vincent moves quickly, grabbing Eric's hand before he can strike Haven again. "Calm down."

A strangled cry escapes Haven. A tear slides down her cheek. Eric has taken the first step to breaking her down again. And, if he's to be believed, I am next. Farren will kill him for this. Eric may be waiting for Farren—and now Vincent is here to probably help him—but my money lies on the man I've fallen for: Farren Shaw.

Just as I'm thinking these thoughts, with my heart racing so fast I feel as if I may die, I hear footsteps upstairs.

We all hear the noise.

Eric suddenly forgets all about Haven. Vincent drops his hand from where he was preventing Eric from hitting her again. Everyone's eyes lock in on the door at the top of the stairs as the doorknob begins to slowly turn.

Suddenly, all hell breaks loose, everything seemingly happening at once.

Eric pulls his gun from the back waistband of his pants.

The door at the top of the stairs swings open.

And Haven screams, "Farren, watch out! Eric is here, and he

has a gun."

Meanwhile, I struggle to make warning noises of my own.

And then my warning noises become actual screams, because Vincent, of all people, suddenly rips the duct tape from my mouth.

"What…" I utter as I spit out the cloth gagging me. I look up at Vincent, confused, and he gives me a small smile. But then his focus moves to Eric, who is already at the bottom step, gun at the ready.

He's about to shoot Farren.

In an instant, Vincent presses his gun to Eric's head. *What is going on?*

"Hold it right there," Vincent says to Eric. "Drop your weapon."

# CHAPTER
# TWENTY-THREE

"WHAT the hell is going on?" I ask in a loud voice. I have my voice back, and I sure as hell intend to use it.

But no one answers me.

Haven glances from me to where Vincent is pressing his gun harder to Eric's temple.

"Do as I say," Vincent urges, "or I will shoot you."

Eric drops his weapon. It clatters to the cement floor. "What's wrong with you?" Eric grinds out. "Get that fucking gun away from my head."

"I don't think so," Farren says as he calmly starts down the steps.

*Wait, Farren is with Vincent? He said they didn't work together.*

Farren reaches the two men. He nods to Vincent in some kind of understanding. Then, he bends down and picks up the gun Eric dropped.

Okay, I guess there is some kind of working relationship there. *Crazy.*

Farren's vibrant emerald-green eyes, eyes that I've missed so much, find mine. He smiles reassuringly, as if to let me know everything is going to be fine now that he's here. I know it will, and I relax.

Farren's smile falters, though, when he notices the swelling on my cheek. When his gaze moves to his sister and he sees she's been struck recently as well, he moves swiftly. In a flash, Farren takes Eric out with one hit. Not with the gun in his hand, but with a solid hit using just his elbow.

There's a loud snapping noise, and Eric drops to the ground. His hand shoots up to his nose as blood begins to flow. "You broke my nose," Eric wails in a wet voice that makes him sound like he's underwater.

Vincent's eyes flash fearfully to Farren. He appears worried that he might be next. "I did as you requested," Vincent says. His tone is placating. He clearly fears Farren. "I got here as soon as I could," he continues. "And if I hadn't stepped in immediately, like I did, Eric would have shot you."

"He would have tried," Farren corrects. "But, yes, you did well. And for that, I thank you."

Farren extends his hand, and Vincent shakes it. I can't help but ask incredulously, "You two know each other?"

Haven echoes my sentiments and adds, "Yeah, what the hell?"

Farren explains. "Vincent works for the government. He's on a special task force that's trying to take down the same organization I've been working on destroying. That means he's on our side."

"You've known this all along?" Haven asks, sounding

wounded.

Farren's expression softens. "Of course not, Hav. I became privy to that information only a couple of days ago."

I have so many questions, but just then Rick moans from where he's still tied to a pipe on the other side of the room.

"What the fuck?" Farren grinds out. He hadn't noticed Rick until now. While Vincent keeps his gun trained on the fallen Eric, Farren walks over to his friend. Rick is coming to, and Farren asks him a few questions as he unties him. They speak in tones too low for me to catch any words, but I assume Farren is making sure Rick is okay.

A few minutes later, Farren returns to where Haven and I are bound. "Will Rick be all right?" Haven asks her brother.

"Yes," Farren replies, kindness in his tone, "he's going to be fine."

Haven lets out a breath, while Farren squats down behind our chairs. He unties the ropes holding us, quickly and adeptly. Seconds later, Haven and I are free. After standing and stretching out our arms and legs, we turn to Farren. He pulls his sister to him, hugging her gently. I receive a hug next, one that is more intimate and lasts a little longer.

"I missed you," I whisper.

Farren is holding me close, so close, and I take the opportunity to inhale his delightful scent that I missed so much. He leans back so he can kiss my lips lightly.

"We have a lot to talk about, Essa." He sighs. "But not here. Not now."

There's warmth in his gaze, and if I didn't know better, I'd say it is warmth born of love. But then again, maybe Farren does love me. I've felt as if he does—especially the night before he left.

But I've not yet heard it from his lips. In any case, I hope he loves me. Because if I wasn't 100 percent sure before, I am now—I love Farren beyond a shadow of a doubt. I want nothing more than to tell him, like, right this second. But like he just said, this is not the time or place to be professing feelings.

Eric makes a noise, like a labored breath, and I glance his way. His nose is askew but no longer bleeding, mostly due to the fact that he's grabbed up the rag that was in my mouth and stemmed the flow of blood with it. He tries to sit up, but Vincent makes him remain as he is, lying prone on the cold, hard floor. *Serves him right*, I think. *Bastard*.

It's then that I realize Farren has divulged Vincent's identity to Eric. "That can't be right," I mumble to myself.

Farren cocks an eyebrow. "What can't be right, Essa?"

"Eric knows who Vincent is now," I reply. "Why would you let him know that?"

Farren smiles sadly. He trails a finger down my injured cheek, so lightly I barely feel a thing. "We need to get you some ice," he whispers.

He's deflecting, and I know the reason. Eric will not be leaving this room. He's going to die in this basement. "Are *you* going to kill him?" I ask Farren, my voice barely audible. I just don't know if I can witness that.

From over on the basement steps, a man answers, "No, I am."

I peer past Farren, who doesn't bother to turn around. That action indicates to me that this man I just now noticed has accompanied Farren. He must have been waiting at the top of the stairs until Eric was subdued.

"Who is that?" Haven asks, reminding me that she's watching this drama unfold just as I am.

"I know who it is," I reply softly.

I feel Haven's eyes snap to me after the words fall from my mouth. Vincent's head jerks my way as well. His eyes are questioning. But it's Farren who appears the most surprised by my admission.

I lift my eyes to him. "It's Mr. Barnes, right?"

Farren nods, confirming my statement. But his confirmation is unnecessary. I would have recognized the man who is now at the base of the stairs anywhere. Hell, I was just gazing at his picture yesterday. Quinton Barnes looks the same as in the glossy photo. He's a sophisticated man of roughly sixty, dark hair streaked with gray, classic features.

"He's here to avenge the death of his daughter," Vincent states, as if to inform anyone who hasn't figured it out yet. "In fact, he flew in last night for this express purpose."

Haven and I glance over at each other at the same time. Her aquamarine eyes convey what I am thinking: *Wow, Farren is going to allow this powerful man he works for to commit murder. Mr. Barnes is about to take out one of the bad guys who hurt and ultimately killed his Annemarie.*

And we are right—that is exactly what Farren is planning to do. He steps over to Mr. Barnes and hands him Eric's gun. Barnes takes the gun and walks over to Eric. He kneels down next to him.

"Just do it," Eric grinds out, defiant to the end.

Farren says to me and Haven, "Don't look. Turn away." Neither of us listens. The scene before us is much too riveting.

Vincent steps back, but not before handing Mr. Barnes a large folded towel from a rack nearby. Barnes places it over Eric's face and says, "You should suffer for what you've done, but this needs to be over."

And then he fires the gun.

The report is muffled by the towel, but the white material turns red swiftly. Vincent says grimly to Farren, "I'll clean up."

Rick, whom I forgot was in the room, stands. He walks over. "I'll help," he says to Vincent.

Farren places a hand on his friend's shoulder. "Are you sure you're up for that? You took a nasty hit to the temple."

Rick replies, "No worries, man. I'm good."

Vincent and Rick get to work on cleaning up and removing Eric's body from the basement. I have a feeling he'll end up in an unmarked grave deep in the desert, which almost seems too good for him, considering all he's done.

Farren whispers a few words to Mr. Barnes, and then the two men step over to where Haven and I are standing. "I'd like to introduce you to someone," Farren says to us, though I note he addresses Haven more than me.

After the introductions are made, Barnes stares hard at Haven. Not in any bad sort of way, but in a very curious manner. I glance from one to the other, perplexed. When my eyes land on Farren, he looks away.

What am I missing here?

Haven, always forward, says to Mr. Barnes, "You wanted to be the one to do it, didn't you? You wanted to kill Eric yourself."

Mr. Barnes nods solemnly. "Yes, I wanted to be the one to kill him. This is true."

"You must have loved your daughter very much," Haven murmurs wistfully, never having known her own father, since he left when she was three.

"I did," Barnes confirms, his voice catching. "But she's not the only child I was avenging."

Farren clears his throat. "Barnes," he snaps warningly.

Paying no heed to Farren, which is kind of a shock, since everyone concedes to Farren Shaw, Barnes says, "I shot him for the things he did to both my daughters."

Haven knows, the same as I do, that Barnes had only one child. She tilts her head, curious, and says, "What do you mean you shot him for both your daughters? Annemarie was your only child."

Mr. Barnes takes a tentative step toward Haven. "That's not exactly accurate," he says softly.

"What are you saying?" Haven whispers, her voice trembling.

Barnes, choking back a sob, says, "I'm telling you that you, Haven, are also my daughter. I'm not just Annemarie's father. I am your father, too."

Haven reaches for and practically falls back on the chair she was tied to earlier. Farren places a steadying hand on her shoulder. She reaches back and holds onto her brother's hand tightly. "What's going on?" she asks weakly.

Mr. Barnes, his voice choked with emotion so raw that tears spring to *my* eyes, says, "You and Farren are my children. You're the children I was forced to leave nineteen years ago."

Oh my God.

# CHAPTER TWENTY-FOUR

HAVEN glances back at Farren. "How long have you known that this man is our father?"

"I've known since he hired me a year ago. He looked different—"

"Plastic surgery," Barnes chimes in.

"—but I knew immediately when I saw him."

"And you never thought to tell me!" she shouts. "All this time our father has been alive, and you've been *working* for him?"

"Only for the past year," Farren tries to explain. "I didn't know until then, Hav. I swear."

I glance around. I'm glad Vincent and Rick are gone. They're out burying Eric's body somewhere, which is better than their being here to witness the family drama.

"This is why I was targeted," Haven says, sighing. "Eric knew, didn't he? He found out somehow and decided to go after his"—

she gestures to Barnes—"other daughter."

*Answers*, I think, *here is one*. Haven was taken because of Quinton Barnes, not as a warning to Farren.

Mr. Barnes looks over at Farren. A silent communication occurs between them. I watch father and son standing together. Now that I know they are related, I can see the similarities—the same strong jaw, the same aquiline nose. Plastic surgery or not, the resemblance is there. I wish Farren had confided in me, but I understand why it was not possible.

"That's why you are so committed to this cause," I chime in. "That's how Barnes lured you. Annemarie was your half sister."

As if it has finally dawned on her, Haven says, "I can't believe I had a sister all that time. But now she's dead, and I'll never get to meet her."

Haven begins to cry, and Farren wraps his arm around her protectively and says, "I think that's enough for now. We'll discuss more later on."

A few hours later, everyone is gathered in the living room. We've all had time to clean up and eat something. Haven and Rick are seated side by side on the sofa. Rick has a huge, swollen knot on his temple, but he seems not to be one bit bothered by his injury. I'm sure he's had worse. Haven scoots closer to him. She is still a wreck, chewing on her nails, dealing with the fact that her dad is alive and well.

"I still can't believe it," she says quietly. "I never thought I'd meet my father."

Rick places a comforting hand on her knee, and Farren, seated next to me on a love seat across from them, follows his movement. Mr. Barnes, in a chair to our right, is also watching Rick and Haven. He doesn't seem to be as accepting as Farren.

His expression is far more wary. But what can he say? He's not been in his daughter's life since she was three. Still, I see a longing in his green eyes—not dissimilar to Farren's—while his gaze is focused solely on Haven. He wants to connect with the only daughter he has left; that much is apparent.

Vincent is seated in a chair across from Mr. Barnes, slightly removed from everyone. He clears his throat and says, "We should discuss what's going to happen from here on out."

"Before we get to that," Haven interjects, "I want some answers." She narrows her eyes at Barnes. "What happened to you? You said in the basement that you were forced to leave us."

"I was," Barnes says gently. "When you and your brother were kids, I witnessed a crime. We were living in New Jersey at the time. I didn't know when I watched two men dump a body into the Passaic River that I was witnessing a hit. I only found out when federal agents contacted me. They needed my testimony, desperately. And they offered protection—"

"Oh, that's nice," Haven interrupts. Her tone is contemptuous. "Just hang the rest of your family out to dry."

"Haven," Farren says sharply, "that's enough."

Haven's anger redirects to her brother. "No, Farren, it's not enough. Our father left us to the wolves nineteen years ago, and you're okay with that?"

"That's not exactly what happened," Mr. Barnes interjects. "I never wanted to leave any of you." His voice cracks. "I had to leave in order to protect my family. I knew the men who'd dumped the body would ID me eventually. I knew they'd go after my wife and children," he adds, eyeing both Farren and Haven pointedly. "The agents convinced me that my testimony could take those bad guys off the street...for good. My family would be safe then. The only catch was that I had to disappear."

He sighs, takes a moment.

After a beat, he continues. "Everything happened so fast. And, of course, I couldn't tell anyone. I had to leave immediately. I was given a new identity *before* I testified. My whole past was erased so that the bad guys couldn't trace me back to you, your brother, or your mom. It was the only way I'd cooperate."

Barnes pinches the bridge of his nose, a gesture I've seen Farren do often. "After the trial, my identity was changed again. I became Mr. Quinton Barnes. I was given a large sum of money to start a new life. I invested, made deals, and I soon discovered I had a knack for business. I became successful, enough that I had the money to change my appearance. Still, I knew I could never go home." He pauses and then says softly, "When I received word that your mother died, it just about killed me that I couldn't go comfort you and Farren. But showing up in your lives at that time would've still been dangerous. I knew that you and your brother moving in with your aunt was the better option."

"It seems like too high of a cost," Haven murmurs. "You basically gave up everything."

"It was too high of a cost," Barnes confirms. "But once the wheels were in motion, things couldn't be stopped."

"You got remarried, though. You had another child. You forgot about us."

"Never," Barnes denies vehemently. And then he says quietly, "Not a day passed that I wasn't thinking of you and Farren. I never stopped loving you and your brother, your mother, too."

Farren shifts next to me. He remains stoic, but there's emotion in his eyes. Haven, meanwhile, is peering down at her hands in her lap while biting her bottom lip. Finally, she looks up and asks her father, "Are those men you testified against out of jail now?"

Mr. Barnes clears his throat. "One of them is."

*Dawson, I know it has to be Dawson. He's the right age, and he's a criminal through and through.*

"And the other one?" Haven inquires.

"He died in prison."

"The one who's still alive ID'd you, though. Didn't he?"

"Unfortunately," Barnes replies, "he did."

Haven says pointedly, "So, the criminal organization he and the dead guy worked for finally found out you were alive and well. They wanted revenge for you testifying against them. That's why Annemarie was targeted." Haven is on a roll, putting the pieces together swiftly. "And, somehow, some way, they've now linked me and Farren to you."

No one responds, and Haven flat-out asks, "Is that why I was targeted? I want to hear the truth."

Mr. Barnes looks away and doesn't say a thing. Maybe he can't. He does seem as if he's close to some breaking point.

Farren responds instead. After clearing his throat, he says, "Yes, Haven, that is why you were targeted. The organization knows everything."

"So it was never about Mr. Barnes not selling the organization one of his companies," I clarify. "And, it wasn't about you going rogue."

"No, Essa. It was never either of those things. I wasn't sure about the rogue story, how much of it they bought. That's why I needed to see Dawson. You learn a lot when you look into a man's eyes face-to-face. I saw then that Dawson knew the truth. But surely you can understand why I couldn't tell you all of this at the time?"

"I understand," I say, nodding once.

Vincent makes a coughing noise. When everyone focuses on him, he says, "I'm sorry, but we need to discuss what happens next."

"It's over," Haven says. "Eric is dead. Vincent, you're on our side. There's nothing to discuss."

Rick quietly says to her, "It's not over, Hav. Dawson is still out there."

Farren adds, "He's right. The organization is far from incapacitated."

I turn to him sharply. "What does that mean? You're not going after Dawson, are you?"

Icy fear nips at my spine.

Farren shrugs one shoulder, and I add, "You told me he's untouchable. You said he has highly placed connections." I take a breath. "Jesus, Farren, if your father couldn't stay hidden, how can you?"

Farren tries to soothe me, turning to me like I'm the only one in the room. "We discussed this before, Essa, and nothing has changed. I can't give up and walk away. Dawson is the man who needs to be taken out. If he falls, the whole organization crumbles."

"Why didn't you just shoot him at his estate," I whisper.

"I couldn't," Farren says, pained. "I wasn't going to take a chance with Haven not yet in my care. And I wasn't about to take a chance with you being there."

He holds my gaze and so many emotions pass. I want to tell him how I feel. I want to hear him say what I think I see in his eyes. But there are too many people present.

So instead I stick to the topic. "Dawson is the man who was

in prison. Am I right?"

Barnes would have the answer, but my question is directed to Farren, since he seems to know everything. "Dawson is one of the men your dad testified against," I continue. "He's the one who lived."

"He is the one," Farren confirms.

"It's too dangerous, then," I say, closing my eyes. "God, please don't go after him."

Farren doesn't assuage my fears. He just says resignedly, "Essa, I don't have a choice here. Can't you see that?"

I open my eyes and quietly inquire, "It's because of Annemarie, right?"

"It's not just about her anymore." Farren's eyes move to Haven, to his father briefly, then back to me. "I have to protect the people in my life that are still alive, the people I love."

# CHAPTER TWENTY-FIVE

THE plan is set. Farren, Haven, and I are flying to New York City in the morning. Mr. Barnes will return to the estate he owns in Connecticut. He invited Haven to stay with him for a while, but she declined.

"I'm not ready for that much closeness with a man I barely know," she confides to me as she's climbing into bed the night before we're to depart New Mexico.

The men are downstairs discussing a few business items. Haven and I are upstairs in her bedroom. We've been talking for a while. But I'm now halfway out the door, ready to head to the room I share with Farren.

Turning back around to face her, I lean my shoulder on the doorframe. "I know, Hav," I say. "I understand."

"I want to get to know my father, I do," she insists as she flops on her back. "It's just that I've never had a dad. I don't remember him at all. He left when I was three."

"Just take it slowly," I advise. I know my friend. I believe she wants to build something with her father. "See how things go," I add.

"Yeah." She nods. "You're right."

"Good night, Hav," I say before I close her door.

"Night, Essa."

Ten minutes later, I'm in bed. When Farren comes in, he gets ready for bed and joins me. With me in his arms, he brings me up to speed on what was discussed after Haven and I left the living room.

"So Vincent and Rick will remain here in New Mexico?" I say.

"Yes. They need to figure out where Dawson slunk off to."

"He's not at that house we went to"—I shudder at the memory—"anymore?"

Farren tightens his arms around me, and I feel better. "No, he's gone," he says.

"When they find him...is that where you'll go?"

"Yes." He shifts and adjusts us until I'm lying on top of him. "I'll go wherever Dawson goes. And then I'll find him."

Unclothed as we are, Farren's skin is warm and damp against mine. Even with the air conditioning back up and running, it's still hot upstairs.

"I'm so afraid, Farren," I whisper.

"Don't be," he murmurs.

He's hard beneath me. One shift of my body and he could be sheathed within me. "I want you," I groan.

"So, take me," he says playfully.

I do.

I shift.

He groans.

We move.

Our sex becomes urgent and raw, reflective of the day we had. Afterward, I remain wrapped up in Farren's strong, capable arms. He kisses the top of my head, and I nestle in closer. "Are you still afraid?" he asks.

"How can I not be?" I say.

Sighing, he says, "I told you once before that I would be fine. And I was. This time, I'll be fine as well, Essa."

"Promise?" I ask him.

"I promise, darling."

I intertwine my fingers with his, bringing them to my mouth. Brushing my lips over our joined hands, I say, "And what about us? Will we be fine, too?"

I feel Farren peering down at me, but I don't look up. I can't. "What are you asking me, Essalin?"

I shrug. "I don't know. Nothing, I guess."

I don't want to pressure Farren into saying something he doesn't feel. But I can't stand it any longer. My feelings for him are boiling over. He included me in his statement about protecting the ones he loves, but I need to know where we stand, especially since he'll be leaving me at some point.

Farren is watching me; I feel his eyes on me. I can't bring myself to meet his gaze, though. He'll see right through me.

Farren, however, isn't stupid. He knows.

"Ah," he says, "you want to know how I feel about you. You want the words."

"Well, yeah. You give me nothing, Farren. You're so"—I search for the right word—"*withholding* when it comes to relationship talk."

"Withholding?" He laughs, and his chest rumbles beneath me.

I lift my head, finally glancing up. He's smiling, confident, sure. "I give you everything, Essa. How can you not see that?" He loosens my grasp on his hand and reaches for my cheek.

I swat him away, but not because I don't want his touch. "You're leaving," I say, choking up as I express what's really weighing on me.

"Essa, Essa."

He touches my cheek again, and this time I don't swat him away. "I wish your hand could remain on me forever," I say.

"I just promised you that I'll be back," he reminds me. I say nothing, and he adds, "And do you know why?"

I shrug and try to look away, but his hand on my cheek ensures I remain looking at him. His expression softens as he says, "I'll be back because nothing will ever keep me away from the woman I love."

"What?"

He chuckles and cups my face. "I said I love you, Essalin. Somewhere along the way, throughout this crazy journey, I fell in love with you."

I'm still in shock. "How long have you known?"

"For a while now," he admits.

"You love me," I echo, amazed. I can't believe Farren has said the words, words I've longed to hear. I've felt his love, but hearing him say it out loud leaves me happy and elated…and every other good thing you can think of.

"Essa, do you love me back?" he asks.

I touch his face, my fingers gliding along his day's-end

stubble. "You know I do," I whisper.

"Say it," he rasps.

His hand moves down to my lower back, caressing and soft, promising more.

"I love you, Farren," I whisper.

"And I love you," he tells me again.

Then, Farren Shaw shows me how much he loves me.

Let's just say it's a lot.

# Epilogue

Lead-in to *Inevitable Circumstances*
(Inevitability #2)

Aᴛᴇʀ Farren, Haven, and I arrive in New York City, I keep waiting for the ax to fall, for Farren to be pulled away from me. I fear Dawson, and I loathe the thought of Farren leaving to go hunt him down. But I know Dawson and his organization must be stopped. If not, we will always be in danger.

As Farren helps Haven and I settle into his spacious, luxurious apartment—the one with the amazing view of Central Park—my worries are temporarily assuaged. Rick and Vincent are unable to pinpoint a location on Dawson, so Farren gets to stay…for now.

Farren tells me, "Let's make the most of it." And we do.

Farren shows me and Haven around the city. Our first two weeks are spent sight-seeing, going to museums, eating in a variety of restaurants. We even take in a couple of shows. Haven loves those nights most of all.

When Farren and I are alone, we stroll over to Central Park. We walk, and we talk. Sometimes we pack a picnic lunch and eat in Sheep Meadow. And every day I fall more in love with Farren. He loves me as well. Apart from telling me often, his love shines in his emerald eyes.

Haven, who recovers fully from her traumatic experience, becomes more and more interested in Rick. He seems to definitely like her, too. They speak whenever they can and text often. She tells me he plans to spend some time in New York City, once the situation with Dawson is resolved. Haven also stays in contact with her father. Mr. Barnes again invites her to his mansion in Connecticut, but she politely informs him she's still not ready.

She confides in me that there are other things weighing on her mind, like deciding where she wants to finish her degree—in Pennsylvania or here in New York. When Farren gets word that she may return to Oakwood College, he abruptly takes off one afternoon, on what he terms "personal business."

The next day, a friend of mine and Haven's calls to let us know Professor Walsh has resigned for no apparent reason. *Good riddance*, I think.

That night, in bed, I ask Farren, "Was that your doing?"

Farren never lies to me, not after all we've been through, and now is no exception. He turns on his side to face me and says, "That asshole fucking broke my sister's heart. If she decides to go back to that school, I don't want him anywhere near her."

Not that I am concerned for Asshole Walsh, but I do have to ask, "You didn't, um, hurt him, did you?"

Farren laughs and rolls to his back. Staring up at the ceiling, still chuckling, he says, "No, Essa. I didn't have to *hurt* him. He was easy to persuade."

"Well, for the record," I begin softly, "I'm glad he's out of Oakwood. For Haven's sake, if she does decide to return. But also for the other girls he took advantage of."

"Hmm…" Farren murmurs.

I don't ask him for specifics of how he "persuaded" the prick to quit. It doesn't matter. Some things are best left unknown.

Farren peers over at me, and, after a minute, I say, "What?"

"Just wondering what *your* decision is going to be." Brushing a swatch of my blond locks over my shoulder, he continues. "Are you going back to Oakwood in the fall, or are you staying here?"

Farren already informed me that with a few phone calls—from him and, not surprisingly, his influential father—I can attend Columbia this fall if I want. Farren doesn't know that I made my decision on this subject a while ago. Without further ado, I tell him my decision. "I'm staying, Farren."

Farren scoops me up and settles me on top of his hard body. He winds his hand through my hair and brings my face close to his. "Kiss me, Essa," he demands huskily.

I kiss him with fervor, and he kisses me back with even more intensity. He kisses me with heart, soul, and finesse, making me gasp when we stop. I take a breath, and then say, "Wow. Guess you like that decision."

"You think?" he teases in a sultry tone.

His hands travel down my back till he's cupping my ass. I wiggle into place, straddling him. As always, he's up and ready.

When I mention this to him, he laughs. "I am a soldier, Essa. I'm always prepared for action on a moment's notice."

"Hey…" I smack his shoulder. "You're supposed to say you're always like this"—I press my core to his sex—"because of me."

More serious now, he says, "It is because of you, Essa."

"I love you," I tell him.

"I love you too, sweetheart."

I start to rub back and forth on him, but he stills me with a hand on my hip. "Wait," he says.

I feel him throbbing—as am I—so I ask, "What's wrong?"

He chuckles, and I know from the timbre that he just wants control. Sure enough, he slides into me unrepentantly, eliciting a throaty moan from me.

"Nothing is wrong, Essa. Everything"—he thrusts up into me and I moan—"is just perfect."

Yeah, everything is perfect. Our love is solid.

The following day, I meet with a career-services counselor at Columbia. She hammers out a schedule guaranteeing that I graduate in three semesters. It puts me a little behind schedule, but I'll end up with a major in journalism and a minor in business.

When I return to the apartment, anxious to share the news with Farren, I find him whipping up dinner in the kitchen. He's hot and adorable in dark dress pants, a white button-down shirt with the sleeves rolled up, and an apron with a rooster on the front. The printed message below the rooster reads, "Kiss the Cock."

"I don't think Haven will appreciate your humor," I say, nodding to the apron.

"What?" He looks down, all innocent. "It means the chicken."

"Yeah," I reply, laughing, "sure it does."

He looks over at the clock on the wall. "Damn," he mutters.

"What?"

"Haven will be home soon. I was thinking if we had more time, you could show me what you think the message on the apron means."

He looks so delicious that I definitely would not mind showing him. But it's true that Haven will be back soon. I sigh and raise a brow. "Later?"

"Most definitely later," he replies with a smile that melts me. He adjusts himself discreetly and then returns to chopping up some green peppers. "So," he begins, "how'd it go today at Columbia?"

"Surprisingly well." I give him the details, and then say, "I think the business minor will keep my parents happy."

Chuckling, he asks, "Yeah, but what do you think they'll say about your living arrangements?"

I plan on staying at the apartment. "I'm twenty-two," I state, "an adult. I can live wherever the hell I want."

With an assessing look, Farren says slowly, "You've changed a lot, Essa."

"I have," I agree.

A little while later, I discover my parents have changed a little as well. When I resolutely declare my intentions for my future—living arrangements, change of school, and all—they are surprisingly accepting. The newly assertive me can be persuasive, I suppose. They don't even cut me off financially.

Still, if I'm going to be an adult, it's time to start earning some of my own money. I resolve to find a job for the summer. Haven is signed up for an acting workshop that meets every weekday morning, and Farren has frequent meetings with his father. I need something to do, too. There's still no sign of Dawson, but I know it's only a matter of time. A job will keep me occupied, and it will keep me busy when Farren has to leave. So, on one particularly bright and sunny summer afternoon, I apply at the coffee shop around the corner from the apartment.

"I'm not crazy about you working there," Farren's says, later in the day, when I tell him of my new employment.

"Why?" I inquire, baffled.

He shrugs. "I don't know. I don't have a specific reason." Sighing, he then admits, "I guess I just want to keep you protected at all times." Farren is not immune to worrying about me, same as I worry for him.

I wrap my arms around him. "I like when you're protective," I assure him. "But trust me, I'll be fine." When he huffs, I remind him, "The coffee shop is, like, two minutes from here."

"I know." He nestles me close to his strong body. "Just be careful, Essa. Don't trust anyone."

Three days into my new employment, Mr. Barnes asks Farren to accompany him on a business trip to a third-world country. His father wants him there as protection but also as a consultant. I'm beginning to get the impression Farren's father fully intends to leave his empire to his remaining children at some point. I think that's why he keeps trying to connect with Haven as well.

Before Farren leaves, it's my turn to ask him to be careful. And then I add in a sad voice, "I'm going to miss you so much."

"I'll only be gone two weeks," he replies in a conciliatory tone.

"Still…" I trail off.

He knows this will be hard because we've been together almost every day for more than two months solid. Enfolding me in his arms, he softly murmurs, "I'll miss you, too, Essalin."

And then he leaves.

With Farren gone, I decide to fully immerse myself in my coffee-shop job. I spend time getting to know the other employees. I ask them about their kids, their spouses, their lives.

I get to know all the regular customers, too, and most of them are pretty cool.

One particular guy catches my eye. Not in a romantic way, of course. It's just that my heart goes out to him. He's around my age, a college student. At least, that's what I assume, since he trundles in every morning with a passel of textbooks. The guy is kind of cute, in a nerdy, klutzy kind of way. He wears glasses and has a mop of reddish hair, but it works for him. He gets noticed by women in the shop, but he only talks to me. I guess that's because I am infinitely patient with him. Like, when his books slip from his grasp, I help him adjust them before they fall. When he drops his money on the counter, I pick it up for him. And when he almost knocks over his usual order—iced coffee—I always catch it before it topples.

Our conversations are a series of him saying, "I'm so sorry… Oh, let me get that…Shit."

My responses are "Don't worry about it…I got it…You're good."

One morning, before walking away after paying, he squints at my name tag. "Essa," he says. Looking up at me with soulful brown eyes hidden behind glasses, he adds, "I'm Justin, by the way."

"Nice to meet you, Justin," I say, and then I shake his hand.

And so it goes.

On the day Farren is set to return from his trip, I wrap up my morning shift early. Klutzy, red-haired Justin is walking to the door just as I am. I notice he's completely distracted, peering down at a paperback in one hand, wrapped up in reading. His iced coffee is in his other hand, way out in front of him, almost like he's unintentionally clearing the way. Customers step left and right, avoiding him. But it's too late for me. Justin wrecks right into me, and iced coffee spills down the front of my green work shirt.

Looking aghast, he says, "Oh, hell, I didn't see you there." He puts his paperback down on a table and starts reaching for napkins nearby. "I'm so sorry, Essa."

I take the napkins from him and start dabbing. But they're no match for the soaking I've received. When it's clear the napkins are not helping, I say, "I better go clean up in the ladies' room."

"Wait," Justin says, his voice urgent. "My car is around the corner. I have some auto-detailing towels in there. They're very absorbent."

I shrug. "Okay, sure."

As we're walking to his car, I attempt to make conversation. "So, you keep a car in New York City. That's crazy."

"I know, right." He laughs. "It would be. But I don't live in the city."

"Oh, where do you live?" I ask as we turn into an alley.

"Jersey," he says.

We reach his car. It's just a simple brown Toyota, a typical student car. Justin reaches for the passenger-door handle.

I take a step closer to the car and notice there's someone seated in the passenger seat.

"Oh…" I start backing up, but Justin gets behind me, his moves suddenly swift and sure. "What the hell?" I mumble.

"Not so fast," he says in my ear. His voice is smooth, confident. No more uncertain, nerdy college guy. Who is this Justin? Clearly, he's not who I thought he was.

My heart begins to pound frantically as he nudges me closer and closer to his car. Within seconds I am trapped between the

Toyota and Justin's body. I have no choice but to look inside.

When I see who's sitting casually in the passenger seat, I gasp, "Shit. Dawson."

I try to spin around so I can flee, but Justin holds me in place. No one is around. I am so screwed.

Dawson pops open the door. The man I hoped to never lay eyes on again leans forward.

Pinning me with his cold, hard eyes, he says coldly, "Ah, we meet again, young Essalin. I think I'd like to spend some time with you. Perhaps you should get in the car."

The story continues in *Inevitable Circumstances* (Inevitability #2), the second and final book of the Inevitability duology ~ Spring 2015.

# Acknowledgements

This is always the hardest part. I never want to leave anyone out. So, let's give this a try. First, so much gratitude and appreciation goes out to the readers and fans of my novels. Thank you for your continued support. Next, I must express my thanks to the bloggers who work so hard to get my name and novels out to the world. Every time I see a post regarding my books on a blog—or anywhere in social media—I am humbled. Thank you to every single one of you. Your efforts are amazing. Additionally, a huge, heartfelt thanks goes out to my amazing street team—Team S.R. Grey. You ladies are more than a street team to me, you are my dream team. Also, a special thank you goes to author J.B. Morgan (Jenn) for helping me craft a concise and compelling blurb. We sure had fun with those back and forth emails and PMs, didn't we? And thank you to Ari for a cover that matches my vision of Farren perfectly. You rock, girl!

Finally, love and thanks to Tom.

# About the Author

S.R. Grey is an Amazon and Barnes & Noble Top 100 Bestselling author. She is the author of popular New Adult novels I Stand Before You (Judge Me Not #1) and Never Doubt Me (Judge Me Not #2). Her newest novel, Inevitable Detour (Inevitability #1), is a wild ride combining the New Adult genre with elements of Romantic Suspense. She is also the author of the Harbour Falls Mystery trilogy. Ms. Grey's novels have appeared on Amazon and Barnes & Noble bestseller lists in multiple categories.

Ms. Grey resides in Pennsylvania. Her background is in business, but her true passion lies in writing. When not writing, Ms. Grey can be found reading, traveling, running, or cheering for her hometown sports teams.

S.R. Grey Facebook:
http://www.facebook.com/pages/SR-Grey

Sign up for S.R. Grey's newsletter and never miss an update, cover reveal, or release:
http://mad.ly/signups/106801/join

Follow S.R. Grey on Twitter: https://twitter.com/AuthorSRGrey

Find blog posts on the S.R. Grey Goodreads Author page:
http://www.goodreads.com/author/show/6433082.S_R_Grey

Author Website: http://srgrey.webs.com

Read the prologue of *I Stand Before You*, the first novel in S.R. Grey's other New Adult series Judge Me Not.

# Prologue

*Chase*

I LEAN my head back against the headrest, crank the passenger window down the rest of the way. The June night air rustles through my hair, reminding me I desperately need a trim. I run my fingers through the strands, chasing the path of the breeze.

My grandmother likes to lecture that I shouldn't have hair sticking out at odd angles, strands curling at the nape of my neck.

"You're such a handsome young man, Chase," Grandma Gartner said just this morning, *tsk*ing when I sat down for breakfast. "You look so much like your father did when he was your age. But, you know, *he* always kept *his* hair short and tidy." And then there was a pause, a long, dramatic sigh. She set down a plate of eggs—over easy—in front of me. "My poor Jack. God rest his soul." My grandmother crossed herself.

Her poor Jack, my father with the short and tidy hair—dead

and gone.

I thought: *I am not my dad, Gram. He failed us, he gave up on us.* But the words never passed my lips. And they never will. Hearing them would only hurt my grandmother's feelings and she's too good to hear the angry thoughts poisoning my polluted mind. So I keep all that shit locked deep inside.

This morning was no different. I kept things light, said something like, "The girls like my hair like this, Gram. Got to keep the ladies happy, ya know."

Then I ducked and waited for the inevitable swat with the dish towel. But it never came. Instead, the lines in my grandmother's face deepened.

"You don't need to be concerning yourself with keeping ladies happy, young man. You're only twenty. Messing with women at your age will only lead to trouble."

I knew what she meant this morning, and I know it now too. She's worried I'll end up getting some girl pregnant. Then I'll be fucked, well and good. But I'm always careful, take the necessary precautions. Besides, it isn't my womanizing ways that's becoming a problem. If only. No, unfortunately, it's my ever-growing dependency on drugs—something my grandmother would never suspect—that has me worried these days.

*These days...* Yeah, right. More like these blurry, fucked-up segments of time.

Sighing, I roll the window up just enough to lean my head against the cool glass. *What am I going to do?* I silently ask myself.

What I really need to do is get the hell out of this tiny Ohio farm town I landed back in two years ago. I'm spinning my wheels here in Harmony Creek, hanging with a bad crowd. Problem is I have no plan, no money either. Drugs are my escape and have been for quite a while. My priorities are all fucked up. My life, it's upside down. Every day it seems like getting high—and staying that way—is my only goal. I want to stop—believe me I do—but I don't think I know how to anymore.

A lump forms in my throat at this thought, but I swallow it down. "Hey," I say to Tate, who is driving. "Let's get out of this town."

Tate Cody, my friend…and my partner in crime in everything wild and crazy these days—women, drugs, drinking, fighting—you name it, we do it. And if we're not doing it nowadays, chances are we've done it at least once over the past couple of years. We've yet to slow down; we live on the edge.

I sometimes wonder when we'll fall.

"What do you think we're doing, Chase, my man?"

I take in and process Tate's reply, while he lifts a bottle of cheap gin to his lips and hits the gas. And for this one long, tortuous drawn-out second, I can't make a distinction between what I asked Tate and what I was only thinking. I panic, assuming my partner in crime's response is to let me know it's finally happening, we're really falling.

But then Tate adds, "I'm getting us out of here as fast as I can," and I breathe a little easier. He just means we're leaving Harmony Creek. Not falling, after all. *Shit, I need to ease up on the drugs.*

I glance out the window, and though it's dark I can see we're heading east, nearing the state line. Soon we'll be out of Ohio completely, and in the neighboring state of Pennsylvania. That's where we're supposed to hook up with two girls tonight. They're from New Castle, and we're meeting at a lake across the state line.

I don't really care about all that, though. What I'd really rather do is keep on going. Hop on Interstate 80 and clock the miles to

Jersey. Better yet, Tate and I could go farther. We could drive our asses straight into New York-fucking-City. Now that would be sweet.

So while Tate barrels down a back road the police rarely patrol—until you get into Pennsylvania, that is—I pretend we're leaving Harmony Creek for good. No looking back, no regrets, just flying the fuck out of this lame-ass small town.

And speaking of flying, I'm flying a bit now too, feeling fine, baby, fine. I close my eyes so I can savor the s-l-o-w creep of numbness that cocoons me like a warm and fuzzy blanket.

I feel nothing, yet I feel everything.

My skin tingles a little, but when I touch my hand to my face it feels detached, like these parts of my body belong to two different people, neither of them me. That thought makes me happy, escape is exactly what I crave.

Needless to say, I've smoked—a lot—and not just weed. But it's the pills I swallowed a while ago that are starting to wrap me up and spin me the fuck out.

A bottle hits the back of my hand and my eyes fly open. Shit, I forgot I am not alone in this car.

"Drink, fucker," Tate urges.

I take the gin, despite the fact I can barely see straight. *No* isn't part of my vocabulary when I'm like this. And, sadly, more often than not, this is exactly how I am. This is who I am becoming: Chase Gartner, burgeoning drug addict.

As per most nights, Tate and I stopped at Kyle's before embarking on *this* night's little adventure. Kyle Tanner supplies us with more drugs than we could ever hope for. And the quality is always top notch. Kyle takes a certain kind of pride in dealing only primo product. But you'd never guess such a thing if you saw the rundown shithole he lives in.

Our dealer resides on the *other* side of town, over by the closed-down glass factory, in a clapboard house he shares with his meth-addicted dad. Lately, going there has been a contradiction of emotions for me. I love and hate concurrently when Tate and I cross over the railroad tracks that mark the end of the safe neighborhoods of Harmony Creek. Then, I vacillate between love and hate as I watch the Sparkle Mart grocery store appear... then disappear. I lean a little more towards hate when we reach the run-down apartment building where the junkies hang out, where their emaciated bodies lean lazily against the dirty brick exterior.

I sure as fuck don't want to end up there, God, no. But maybe I'm powerless to stop my downward spiral. Lord knows, by the time we start down the long dirt road that leads to Kyle's place, I crave and I want. And love trumps hate by that point. Even the junkies seem less scary. So we go...and we go...and we keep going back.

Tate tells me the road to Kyle's house is the road to salvation. *Salvation, my ass.* I'd be more inclined to say Tate and I are traveling a path to hell. We're in the express lane to damnation, and one step closer to burning every time we travel down that fucking dirt road. I know it, he knows it, but do we ever do anything to stop? Do we try to crawl out of the hole we're wallowing in? No, never.

In fact, Tate wants us to delve in deeper—start selling. He says we'll make, at the minimum, enough money to help pay for the copious amounts of shit we ingest...snort...smoke. Yeah, we do it all, everything short of needles. I somehow know if I ever cross *that* line, there will be no going back.

But I'm considering the selling thing, albeit for a different reason than my friend. Tate hopes to eventually make enough cash to buy his own wheels. He hates borrowing the piece of shit we're currently in—his mom's old, rusted Ford Focus. I just want to make enough money to buy a ticket out of this place. The little bit I earn painting people's houses, picking up construction work here and there—it's not adding up fast enough for my liking.

Hell, I still live at my grandmother's farmhouse out on Cold Springs Lane. Granted, I recently fixed up the little apartment above the detached garage, moved from a bedroom in the main house to an area not too much larger. But that little apartment provides privacy, and that's what I need. I am no longer a teenager, like when I first moved back two years ago. That's why I want, more than anything, to just get the fuck out of here. I'm thinking the money I make selling will make escape a reality, not just some pipe dream. No pun intended.

I raise the bottle of gin to my lips and tip it back. Alcohol heats my throat. "I think I'm going to take Kyle up on his offer," I say after I swallow the burn, the resulting grimace distorting my voice. "I need the money and it's going to take forever to earn it legit."

"You're making the right decision, my friend," Tate replies as he reaches over to take back the bottle.

*Whoa...* My vision turns wonky. There are three overlapping filmy images of my friend, and then just two.

"It's all about the numbers, man," two filmy Tates tell me.

I tell myself I need to slow down, and then I say to Tate, "That it is." I squeeze my eyes shut to keep from swaying in my seat. "That it is," I repeat.

The irony is that I once had money. Well, my family did,

enough that my parents had a trust fund set up for me. Not a big one, mind you, but enough that it would've allowed for me to go to a decent college, get set up in a new city, shit like that.

I have no idea what my future holds nowadays, but I know it's been tainted by my past.

Back when I was around eight my parents moved from this town out to Las Vegas. My dad, who'd been successfully building houses here for a while, started a similar construction business out in Nevada. The timing was right, the stars aligned. We caught magic in the early days of the housing boom. Everything was golden and money poured in. It was happy times. For a while.

During those good times, Mom got pregnant. She gave me a little brother named Will that I still love like crazy and miss every fucking day. We used to talk on the phone all the time, but now I'm lucky if I get a two-word text from my little bro. I suppose when you're eleven years old—and haven't seen your big brother in two years—memories become a little hazy.

That's another thing the extra money from selling drugs will help with: I'll have enough funds to fly out to Vegas to see Will. Or I can just buy him a ticket to come here. As it is my mom, Abby, barely makes enough to get by out there.

But, like I said before, it wasn't always that way. In the early years, my father's construction company grew and thrived, so much so that I once entertained dreams of taking over the business. I used to imagine following in my father's footsteps, as sons are apt to do.

One afternoon, when I was about thirteen, I told my dad I wanted to build homes, same as he did. I showed him some sketches, just some basic designs and floor plans I'd thrown together. My dad was impressed. And not the false kind of fawning parents often try to sell to their kids. No, my drawings truly floored Jack Gartner. I could tell he couldn't believe his eldest son possessed that kind of crazy talent. He told me I should aim high, the sky was the limit. My sketches were incredible, he said, especially for my age. I could be an architect if I wanted, design skyscrapers even.

I had no reason not to believe him.

When you're thirteen you think you can have it all. Life hasn't roughed you up so very much…yet. At least it hadn't for me. So I told my father I'd do both—I would design the skyscrapers, and then I'd build them. My buildings would sell like hotcakes, and I'd be as rich as Donald Trump. No, richer even.

"The sky's the limit," I said, echoing my father's words back to him.

Dad smiled and patted me on the back.

Jack Gartner wasn't patronizing me, he truly believed in my possibility. "You have talent, Chase," he said. "Just don't ever lose yourself. If you can stay true to your dream…to who you are… then you'll do more than fly. Someday you'll soar."

Yeah, right. I sure am soaring at the moment, but I have a feeling this isn't what Dad had in mind.

Tate tries to pass the bottle back to me, but my mood has dampened. The pills, along with the memories, are doing a fucking number on my emotions. I'm sad one minute, reflective the next, mad at everything, contemplative over nothing. I guess I am officially fucked up.

I push the bottle away, harder than necessary, and clear liquid sloshes over the side. "Asshole," Tate mutters.

"Sorry," I say.

Do I really mean it? No, it's just a word, an empty string of letters. Empty, like me.

I tune Tate out. I am high as fuck and lost in my mind. We idle at a swinging red light hanging over an empty, dark stretch of road, and I sit waiting on an imaginary red light in my head, one on memory-fucking-lane.

When I blink, both lights turn green…

My dad started taking me to work the summer I showed him the drawings. I learned how to wire a home, how to put in plumbing, how to lay insulation. And that was just the beginning. I used to watch how my dad talked to the guys. He treated them with respect, and in turn they went the extra mile for him. It was all "Yes sir, Mr. Gartner," "Consider it done, Jack."

When I turned fourteen, my dad bought me a drafting table, a bunch of fancy software too. The kind real architects use, or so he said. I practiced all the time, got pretty damn good. I was building my wings, you see, preparing to fly.

Will was only five, but damn if that kid didn't love to sit around and watch me sketch. For him, I'd draw all kinds of ridiculous structures.

"Dwaw me a house, Chasey," he asked this one day.

I laughed while I tousled his blond hair. I remember the fine strands looked so light in the sunlit room. Hell, they were almost white. "All right, buddy, what kind do you want?"

"A house like a tweeeee," Will sing-song replied, green eyes innocent and wide as he focused on the sketch pad I'd picked up from my desk.

I readied a colored pencil and asked for clarification, "Okay, a tree house, right?"

"No-o-o." Will shook his little head vociferously. "A house that *is* a twee, Chasey."

"Aha, got it," I said.

And I did. I drew Will a tree house shaped exactly like a tree, big, sturdy, loaded down with bushy branches. The leaves I shaded in the color of my brother's eyes. I sketched a door at the base of the trunk, then drew a Will-sized truck and parked it under a low-lying branch. After I finished with some final shading, I held the drawing up for my brother to see.

Will's house looked like one of those tree houses in the commercials with the elves and the cookies, only this one I'd drawn was far better. There was a lot more detail, and I'd drawn the tree in 2-D. In among the branches and the leaves all the rooms were in cross-section, done up in varying shades of blue, Will's favorite color. I also made certain every last blue-shaded 2D-room overflowed with toys.

Will threw his arms around my neck and told me he loved his *twee house*. Then, he leaned back and told me he loved *me* even more.

He gave me a kiss on my cheek. That shit always touched my heart, choked me up a little. "I love you too, buddy," was about all I could say as I held on to a little boy who meant the world to me.

Things are never bad when love is abundant. I thought it would stay that way forever, I did. A home filled with love, a happy family, just a good and easy life.

Man, was I ever wrong.

Shortly after I turned seventeen my world began to crumble. The bottom fell out of the housing market. The wave everyone was riding touched the surf and crashed. My dad's business was one of the first to fail. He had overextended himself; all our assets were mortgaged. He made ridiculous deals, attempting to keep us afloat, but his efforts proved futile. We sunk faster than a stone.

I sold the fancy architect software on eBay, the drafting table too. I gave the money to my parents, but it was merely a drop in the bucket compared to what we owed. I watched my once-vibrant dad turn into a shadow of the man he once was. My mom, always so young-looking and pretty, developed dark circles under her eyes—from crying, worrying, not being able to sleep. She even tried her hand at the casinos, we were that fucking desperate. But everyone knows gambling is a loser's game. The house always wins in the end.

One night, my mom was at one of those casinos. It wasn't the first time she'd spent hours and hours away, trying to win back what we'd lost. She came out ahead a little here and there, but it was never enough, never enough.

Will had fallen asleep early that night, so my dad and I were more or less alone. He asked me if I was hungry. When I nodded slowly, reluctant to reveal just how ravenous I really was and cause my father any additional undue guilt, he sighed, picked up the phone, and ordered a bunch of Chinese take-out.

I swear I smelled that food before the delivery man even pulled up to the house. Beef Chow Mein, General Tso's chicken, Hot and Sour soup, and eggrolls, the first real meal I'd eaten in weeks. And even though my dad and I had to sit on the floor— our furniture had been repossessed days earlier—I savored every fucking bite.

Afterward, my dad said he had somewhere to go. There was something he had to do. Would I keep an eye on Will?

"Sure," I told him while shoving white take-out cartons with little metal handles— leftovers I'd saved for Will and Mom—into the fridge.

With my father gone, I had nothing to do. Our TVs were

gone, the stereos too. Video games? Forget it. Those were among the first things to go. So, I wandered around the house barefoot, padding around on neglected hardwood floors. I trudged from one empty room to the next.

Then I took a minute to look in on Will.

My little brother slept on an air mattress in the middle of his now-barren room. The *twee house* sketch, the only thing left on his four stark walls, had fallen. It lay abandoned on the floor, close to Will's hand, close to where his little arm was dangling off the side of the mattress. To me, it looked as if my brother was subconsciously reaching for the drawing. Three years had passed since I'd drawn Will's tree house—and I'd sketched hundreds of other things for him since that sunny day—but that particular piece of made-with-love art was still my brother's favorite. I think to him it symbolized something more. He'd once said my sketch gave him hope. I guess it reminded him of when things were good.

I stepped into his dark room and picked up Will's hope. I kissed the top of his head and gently placed his *twee house* next to his sleeping form. I made my way back down to the living room, feeling solemn and too fucking worn for seventeen. Tears welled in my eyes, but I refused to let them fall. *Hell with that shit.* The paper bag that had held the Chinese food was still on the floor. Frustrated, I kicked it out of my way. A fortune cookie shot out and landed at my feet. I picked the projectile up, ripped the plastic covering off, and slid a tiny piece of paper from the confines of the cookie.

The fortune stayed in my hand, the cookie ended up in my mouth.

Truthfully, I was still hungry. Crunching away and savoring

sugary goodness, I read the words on the little slip of paper I held between my fingers.

*As I stand before you, judge me not.*

It sounded a little hokey and I almost threw the fortune away. But there was something about those words that made me hesitate, something almost prescient. I ended up folding the little piece of paper in half and tucking it in to my pocket. Maybe I needed some symbol of hope just like my brother. I knew the things happening in my life would eventually define my future, and I guess I hoped no matter what occurred those things wouldn't ultimately define me.

My mom came back later that night, but my dad never did.

Jack Gartner had gotten on route 160, heading west to California. But he never made it out of Nevada. His car was found at the bottom of a ravine, below what the officers who came to our door to break the news termed *a treacherous curve.*

Killed on impact, we were told.

Did he lose control, or drive off the road on purpose? Maybe his plan all along had been to leave us and start a new life in California. That's what my mom believed at the time. Still does, in fact.

I, however, am not so sure. My father didn't pack a thing. Sixty dollars and a cancelled credit card, that's all he had on him. I think my dad just gave up. He quit on us, and that was the way he chose to end it. My mom can delude herself all she wants, but I know in my heart that I'm the one who's got it right.

Anyway, the bank took the house soon after my father's death. My mom sold off what little was left. For awhile, we became nomads in the desert. We lived in the only big-ticket item that hadn't been repossessed, a white minivan. The Honda Odyssey was home…until Mom won enough money gambling to move us into a cheap apartment. Our new residence was a dump, but at least it had running water. And it was furnished. Kind of.

When we first stepped across the threshold and Mom caught me scowling at the rusty fixtures, the water-stained ceiling, the musty olive-green carpeting, she tried hard to convince me our new place had its good points.

"Like what?" I asked.

"It's close to The Strip. That'll be convenient."

"Convenient for who?" I sniped. "You?"

"Chase," she said pointedly, "it's better than living in a minivan."

She had a point there, so we moved in the next day. Will's first reaction was to run straight to one of the two back bedrooms and hang up his tattered *twee house* sketch. I followed him and watched as he stood on a soiled mattress on the floor—in a shoebox of a room we were going to have to share—and pinned hope on a wall.

After we were settled, time, as it does, marched on. Will and I attended school, while my mom—still fevered and sick with the gambling virus—spent her days in the casinos.

I turned eighteen that April. But no one really noticed. Well, Will did. Not much got by that kid.

He stuck a candle he found in the back of a drawer in the kitchen on a stale snack cake. He made me sit on the only kitchen chair that didn't rock when you shifted, and then he placed the snack cake on a card table we used as a kitchen table.

Will sang me the most beautiful off-key and from-the-heart rendition of "Happy Birthday" that I have ever heard, before or since. When he was done, I leaned forward to blow out the candle. Will stopped me and told me to make a wish first, so I did. And then I blew out the candle. Will clapped and cheered. He asked me what I wished for and I told him it was a secret. I didn't want to tell him I wished for him to be given a better life than what we were, at the time, living. My brother and I split the snack cake in two, dinner for the night, and ate in contemplative silence.

Summer arrived that year and I somehow managed to graduate. But—with my trust fund long gone—college was no longer on the table. With no real guidance, and a lot of pent-up frustration, my downward slide took hold. I was angry all the time, and ended up getting into too many fights to count. The places in Vegas where I'd started hanging were tough. Early on, I got my ass kicked…often.

But then something happened.

I learned how to use my strength, my quickness, *and* my anger. I started to win. I had a real knack for fighting and rapidly turned into a badass nobody messed with. I earned street cred. All that really meant was guys started showing me respect and girls suddenly wanted to have sex with me. I happily obliged more than a few of the latter.

But all that shit meant nothing, I was empty inside. I had no one to talk to about the mixed-up emotions I didn't know how to deal with. Like, why was I so angry all the time? Why did I like to fight so much? Why did it feel so good to make someone else hurt?

But mostly I wondered why I missed my dad so much.

I missed talking to my father, seeing his face everyday. I had relied on him, I still needed him. But he was gone. He took his own life. Why couldn't I just accept what had happened and forget him?

But I couldn't, and, worse yet, I longed for answers.

Every day, for a while, in my quest for enlightenment, I'd grab the bus outside our apartment and visit my father. Well, I'd visit his grave. At the head of where my father rested eternally, I'd sit under a big stone angel kneeling by his grave—thankful for the little bit of shade she offered under the hot, beating sun of the desert.

Sweaty and lost, I'd ask her if she could tell me why my dad wasn't still alive. Why had God allowed Dad to take himself away? Why did my father choose to leave me? Why would he leave Mom and Will too? Was our love not enough for him? Did he regret his decision when he realized there was no going back?

Of course, the stone angel had no answers, and one day I just quit going. No more sitting in the shadow of the angel, no more hot and beating sun. No more asking questions that could never be answered.

My trips to the cemetery were over, but that didn't mean I wanted to forget that *someone*—even though he'd left—had once believed in me. Despite everything, I still loved my father and part of me yearned to be just like him.

So, July of that year, I had his angel's likeness—the stone one at his grave—inked in profile on the middle of my upper back, between my shoulder blades.

I shift in the passenger seat now.

I can almost feel her back there, watching over me, like my dad's angel watches over him. And like his angel, mine is kneeling. The edges of her heavy robe lie in a puddle of fabric around her. Her wings are folded against her back. Her hair is long, obscuring the side of her face. And her head is bowed. In supplication or in shame, I haven't decided which. But if she's been watching the shit I've been doing these past two years, it's probably in shame.

After the angel tat healed, Mom hit for more money. I successfully talked her into paying for another tattoo, guilted her into it really. In any case, I ended up with big, intricately detailed wings inked up and over my shoulder blades. The top feathers curve onto my shoulders, while the wings dip down the sides of my back, effectively framing the angel.

But the angel and the wings weren't enough. I wanted something more to remember my father, something to remind me always of that final night, when it was just him and me, eating Chinese food on the floor of an empty home, a last supper shared.

I kept coming back to the cookie, the fortune inside, the hope it symbolized.

*As I stand before you, judge me not.*

Words printed on a piece of paper, but really they were so much more. So I had those words inked—in concise and script letters—around my left bicep.

My tats were but temporal attempts to heal my soul, as my heart remained an open wound. There was no solace to be had at home. In fact, things were getting worse. I started to drink and do drugs to ease the pain and fill the void. I hated what had happened to our family. Seeing Will transformed from an energetic little boy to a sullen nine-year-old left me sad and frustrated. And watching my mother try to heal her fractured heart with gambling—and eventually men—just pissed me the fuck off.

But at least Mom wasn't indulging in one-night stands like I'd been doing. Nope, Abby actually went out on dates. Still, her attempt at dating led to a revolving door of boyfriends. Some lasted a week or two, some a little longer, but the one common denominator they all shared was that not a single one liked me.

Mom told me to try harder, give these guys a chance for her sake. I laughed and told Abby her men could blow me. "Chase, don't be crude," was her response.

By the end of the summer Mom hooked up with what turned out to be steady boyfriend number three. I was no fool; I immediately sensed my days were numbered. I would've had to have been blind not to see the writing on the wall, a wall I didn't realize I was hurtling toward. But it wasn't just Abby's lame new boyfriend disliking me that was a problem. There was something else, something she'd never admit to. There was no escaping it though, not really.

I saw Abby's problem every day when I looked in the mirror.

Standing in a cramped and steam-filled bathroom, hot water running, can of shave cream poised in hand, I couldn't deny the truth in front of me. I'd swipe at the misted mirror with my free hand, leaving it streaky, but mostly clear. And it wasn't me I saw in the reflection, it was my father. That's how much I looked like Jack Gartner, even at eighteen. And *that* was my mother's real problem.

*Shit.* Even thinking about it now—two years later—fucks with my head.

I glance over at Tate. He's quiet, taking long pulls from the bottle. I shift in my seat and wind up the window the rest of the way. Time to assess my bleary reflection, time to compare it to what it was, time to compare it to the man who made me...I sometimes do this just to fuck with myself.

When I take in my reflection, I laugh. Hell, the resemblance is still uncanny. And just like when I used to stare at the steamed-up mirror in the bathroom, it's my dad's eyes staring back at me now. But these pale blues are all mine. Yeah, *his* whites were never shot with red like mine.

Still, even with the bloodshot eyes, similarities far outweigh differences. Though it's not *short and tidy*—like Grandma Gartner would like it to be—my hair is the exact same shade as her son's once was, light brown. Jack also blessed me with his straight nose, his square jaw, and his defined cheekbones. Everyone used to say my dad was good-looking, I guess I am too. Girls seem to think so, that's for sure. And my mother sure was smitten with my dad.

Abby used to lean across the front seat of the sporty car my dad bought for himself during the good times. Will and I would be in the back, rolling our eyes at each other. My mom would kiss my dad, making him swerve a little as he drove. She'd tell him he was gorgeous, and that she loved him. Dad would laugh and tell Abby he loved her even more. He'd say his love for her burned hotter than the Vegas sun above us. My mom loved that shit. Will and I, however, would groan in disgust and make gagging noises.

Shit, I feel like gagging now. Not because of the memory, but at how closely I still resemble my dead father. I turn away from my reflection. I can't bear to endure this self-inflicted torture any longer. No wonder I was fucking sent away. Too bad I couldn't disappear completely just as easily right now. Guess, in a way, that's why I live my life the way I do, filling it with drugs…sex… violence.

Back then my very presence in my mom's life must have been a constant reminder of all she had lost. When you're striving to move on, you don't need an anchor to the past. She could move forward with Will, he was just a kid. Besides, he looked like her, not like my father. But I was eighteen, an adult, and far too much my father's son for everyone's comfort. I guess it was just too difficult for Mom to look at me—see *him*—and be reminded of all she'd once had.

So the day steady boyfriend number three, a guy named Gary, told her she could move in with him, I kind of fucking knew the invitation wouldn't be extended to me.

Sure enough, on a blistering hot afternoon, my mom sent Will out to ride his bike and told me we had to talk. She sat me down on the ratty couch in our shitty apartment. I felt like a condemned man waiting to hear his fate, and all the while the noisy air conditioning unit in the window behind me kept blowing gusts of lukewarm air across the back of my neck.

Not that it mattered. I barely noticed. I was mostly numb. In preparation for this "talk," I'd done a couple of lines of coke in my room. Of course, I hadn't brought that shit out until after Will had left. One thing I stuck to was that I never let my little brother see me taking part in any of my newfound vices.

Anyway, that day in the living room, I couldn't sit still. Fidgeting, fidgeting, tapping my foot. Mom took no notice, she was almost as bad. Pacing back and forth in front of me, smoking a cigarette, a new habit she'd just acquired. Gary smoked, so she'd picked up the habit too. *Pathetic*, I remember thinking.

My mother appeared so edgy and wired I almost asked her if she was dabbling in drugs, like me, or if what she had to say was really just that fucking bad. She started speaking before I ever got the chance.

"You're not a kid anymore, Chase," she began, still pacing, ashes peppering the olive-green carpeting.

She took a drag, crinkled her brow, and leaned over to stub

her cigarette out in a plastic ashtray on a low table.

"You have to get started on doing something, somewhere, kid," she said as she spun to face me.

She stood right in front of me, and though my head was down I watched her every move. She blew out a breath and I watched her dark blonde bangs lift up off her forehead. A few strands stuck to her skin. Mom was starting to sweat.

"So, Grandma Gartner called the other day," she continued, her words deliberate, pointed, like a knife. "She said she's got lots of room in that old farmhouse back in Ohio. And she sure could use some company."

I looked up at her in disbelief. This woman who'd given me life tried to smile, but she could not. She knew damn well she was spewing pure bullshit. She just wanted rid of me.

"Just spit it out," I ground through clenched teeth, my voice far from even.

"Okay, of course, honey." She looked everywhere but at me. "Uh, so, Gram thinks moving back to Harmony Creek might do you some good, get you out of Vegas, give you a chance to start over, and—"

"Mom, I'm only eighteen. Start over?" I blew out a quick breath. "I haven't even had a chance to get started *here*."

Her expression grew stern. "Chase, don't act like I don't know the things you do behind my back." I tried to protest, but she shushed me. "I know you use drugs. I know you bring girls back when Will's not around. That shit isn't going to fly once we move in with Gary. He won't stand for it, Chase. He has standards—"

I snorted, "The fuck he does—"

"I'm not going to argue with you about it," she said, her voice tired and cracking.

When she reached for her pack of cigarettes, I noticed her hands were shaking. "Honey, I just think Grandma Gartner's is the best place for you right now, okay?"

I picked at a hole in my jeans. "Do I have a choice?" I asked, defeated, and, truthfully, feeling like I'd just been set adrift.

She shook her head no.

I'd known it was coming, but her words still flayed me up the middle and pierced my already damaged heart. I was shocked that my heart could continue beating, since it felt all smashed to hell. But beat it did. In fact, my heart pumped faster and faster, like it was going to burst right out of my fucking chest. Whether my reaction was from cocaine...or despair...I couldn't quite figure.

With my heart pounding like a sped-up death knell, I tried to push some words out of my cotton-dry mouth. "Mom..." I croaked, my voice catching.

I just couldn't finish.

Verbal communication failed me, so I tried to meet her eyes, speak to her soul. Was this really what she wanted? Send her eldest son away? Give up on me? Just like Dad did with all of us.

I searched and searched, but my mother had no answers in her big green eyes, no more than the stone angel had at my father's grave.

Abby took in a stuttered breath and turned away. She swiped at a tear. "It's for the best, Chase," she mumbled.

And then she left me sitting there, all alone, warm air blowing across the back of my neck.

I went back to my room and cut up three more lines.

That was nearly two years ago and here I am. Mom is still in Las Vegas with Will, on steady boyfriend number six, last I heard.

She's still chasing the elusive jackpot too, hoping to recapture the life she once knew.

*Good luck with that*, I think bitterly. *Jackpot, my ass.* If anyone needs to hit a fucking jackpot, it's me.

Suddenly, drug-induced visions of flashing pots of gold swim lazily into my head, along with some break-dancing leprechauns, and I can't help but chuckle.

Tate looks over. He must think my mood has improved, 'cause he starts talking all excitedly about how much money we're going to make from our new business venture with Kyle. I listen to his voice, not really hearing any words, but then the cell buzzes and I am alert, very alert.

Tate tosses it my way. "That there would be the ladies," he says—all smooth like—as I catch the cell with one hand. Even impaired, my coordination is impeccable.

"Ladies, my ass." I roll my eyes.

Tate laughs, knowing as well as I do that the two girls we're meeting up with tonight are no ladies. They're looking for the same thing we are, but therein lies the beauty.

"What's it say?" he asks, nodding to the cell.

The text is kind of blurry, but, then again, everything is. I blink a few times and my vision clears. When I read it out loud, I mimic a high-pitched girl's voice, just to be an ass. "Crystal and I are almost at the lake. Come prepared. Tammy. Laugh out loud, winking smiley face."

"Dude-e-e." Tate shoots me a knowing sidelong glance. "You know what *come prepared* means, right? You got that covered, yeah?"

As reckless as I am—and that's pretty fucking reckless—I always make sure I wrap my shit up. Better safe than sorry. But as I feel around in the pockets of my jeans I realize I've left the condoms at home. "Fuck," I mutter.

The blue *Welcome to Pennsylvania* sign looms ahead, our headlights flashing off the reflective letters.

Tate asks, "What?"

I rake my fingers through my hair. "I forgot the goddamn things at home."

"Not a problem. We'll just stop at the convenience store across the state line."

"Bad idea," I counter. "Cops are always hanging out in there. You think they won't notice how fucked up we are?"

"How fucked up *you* are," Tate corrects, laughing. "I didn't smoke nearly as much as you."

"You smoked plenty," I mumble under my breath.

But Tate is right, I smoked more. And Tate smoked only weed. Plus, my friend didn't see the pills Kyle slipped me before we left.

Still, I nod to the almost-empty bottle. "You pretty much drank that whole thing, dickhead. You'll never pass a field sobriety test."

"Yeah, but I don't plan on taking one, my friend. And, I hide it better than you." He shrugs. "Trust me, I got it covered. Just wait in the car. It'll only take a sec."

Tate's always confident like this. He can talk anyone into just about anything. I always tell him he's a natural-born salesman. Maybe if we ever get our shit together he can do something legit using his smooth ways. It's cool, it's Tate's thing, and it helps make him popular. He's an okay-looking guy—brown hair, brown eyes, kind of skinny—but it's his smooth talk that gets him in with the girls. They eat that shit up.

We cross the state line, turn into the convenience store. No cop cars. "See, we're good," Tate says, still as confident as ever.

I flip up my black hoodie hood and slouch down in my seat. "Just be quick," I mumble.

Tate hesitates, and I know something is up. "What the fuck are you waiting for?" I ask.

He begins his sentence with "Don't be pissed—" and I cut him off right away, hoping I won't have to kick my good friend's skinny ass. It would be a damn shame really, since Tate wouldn't stand a chance against the likes of me. I am way bigger and far stronger, and the rage within me has no match.

"What?" I spit out, clenching my jaw.

Tate ignores my attitude; he's used to it. "I kind of need you to hold on to something while I go in there. Just in case."

"Just in case of what?"

I am running out of patience. I scrub my hand down my face, wary to hear what Tate the salesman is up to now.

He smirks, and I tell him to knock that shit off, save it for the "ladies."

"Okay, okay." He raises his hands in mock surrender. "I may have kind of asked Kyle to give us a little something to get our entrepreneurial gig started."

"Us?" I say, feeling the anger rise up. "You didn't even know I was going to sell with you until about ten minutes ago."

"What can I say, man." Tate places his hand over his heart. "I had faith."

"Whatever."

I try to stay pissed, because what he did was really out of line, but my anger fades fast. High as I am, these strong emotions are too fucking slippery to hold on to for very long.

Tate hands me a plastic packet filled with little pills, a rainbow of color. "Jesus." I know all too well exactly what this shit is. "X? You're fucking higher than I thought. We're supposed to start small, bitch. Move a little bud, see how it goes."

Tate shrugs. "We'll make more money this way. Like, I know we can sell to the girls tonight. Hell, I bet we can talk them into buying *our* hits."

He's laughing at his own ingenuity, but I ignore him. I'm too busy trying to count the pills in the packet. But being in the condition I am in, it's a bit of a challenge.

"How much is this anyway?" I ask, giving up on figuring it out for myself.

"Twenty hits," he tells me, and then he has the balls to throw another packet in my lap. "Make that forty…maybe a little more."

"You're fucking crazy. If we get caught, Tate, this isn't possession. This is possession with intent to sell."

"That's why I'm leaving the shit here with you."

"Oh, that's real fucking cool." Back to being pissed, even my high can't calm me now. I whip one of the packets back at Tate. "I am so not getting caught with forty hits of Ecstasy, asshole."

"Calm down, man." He gingerly picks up the packet I've just thrown and holds it out for me to take back. "If a cop shows up just hit the road."

"What about you?" I ask as I grudgingly accept the X.

Tate grins. "Don't worry about me. You know I can play it cool. Just swing by after the heat's gone, and we'll be back in business."

"The heat? What is this, the seventies?" I ask, laughing, but Tate's already out the door.

I tuck the two packets of Ecstasy into the back pocket of my jeans and think nothing more of it. Until a few short minutes later when a state cop pulls into the lot. Then, I panic.

I start climbing over the console to get the fuck out of there, but, suddenly, with every fiber of my being, I know I've just made the dumbest mistake of my life. That, however, doesn't stop me from slipping down into the driver's seat, throwing the car into reverse. I hit the gas, peel out of the parking lot, and leave a cloud of gravel and dust in my wake.

I've got the Focus up to eighty, music playing…loud, loud, fucking blaring. Maybe I can outrun this cocksucker? I'm tapping my hands on the steering wheel along with the beat, flying so fast it's amazing I don't lose control and crash.

But I don't, I stay steady.

I even make it a good five miles down the road before a cop heading my way—backup, I'm sure—screeches to a wide arced stop in front of me. His patrol car blocks the entire road, so I have no choice but to hit the brakes and squeal to a halt.

My car ends up parallel to the cop car, both of us straddling the lanes, engines idling like we're in some fucking action movie. The air reeks of burning rubber, and smoke billows around us. The speakers beat out a song from 50 Cent that is frankly ironic at this point.

When all the smoke clears, the sign for the lake is right smack dab in front of me. I can't help but laugh. The shit situation I'm in, and all I can think of is that Crystal and Tammy are out there, waiting, for two boys who are never going to show.

Two more cops—including the one from the store—pull up behind me. I pitch the door open, tumble from the seat. I hit the warm pavement and try to stand. Someone yells, "Hold it right there, hands on your head."

I hear guns being drawn, cocked. This isn't a movie, I know they're loaded. I squint to try to see what's happening, but all the flashing lights leave me blinded. Before I can think another drug-muddled thought, someone tackles me from behind. My face smacks right into the yellow center line, but I don't feel a fucking thing.

Whoever tackles me yanks down my hood, frisks me, and comes up with my wallet. Oh, and the forty hits of X, of course.

It's all ambient noise from that point on, but I do hear, "Chase Gartner, you're under arrest."

I have no idea that, despite the altered state I'm in, these will be the last coherent words I will remember for a very long time.

T HE time following has no sense of structure. Days, weeks, they all blend together. I'm in jail, facing a long, long list of charges. But it's the X that has me fucked.

Bond is set high. I call my mom, but all she does is cry. Like, these horrible wailing sobs that do nothing but make my head ache more than ever. She keeps apologizing for not having the money and swears she'll help me when she can. I hang up. I won't be holding my breath. The past has taught me not to put too much stock into Abby's flimsy promises. Mirages in the desert are what they are—get too close and they disappear.

My grandmother wants to mortgage the farmhouse, all the property around it. We're talking a good fifty-five acres. It'd be enough to make bail, but I tell her *no way*. She's done enough for me already, and look at how I've repaid her. I don't deserve her money…or her love.

So I'm on my own. And not thinking very clearly. Once all

the illegal shit is out of my system, I find myself in a constant state of agitation. I can't sleep, I barely eat. I sweat bullets even when it feels like I'm freezing.

Eventually all that passes, but then all I want to do is fight. Like beat heads in. It's worse than when I was back in Vegas; I feel so much more fucking rage. I sit around clenching my fists, hoping for a chance to kick some poor unsuspecting soul's ass.

Finally, my wish is granted.

They throw a cellmate in with me and my ass is on him like an animal, beating the hell out of this never-saw-me-coming sap. But then two guards see what I'm doing, pull me off the bloodied and broken man, and promptly return the favor.

Another blur of pain.

This one, though, I welcome. The medical staff gives me plenty of drugs, legal ones this time. And still more before I am put before the judge.

Even in the sedated fog I float around in, I quickly learn the law…and some new math.

MDMA, Ecstasy—X, as I like to call it—is a schedule I narcotic, and carries as stiff a penalty as heroin if you're caught dealing, which they naturally assume I was. Casual users don't tote around forty-plus hits of Ecstasy, but dealers do.

I say nothing one way or the other to dispel their myth, I rat no one out. I just stay quiet and accept my fate.

My math lesson continues…

Ten pills are equal to one gram, and I've been caught with over forty pills. Forty pills equal four grams, which is more than enough to be charged with possession with intent to sell. But I already knew that part, right?

My lesson isn't over though. It's only just beginning.

I learn in Pennsylvania, the state in which I've been apprehended, four grams can easily earn you a prison sentence. This is especially true when you don't have enough money to hire a good attorney. Add to that, your public defender isn't getting paid enough to care. Not that you're doing much to help the overworked, underpaid man do his job. And, oh yeah, don't forget that one prior arrest for fighting last fall. It didn't seem like much at the time, but it sure haunts your ass now.

Are you keeping up?

Some final math…

Four grams buys you a six-year sentence at a state correctional institute when you have no resources, and, really, no heart to fight it.

Twenty years of age feels like ninety when your freedom is stripped away.

It takes one hundred and forty-three steps to walk down a long, noisy corridor to reach cell block seventy-two.

And when they turn the key, you hear one life—the only one you've ever known up until now—ending.

"It's all about the numbers, man," as Tate would say.

It sure is, my friend. It sure is.

*I Stand Before You*
is available on Amazon and Barnes & Noble.

This paperback interior was designed and formatted by

# E.M.
# TIPPETTS
## BOOK DESIGNS

www.emtippettsbookdesigns.com

*Artisan interiors for discerning authors and publishers.*